The TEXAS Connection

CRAIG I. ZIRBEL

WARNER BOOKS

A Time Warner Company

WARNER BOOKS EDITION

Copyright © 1991 by Craig I. Zirbel
All rights reserved.

This Warner Books Edition is published by arrangement with the author.

Cover design by Gerald Pfeifer
Cover photos courtesy of Tri Studio and Wide World Photos

Warner Books, Inc.
1271 Avenue of the Americas
New York, NY 10020

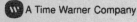 A Time Warner Company

Printed in the United States of America

First Warner Books Printing: November, 1992

10 9 8 7 6 5 4 3 2 1

This book is dedicated to my mother, who supplied me with human insight; to my father, who taught me rational thinking; to my teacher Mrs. Harriet Joy Quinn, who instilled in me self-discipline; and to my wife, who has patiently lived with me.

Table of Contents

Foreword

The assassination of President John F. Kennedy puzzles and disturbs the American public today as much as it did in 1963. New books and explanations continually appear, offering differing views of the evidence and many explanations for the killing.

Since my youth I have read and collected every major book and news article relating to the assassination that I could discover. The Sources in the back of this book recount only in part the material that I have read and studied.

Eventually, I came to the realization that everyone seemed to be tip-toeing around the crucial issue . . . whispering, rumoring, and suspecting, but never speaking or writing about the one obvious possible explanation . . . *The Texas Connection*.

This book is the distillation of my thought into a straightforward criminal investigation of the assassination which should have been conducted in 1963. It is not presented as the final answer, since the solving of a premeditated murder rarely results in certainty, only guilt beyond a reasonable doubt, and the decision as to reasonable doubt is made by each person who serves on the jury.

Therefore, what I have done is to present to the reader as much of the evidence that I have summarized over the years, which is relatively indisputable and not subject to reasonable debate, in a logical form much as is presented to a jury, and then ask you, the reader, to make your own decision.

I have made mine. What will yours be?

Craig I. Zirbel

SECTION 1

Background

1

Introduction

President John Fitzgerald Kennedy was assassinated Friday, November 22, 1963 at 12:30 P.M. That same afternoon, Vice President Johnson went to the airport, transferred his own luggage to the President's plane, put the dead President and the widow in the back, took his oath of office, and then flew back to Washington. The assassin was arrested, charged, and then executed on national television before an audience of millions. On Sunday, shortly thereafter, Texas officials in charge of investigating the assassination declared the case closed. The following day the President was buried and America had a new leader, a bitter enemy of the former President, sitting in the oval office waiting to go to work.

In any country of the world, except America, this event would have been viewed suspiciously as a bloody "coup." Here, while the transfer of power was initially accepted without rioting and rebellion, rumors of conspiracy and mystery surrounding the assassination soon began to circulate and have continued to this day, despite the "official report" of the United States government following its investigation of the assassination.

This book is an attempt to fill the black hole of mystery still remaining as to why President Kennedy was killed. It proceeds on the assumption that finding a motive often exposes the killer. It is a fresh look at the known facts of the assassination rather than a revelation of new and startling discoveries. This book is a distillation of thoughts collected over 25 years of reading, studying, and re-reading other assassination works. It attempts to present the assassination story in a readable form offering a common sense, believable explanation why the President was killed. The book explains why the assassination theories advanced by both the Warren Commission and others who disagreed with the Commission are not credible. It then re-evaluates the details of the assassination including the pre- and post-assassination events to arrive at a logical conclusion as to who was really responsible. However, the reader should be advised that the most likely solution to the assassination and its mysteries may not be the most complex and may in fact be the most obvious.

With this in mind, a journey into the assassination maze should begin with these common sense questions:

Question One: Of all persons closest to President Kennedy, who was known to have despised him the most in the last years of Kennedy's life?

Question Two: Who planned and knew the details of President Kennedy's fatal Texas trip?

Question Three: Who gained the most by President Kennedy's death?

2

Basic Facts

Those who were living at the time of Kennedy's assassination probably vividly recall where they were at the exact time of his shooting. However, most people have only a general memory of the rest of the details of that weekend (except for the prime time televised execution of Lee Harvey Oswald). For this reason, an outline of what happened that weekend in the fall of 1963 will be recounted to supply a fresh memory of the events and avoid needless repetition in later chapters.

Prior to President Kennedy's murder on Friday, November 22, 1963, the President's trip had been under consideration for almost a year. By April 23, 1963 Vice President Johnson had already publicized the fact that President Kennedy was going to make a Texas trip. On June 5, 1963 the final decision to go to Texas and an outline of the trip plans was agreed upon in a meeting at the Cortez Hotel in Texas. The participants at the Cortez Hotel meeting were Vice President Lyndon B. Johnson, Texas Governor John B. Connally and President John F. Kennedy. It was initially proposed that the President go to Texas on Johnson's birthday in August. However, Connally objected. After discussion, the President agreed with Connally to make the trip later in the year.

By September of 1963 the trip had expanded from one day

to a several day affair. Once White House approval for the expanded visit was given, Connally suggested a Presidential motorcade through downtown Dallas. Governor Connally then set into motion plans for: the motorcade; arranged a luncheon date and place; a separate trip to Austin; and a visit to the LBJ ranch.

On October 4, 1963 Connally traveled to the White House to personally discuss more details of the trip and to confirm the plans with the President. According to sources, Kennedy's aides wanted him to avoid the trip entirely and Kennedy himself voiced some concern about making it but eventually agreed to go.

On the same day of the Washington visit, October 4, 1963, Lee Harvey Oswald returned to Dallas from Mexico even though he had no apparent employment prospects in Dallas.

On October 16, 1963 Oswald started his new job at the Texas School Book Depository in Dallas. He obtained his new job even though there were no advertised job openings. The Texas Book Depository had no official connection with the state, but it was the name given to an office/warehouse building where a number of book publishing companies were located. These book companies leased various spaces in the building to store books which were sold to Texas schools. Coincidentally the building location put Oswald on the direct path of the motorcade route that the Texas planners had suggested for Kennedy's Dallas parade.

On Monday, November 18, 1963, President Kennedy spoke to audiences in Tampa and Miami Beach, Florida. That same Monday in Dallas, Police Chief Jesse Curry drove U.S. Secret Service agents over the President's planned motorcade route for the first time. Chief Curry was in charge of the City of Dallas Police Department. The Dallas Police Department was to be in charge of crowd control for the President and jointly responsible with the Secret Service for his safety while in Dallas.

On Thursday, November 21, 1963, President Kennedy flew to Texas to begin the trip. Kennedy attended receptions in

San Antonio, Houston and Fort Worth and ended the day in Fort Worth at a hotel approximately 30 miles from Dallas. The trip was scheduled to continue to Dallas the next day. During that Thursday in a private conference President Kennedy and Vice President Johnson got into a heated dispute about some upcoming event on the trip. It was resolved to Kennedy's satisfaction.

Friday, November 22, 1963 was President Kennedy's last day alive. It began with Kennedy awakening in his 8th floor hotel suite and shortly thereafter attending a Chamber of Commerce breakfast. After breakfast the Presidential party went to the airport for a short flight to Love Field in Dallas. Air Force One touched down in Dallas at 11:37 a.m. (c.s.t.). The temperature was 76 degrees. A light morning rain had stopped bringing out a sunny day in Dallas.

The Presidential motorcade left Love Field at 11:50 a.m. and headed toward the planned motorcade parade route on its way to the Dallas Trademart for a planned luncheon. The lead car was driven by Dallas Police Chief Jesse Curry. Curry's car contained the local Sheriff and two Secret Service agents. Curry's car was to operate as the lead command post with the occupants scanning the crowds and buildings attempting to spot trouble. Immediately following the lead command car was President Kennedy, Mrs. Kennedy, Governor Connally, and Mrs. Connally sitting together in the open top Presidential limousine. The limousine also carried its driver and a Secret Service agent. Closely trailing the Presidential limousine were Secret Service agents in another car, followed further back by LBJ, Senator Ralph Yarborough and their wives in yet another car.

The motorcade proceeded down Main Street passing huge crowds standing on the sidewalks and waving from windows in high rise office buildings. At the intersection of Main and Houston streets the motorcade slowed to make a right turn onto Houston. It proceeded down Houston for one block and then made a slow wide turn angling onto Elm Street in front of the Texas School Book Depository. It then traveled towards a railroad underpass heading for the Stemmons Expressway.

After the motorcade made the turns and proceeded down Elm Street traveling away from the Texas School Book Depository it passed before a grassy knoll. Shots rang out. It was 12:30 p.m. Two shots struck President Kennedy and another shot struck Connally. The exact number of shots fired is still disputed since some witnesses heard three, others four, and others believed that even more than four were fired. One shot hit the President in the neck and another his skull, leaving brain matter splattered inside the limousine and on a trailing motorcycle policeman.

After the shootings the Presidential limousine raced to Parkland Memorial Hospital. President Kennedy and Governor Connally were rushed into Emergency Room One. The doctors took Kennedy to bay 13 where they attempted to revive him. At 1:00 p.m. (c.s.t.) President John Fitzgerald Kennedy was pronounced dead.

At approximately 1:13 p.m. Lyndon Johnson was informed of the President's death and the Secret Service transferred their full security attention to Johnson as the new head of the U.S. Government. Total confusion and fear existed. There were concerns about the beginning of a nuclear war as well as thoughts about a revolution to overthrow the government and wipe out its leaders. This caused the Secret Service agents to believe that Johnson might be the next target. The agents strenuously urged Johnson to leave the hospital, go to the airport and take off immediately. Although Johnson agreed with the Secret Service that he might be the next target and that perhaps "a worldwide conspiracy existed," he still refused to leave.

Dallas Police Chief Curry remained with the uninjured Lyndon Johnson at the hospital. When Johnson finally decided to leave the hospital, the Chief went along. When Johnson, Curry, and the Secret Service arrived at Love Field, the new President again refused to follow security advice. He refused to immediately get airborne and away from the troubled city. Rather, Johnson first delayed the departure by demanding that Kennedy's plane be commandeered and used for himself and insisted that his luggage be brought aboard. But when the transfer of luggage was completed, Johnson made another demand that delayed departure. He directed that he return to Washington with President Kennedy's body in his plane even though it could have been flown back later in another plane. After arrangements were made to carry out this order, Johnson issued another order necessitating further delay. He insisted on taking his Presidential Oath of Office on Texas soil contrary to all security advice and against the legal advice of Attorney General Robert Kennedy. Robert Kennedy told Johnson to get airborne as quickly as possible and to take the oath either in the air or in Washington.

After the presidential oath was completed, the local Dallas police, assorted citizens, and the news media were ushered off the plane. Johnson gave them instructions to see that photographs of his swearing in ceremony were immediately distributed to the world. After that last command on the ground, the new President shouted to the pilot "let her roll" and at 2:58 p.m. the plane headed for the White House with Johnson in the front and the dead President and his widow in the back.

At about this same time in Dallas, Oswald had been arrested (1:50 p.m.) and confined to jail by the Dallas police. Oswald's first attempt to reach a lawyer resulted in a 1500 mile telephone call to an attorney in New York City. When the lawyer could not be reached, Oswald was then interrogated without a lawyer for the next two days. Throughout these grillings and, in fact, during his entire incarceration Oswald repeatedly requested a lawyer and continually denied killing the President.

Late Friday evening November 22, 1963, while Kennedy's body was being dissected by doctors in Washington, the Dallas police exhibited Oswald at a silent "press conference".

The purpose for the exhibition has never been explained since it served absolutely no police purpose. Oswald's executioner, Jack Ruby, was at the "press conference" standing only a few feet from Oswald with a loaded gun in his pocket. However, Ruby did not open fire that night.

On Sunday, November 24, 1963, the transfer of Oswald from the Dallas City Jail to the County Jail was attempted. Police Chief Curry put himself in charge of the transfer arrangements. At 11:19 a.m., Oswald was led to the basement of the City Jail without the protection of a human police shield or any other protection to shield him from an assassination. He was taken from an elevator and shot in the presence of over 70 uniformed Dallas police officers, dozens of reporters, and a television audience of millions. Ruby shot Oswald once, firing into his abdomen. At 1:07 p.m. Oswald was pronounced dead at Parkland Hospital from internal bleeding. Within an hour of Oswald's death the Dallas police announced that the case was now "closed".

When the Dallas police "closed" the case, public suspicion opened, and demands were made that the case continue to be investigated until fully solved. Five days later, November 29, 1963, President Johnson created the Warren Commission, personally selected its members, and ordered that they report to him. The Commission evaluated the evidence and less than 60 days before the 1964 Presidential election, with Johnson seeking election as President, the Warren Commission issued its findings which were immediately made public.

The basic conclusions of the Warren Commission were: no conspiracy existed; Lee Harvey Oswald was the lone assassin; Jack Ruby killed Oswald out of empathy for the slain President and his family and for no other reason; and, the Commission was not able to discover a motive for Oswald's act.

Within weeks after the release of the Warren Report, President Johnson defeated Republican Senator Barry Goldwater for the Presidency. Johnson then served as an elected president for one term, choosing not to seek re-election. Johnson's decision of not running for re-election was strongly based upon his inability to control domestic violence, responsibility for the nation's division over the war in Vietnam, and public perception branding him as originator of the ''Credibility Gap'' caused by repeated public lies.

3

LBJ'S Power to Control

After a building is built the usual last work to be completed is the work by the clean up crew, to clean up the mess left behind. In parades and sporting events, maintenance crews are used solely for the job of clean up. Clean up crews are even used after military battles,[1] so the use of a clean up crew after an assassination should not be that unusual. A well planned assassination probably has a clean up crew standing by to tie up loose ends. "Clean up" and "cover up" are probably interchangeable when applied to criminal acts, since a good "clean up" is an effective "cover up".

A major problem in using a "clean up" crew after a crime is that if those involved in the "clean up" know the purpose they might talk. And, of course the more people in a clean up crew the more likely someone will talk. This is one of the strongest arguments advanced by those supporting the lone assassin theory in Kennedy's death, that no one could have directed all the people possibly involved to never talk about a cover up.

It is claimed without reasonable dispute, that if there was a government cover-up of a conspiracy relating to the assassi-

---

[1] Remove or bury the dead, salvage usable military hardware, and remove land mines.

nation, many individuals, government agencies, and government employees would have to have been involved. And, because after all of these years no one from the F.B.I., the CIA, the Secret Service, Army, Navy, or anywhere else has ever come forward with any credible evidence that a government conspiracy existed and was covered up, it can be reasoned that no clean up crew ever existed. However, the fact that no one has admitted being involved in a clean-up may not necessarily mean that one did not exist. Individuals or government departments may have unwittingly performed the role of a "clean up crew" by just following orders allegedly issued for national security purposes. They may have altered, destroyed, or even disposed of evidence without knowledge of the true purpose for their actions. By just following orders people may have unwittingly distorted the truth without knowing what the real truth was.

For example, one photograph of the assassination site showed a road sign that appeared to have been struck by a stray bullet. This was observed by the investigators and was even noted by Warren Commission staffers. This piece of evidence was of great importance because the existence of another stray bullet would prove that at least 4 shots were fired. Since it was impossible for Oswald to have fired four shots during the time Kennedy was within his possible target area, and the three shots Oswald allegedly fired were all accounted for, the road sign was evidence of a fourth bullet and it would have completely destroyed the lone gunman theory. It would have proved a conspiracy existed. It would have opened "Pandora's Box" as to who else was involved.

However, shortly after the assassination the road sign was removed and disappeared. Obviously the removal had to have been ordered by someone. Those involved in the actual removal of this potentially relevant evidence may not have known the purpose for what they were doing, they just did it. All that was required, was for one order or even a suggestion, made by one person with political power to seize all assassination evidence and to deliver it to one place and the "clean up" task would be accomplished.

Another example that such a "clean up" order had been issued in the Kennedy assassination by someone ·was the handling of the medical evidence relating to the Kennedy death. The doctors who attended the President at Parkland Memorial Hospital noted a small wound in John Kennedy's throat and a massive wound in the rear of his skull. The doctor who first treated Kennedy at Parkland Hospital drafted a hospital report describing Kennedy's throat wound as an entrance wound. This wound, caused by a bullet entering from the throat would have been strong evidence that Oswald did not act alone because it would have been impossible for Oswald to fire from that direction. The Dallas doctor who was in overall charge of Kennedy's care, and another doctor who actually pronounced JFK dead, both told the press at a post-treatment press conference that "there was an entrance wound below his [JFK's] Adam's apple". The medical opinions of these men had barely surfaced publicly when the Secret Service, under orders from someone, seized all tapes of the press conference and refused to release them.

Further evidence that a "clean up" order had somehow been issued is also demonstrated by the final autopsy procedure performed on the President at Bethesda Naval Hospital in Washington on the evening of his murder.

Three Washington, D.C. doctors, all military officers, were selected to perform the most important autopsy of the century. They were selected in spite of the fact that none were forensic pathologists, doctors who specialize in determining the cause and scientific basis of a traumatic death. The doctor placed in charge, Dr. James Humes, had taken only a single medical school course in forensic pathology. Yet, in spite of the lack of skill and the inexperience of the selected team, the doctors attempted to do their best to examine the deceased President's wounds. But when the doctors went to dissect Kennedy's throat wound, they were not permitted to do so. When the doctors made a request to examine Kennedy's clothes to look for bullet pathways, they were denied access to the clothes. When the doctors tried to track the bullet wounds in Kennedy's body to determine the exact path of the bullets, they were stopped. And, when the doctors wanted to study the photographs that their own staff had taken of Kennedy's wounds (10 to 15 in number), review their own x-rays (10 to 12), and inspect another roll of photographs taken by a medical corpsman assisting in the procedures, these materials were seized by the Secret Service even before they were developed. Even the original autopsy report by Dr. Humes was subsequently "rewritten" and the original was burned in a fireplace. And Dr. Humes was never allowed to explain his opinions nor describe the contents of his original burned autopsy report because he was "forbidden to talk".

It is clear that somehow an arrangement to seize and control evidence in the immediate post-assassination stage occurred. While the doctors, newsmen, and even the Secret Service, may later have had doubts about why they participated in these now apparent "cover up" actions, these later doubts, without proof as to what evidence actually existed and what it actually showed, would only be unsubstantiated opinions.

But the fact that a secret order, suggestion, or directive, was issued is obvious from the activities of Lyndon Johnson and his aides which took place immediately after the murder. For instance, Johnson's aide, Cliff Carter, for no discernible reason, sent Secret Service Agents to retrieve and launder John Connally's bloody and bullet ridden clothes destroying the usefulness of this evidence. On the evening of Kennedy's death and immediately upon returning to Washington, Johnson directed Carter to place three separate telephones calls: the first call was to Dallas District Attorney Henry Wade *ordering him not* to allege a conspiracy—whether "he could prove it or not" and to "just charge Oswald with plain murder." Wade charged Oswald alone with the murder. The second and third calls were to Dallas Police Chief Curry and Captain Fritz. Each man received similar telephone calls from Carter insisting that all local evidence be immediately turned over to the FBI in Washington (who had no jurisdiction in the case). Chief Curry later would only disclose that the order came from someone in "high authority in Washington". According to others, when people refused to obey Cliff Carter's orders, a follow up demand actually came via a personal telephone call from President Lyndon B. Johnson. The persuasion obviously worked because within less than 12 hours after Kennedy's murder all evidence collected in the case to that point was sent to Washington, D.C., including Oswald's gun and the "miracle bullet".

The sending of all the important evidence to Washington the night of the assassination and *after* Oswald was charged with the state crime of murder in a Texas court is another of the unsolved mysteries relating to events surrounding the assassination. Since Johnson and his aides demanded that Oswald alone should be solely charged with murder irrespective of the evidence, this type of charge was a state violation and not a federal crime. It would have resulted in a state court trial prosecuted with the evidence in the State of Texas. If it was really intended to prosecute Oswald in a Texas court, what good would the evidence do in Washington, D.C.? One suggested answer is that it was never part of the plan to let Oswald live long enough to be tried—at least that is what happened and the shipping of the evidence out Friday night at Lyndon Johnson's request is consistent with such a plan.

Other mysteries include questions about why President Kennedy's brain and microscopic tissue sections (that could remain helpful today in another autopsy) have turned up missing from the National Archives in Washington, D.C.? And what happened to Oswald's rifle? After the Commission completed its tests on Oswald's rifle, it was returned to Oswald's widow who sold it to a gun collector. There was no law to prevent the transaction, but suddenly, as the gun collector was about to take possession and perhaps independently test the weapon again, the federal government filed a "tax lien" on the weapon which delayed the transfer. Then Congress quickly passed a bill to retain the weapon in government hands, the bill was flown to Johnson at his ranch for his signature, and the federal government ended up retaining control of the evidence.

After President Kennedy was killed, the only person in the country with power to issue sweeping orders, obeyed without question, was the next President, Lyndon B. Johnson. Perhaps, as Johnson later claimed, his orders: to District Attorney Wade to charge Oswald only for the murder and not conspiracy regardless of the evidence; to Police Chief Curry to turn all evidence over to Washington (permitting him to control the evidence in advance of the Warren Commission); and to the Commission to "quell rumors of the most exaggerated kind", were actually for security purposes. But, whose security? Neither a war nor a civil uprising followed the assassination. It is reasonable to at least consider whether Lyndon Jonson's orders were made for his own security and protection.

4

The Commission's Report Cannot Be Trusted

Most of us alive in 1963 have some vague recollection of the "Warren Commission" and at the time probably believed that it was a prestigious impartial fact finding committee. That belief was wrong. The truth is the Warren Commission was a politically biased entity created solely by Lyndon Johnson in order to extricate himself from another political scandal, this one emerging as the worst of his career.

At the time of the assassination, the murder of a U.S. President was *not* covered by Federal law unless it involved conspiracy crossing state lines. Therefore, Texans, applying Texas law, had the exclusive jurisdiction to investigate the murder of John Kennedy as long as there was no evidence pointing to a conspiracy. Understanding this state of the law in 1963 is of critical importance to understanding why Texas officials, immediately after the assassination, insisted that the killing had to have been caused by a lone gunman. It also explains why Johnson's aide (Cliff Carter) was so adamant in demanding that Dallas District Attorney Henry Wade only charge Oswald with the murder, irrespective of whatever else he could prove.

As long as the single assassination position was taken and maintained, Texans had the legal right to control the assassination investigation and prosecute and jail any suspect. Because of the state of the law in 1963, if a group of Texans had conspired together to kill President Kennedy to help elevate Lyndon Johnson to the Presidency, as long as they arranged for a single assassin to appear to do the killing, it could become the perfect vehicle to hide their crime. "Texas justice" would then be in control and they all knew that they could control Texas justice.

However, things did not work out that way. The declaration on Sunday, November 24, 1963, by the Dallas Police Department that the case was now "closed" because the lone assassin was killed did not end the public outcry. Rather, it increased it. By Monday the groundswell of public demands for a complete investigation began to snowball and Lyndon Johnson faced a serious dilemma. To keep control of the case in Texas, the prospect of convening a Texas Grand Jury or initiating a Texas Court of Inquiry was publicly suggested. However, once again the public outcry against a Texas investigation was tremendous since there were strong suspicions about "Texas justice" producing a whitewash. While a Texas Grand Jury investigation may have been legal, it would have politically destroyed Johnson even before he started into his new presidency. Realizing this, but hoping to keep control of the matter in Texas while still appeasing the American public, Johnson came up with another alternative. He proposed a special Texas Commission to investigate the crime composed of distinguished Texans whom he personally would select. The public hostility to this proposal was even stronger.

As long as Texas officials maintained that a lone gunman murdered President Kennedy, then Texans had the exclusive legal right to investigate the case. But, Johnson quickly realized that the American public would not accept this without political retribution against him. On the other hand, things could be much worse. If a conspiracy to kill Kennedy was admitted as a possibility, or if the State of Texas abandoned its legal right to investigate the crime, then the Federal government, through the Attorney General's office, would gain control of the matter. The Attorney General was Robert Kennedy. He was the slain President's brother. Robert Kennedy and Lyndon Johnson hated each other. If the slain President's brother got control of the investigation there was no telling where it would lead or who might be indicted. Thus, Johnson knew that if Texans investigated the case he would be politically destroyed; but if Robert Kennedy got his hands on the investigation, Johnson or his friends might be criminally indicted.

Lyndon Johnson resolved this dilemma as only he could. Within less than a week after the assassination, after publicly losing out on all of his Texas investigation suggestions, Johnson created what became known as the "Warren Commission". It was not a Texas Commission composed of Texans and therefore public concerns about a whitewash were eased. It was also not a Justice Department investigation which kept the case away from Attorney General Robert Kennedy. The Commission was a hybrid. It was a federal investigative body independent of the Attorney General's office. This hybrid kept Johnson in control while still pacifying the public.

By Executive Order #11130 President Johnson created the "Warren Commission". However, issuing the Order creating the Commission was the easy part. Obtaining credible Commission members was a much harder task for Johnson. He first offered the Chairmanship position to Chief Justice Earl Warren of the United States Supreme Court. Warren flatly refused. But, as rumors began surfacing that the murder involved a conspiracy of Texans and after a private meeting with Johnson, Warren reluctantly agreed to serve. It was reported that as Warren left Johnson's office following the meeting when he agreed to serve, he had tears in his eyes.

Once he got Earl Warren to serve as Chairman, Johnson added ex-CIA Director Allan Dulles as one of the important "name" members. It should be noted that shortly prior to his death, President Kennedy had fired Dulles (or forced him to "resign") because of his agency's gross mishandling of the Bay of Pigs Invasion. Despite the potential personal hostility that Dulles may have had against Kennedy, Johnson put him on the Commission because of his "expertise" in CIA matters. But Johnson's real intent with this appointment may have been more biased. Dulles' conduct as a Commission member subsequently involved charges that he deliberately withheld important CIA information from the Commission. It was also reported that Dulles worked to influence the other Commission members as to the validity of the lone gunman theory.

Dulles started the lone gunman influencing effort at the very first Commission meeting. There he passed out booklets which claimed that all past Presidential assassinations were the result of crazed gunmen acting alone. It was also later learned that when the Commission was considering a Castro conspiracy to kill Kennedy, it concluded that it was not plausible, all while Dulles sat in silence knowing that there might be reason for concern. He said nothing about the possibility of a Cuban conspiracy theory when he knew that CIA agents under his direction repeatedly tried to kill Castro, that Castro knew of this, and had warned the CIA to stop. Obviously, silence was golden because the Commission's consideration of any conspiracy theory was dangerous and could have led anywhere.

The other members of the Commission were: Senator Richard B. Russell; Senator John S. Cooper; Congressman Hale Boggs; Congressman Gerald R. Ford; and John J. McCloy. While these men were political or public figures, they had no experience as criminal investigators, criminal jurists, or even interested evaluators. Some members did not even bother to show up. One member came only five times. Another made it to only 16 meetings. Out of the 51 sessions the Commission held to reach their conclusions, the majority of the members missed most of the meetings. This resulted in some of the staff becoming so disgusted with the Commission process that they quit. Other staffers, by memo, charged that the Commission was not adequately investigating any of the important issues. When the Commission ignored the memo, one of the staff lawyers quit in disgust.

The Commission spent days questioning non-important

IMMEDIATE RELEASE   **NOVEMBER 30, 1963**

Office of the White House Press Secretary

- -

THE WHITE HOUSE

EXECUTIVE ORDER
NO. 11130

- - - -

APPOINTING A COMMISSION TO REPORT UPON THE
ASSASSINATION OF PRESIDENT JOHN F. KENNEDY

Pursuant to the authority vested in me as President of the United States, I hereby appoint a Commission to ascertain, evaluate and report upon the facts relating to the assassination of the late President John F. Kennedy and the subsequent violent death of the man charged with the assassination. The Commission shall consist of --

The Chief Justice of the United States, Chairman;

Senator Richard B. Russell;

Senator John Sherman Cooper;

Congressman Hale Boggs;

Congressman Gerald R. Ford;

The Honorable Allen W. Dulles;

The Honorable John J. McCloy.

The purposes of the Commission are to examine the evidence developed by the Federal Bureau of Investigation and any additional evidence that may hereafter come to light or be uncovered by federal or state authorities; to make such further investigation as the Commission finds desirable; to evaluate all the facts and circumstances surrounding such assassination, including the subsequent violent death of the man charged with the assassination, and to report to me its findings and conclusions.

The Commission is empowered to prescribe its own procedures and to employ such assistants as it deems necessary.

Necessary expenses of the Commission may be paid from the "Emergency Fund for the President".

All Executive departments and agencies are directed to furnish the Commission with such facilities, services and cooperation as it may request from time to time.

                                        LYNDON B. JOHNSON

witnesses over unimportant details. It amassed thousands of pages of irrelevant documents. It was almost like the Commission's goal was to concentrate on the obtuse and ignore the important. For example, the Commission made no credible attempt to determine whether Oswald had in fact shot Kennedy. It started with the assumption that he did and it refused to deviate in spite of evidence to the contrary. When the Commission was unable to establish a motive for Oswald killing Kennedy, rather than explore other possible avenues, including other logical suspects with strong motives as an astute investigation team would do, the Commission chose not to proceed in this direction. Rather, it chose to determine that Oswald was ''a killer without a motive''. The Warren Commission did not look at the autopsy x-rays and photographs of Kennedy's body that had been seized. It chose instead to put this and other important evidence into a box under seal and then ordered that it not be released for public scrutiny until the year 2039.

Even though the Commission questioned 551 witnesses, it avoided questioning those whom any reasonable investigator might have considered to be logical criminal suspects. For instance, one of the principal witnesses ignored was Lyndon Johnson, despite the fact that Johnson, in a trailing car, was in fact a witness. He could have told the Commission what he saw and heard at the assassination site, but more importantly, he could have explained why he refused to leave the city. However, rather than question their creator about his involvement and thereby make an effort to quash the assassination rumors circulating about Johnson, the Commission chose to ignore the matter in its entirety.

The Commission members were well aware of the terrible undercurrent of rumors circulating about Lyndon Johnson's possible involvement in the assassination. As members of the criminal investigative body handling the most important crime of the century, and with a staff of professionals to counsel and advise them, they had to have been keenly aware that Johnson was technically a prime suspect. Yet, the Commission did not bother to interview him as a witness, nor take the time to have him supply a sworn statement. Instead, they merely accepted a short typewritten statement drafted by Johnson's lawyers for him. Why did this occur?

The painfully obvious answer is that if the Warren Commission could have easily and satisfactorily resolved and destroyed any possible allegation relating to Johnson's involvement in the murder, it would have aggressively done so. This is especially true when one considers that many Europeans, at the time, were publicly commenting about Johnson's potential involvement. Since the Commission avoided this issue and made no mention of Johnson's possible involvement, the only rational conclusion that can be drawn was that it was agreed by the members that complete avoidance of the issue would be better for America. The Commission members surely realized the repercussions that would result from attempting to investigate Johnson if the evidence that was uncovered even hinted of an internal political coup. This would not only have tarnished the American political system for decades, but, more importantly would have dishonored democracy throughout the world at a time when the "cold" war was "hot" in the battle of ideals in the world. Therefore, while the Warren Commission's public goal was to be a "servant of history", its unspoken credo had to have been preservation of the American political system above all else.

Years later, one of the conclusions reached by the Senate Intelligence Committee when re-investigating the assassination was that the White House exerted extreme political pressure on the Warren Commission to issue a report finding that Oswald was the lone assassin. Of course, the exertion of extreme pressure can bend the will of the most moral man, especially if he believes it helps in achieving a more altruistic national purpose.

For instance, when the Warren Commission finally got around to examining Jack Ruby in Texas, Chief Justice Earl Warren as the Commission's head actually told Ruby *not* to talk. A review of the transcript of the verbal exchange between the Chief Justice and Ruby reveals that Warren, as a lawyer, and more importantly as the Chief Justice of the American Court System, committed such a gross error in fundamental witness examination that his conduct had to have been a deliberate choice.

* * * *

Ruby: "Gentlemen, unless you get me to Washington, you can't get a fair shake out of me . . . unless you *get me to Washington, and I am not a crackpot*, I have all my senses—I don't want to avoid any crime I'm guilty of."

Ruby: "Gentlemen, *my life is in danger here.*"

Chief Justice Warren: *"I understand you completely. I understand what you are saying. If you don't think it wise to talk, that's okay."*

Ruby: *"No, I want to talk, I just can't talk here."* [Emphasis Added]

In this testimony, Jack Ruby said he would talk but that he could not talk while in Dallas because his life was in danger. He asked the Warren Commission to take control of him and take him to Washington where he could be protected and talk without danger. In response, the Chief Justice, who could have easily taken Ruby right out of his Dallas jail cell to Washington or anywhere else and questioned him in seclusion, chose instead to *warn Ruby not to talk*. And, of course Ruby was never taken to Washington by the Commission, never did talk, and died in jail under circumstances that some have characterized as suspicious.

Why would the Chief Justice, sworn to investigate the assassination and who had a culprit willing but too scared to talk, not take him to a place of safety to obtain the truth? The "excuse" supplied later to explain Warren's preposterous actions was that it was felt Ruby just wanted a free trip to Washington. So what! The Warren Commission spent millions allegedly attempting to discover the truth. In 1964 it would have cost the taxpayers about $150 more for a first class ticket to get Ruby out of Dallas. It would have cost nothing more if Ruby had been transported back to Washington on a government plane. But this cost supposedly outweighed the potential benefits of getting truth from the person who killed Oswald and may have been involved in more. Does this make sense?

Also lacking sense are the few exhibits that the Commission released for public dissemination since, for some reason, some were altered. For example, an important photograph of the assassination area taken by retired Air Force Major Philip L. Willis was deliberately cropped. Willis' crowd photograph of the assassination area included what appeared to be the face of Jack Ruby. However, Ruby (Oswald's assassin) claimed that he was not at the assassination site. The Commission therefore followed the logic that if the photographic evidence showed the apparent face of Ruby near the assassination site, but Ruby said he was not there, then the photograph was wrong and the evidence had to be "corrected" to present the "truth".

The Commission also misprinted the movie slides taken from the now famous Zapruder home movie showing the President as he was killed. The Commission's "error" involved photographic slides showing Kennedy's head position at the exact time of the slaying. The "error" made it appear as if Kennedy's head was going forward as he was shot, instead of backwards as the movie actually showed. This movie has always been a thorn in the side of those who claimed that Oswald was a lone assassin firing from the rear, because the movie showed his head going backward, not forward at the time of impact. When this switching of the slides was exposed, J. Edgar Hoover of the FBI explained that the Commission's missequence of slides was not deliberate, but was merely an accidental "printing error". Hoover, of course, had been Johnson's next door neighbor in Washington for over 20 years.

The best evidence that the Warren Commission never seriously tried to give the American people a clear picture of what happened is its own report. The first part of the report contains the Commission's conclusions. These twenty-five pages of conclusions are concise and readable. But the remainder of the 700 page report, which supposedly supplied the factual basis for the Commission's clear conclusions, is jumbled and disjointed. Almost one-half of the report consisted of 17 separate appendixes ranging on a variety of subjects and printed in very small type. The report jumps from topic to topic with numerous references to either the appendixes or to the 26 additional, nonattached volumes of the Commission's work (the 26 volumes were not released until after LBJ's 1964 Presidential victory).[2]

It was *not* an accident that the Warren Commission issued its report just before the 1964 Presidential election. Johnson ordered that it be completed by then. It was *not* by chance that the Commission began its report with its conclusions consisting of twenty-five pages of easy to read material. And, it was *not* coincidental that the remainder of the report was jumbled and disjointed. Few Americans have ever read a 700 page novel, let alone a detailed report. It was expected that the American public would not read beyond the initial simple conclusions and many would rely only on the brief newspaper accounts summarizing the report's simple conclusions. Because of the report's style with references to the appendixes and to the 26 nonattached (not released in 1964) volumes, it was obvious that it would take dedicated scholars years of work to analyze the report and reach other conclusions. Also, because of its release date and style, it was expected that any challenges to the report would at best involve technical and confusing arguments that only other researchers and historians

---

[2]If the reader desires to gain a true perspective of what the Warren Commission actually did, attempt to read the 700 plus page report in its entirety.

could understand. By that time it was presumed that if other opinions would be offered, it would be old news to a public who, long ago, had made up its mind from the "news accounts" summarizing the Commission's conclusions.

The Johnson strategy was brilliant! He offered Americans a simple conclusion by an esteemed group of men with a report that made things appear too complicated to fully understand. This strategy is not new. It is used every day across America by lawyers in courtrooms with tough cases (ones they probably cannot win). The strategy is to deliberately confuse issues and complicate matters before the jury, while at the same time offering a simple solution. It is hoped that the jury will believe that the actual issues are too complicated to grasp, but if they were smart enough to understand them, the solution would be the simple one that was offered.

Chief Justice Earl Warren was an astute lawyer and probably used the confusion strategy himself when he tried cases. In any event whether deliberate or not, Warren, as Johnson's appointee to head the Commission, let the investigation get so sidetracked and let the truth become so garbled that staff members not only left in disgust, but one of the seven Commission members refused to sign the final report unless and until a footnote of his own could be added. This demand was agreed to in order to obtain the dissenter's signature but the footnote was omitted from the final report.

The Warren Commission, appointed by Johnson, handed their report directly to him rather than to the public. The report absolved Johnson of all criminal suspicion and insured him of a presidential victory in the election five weeks later. To disseminate the "impartial" report quickly, Johnson had printers standing by ready to print the report the moment he got his hands on it. This resulted in a world record in book publishing by a printing of 700,000 copies of the 700 page report in just 80 hours. Johnson then made special arrangements to airlift the reports all over the world to make sure that everyone had a chance to read the opinions of his own Commission.

And, as should have been expected, Johnson had all of his other "political cards" in order, ready for the public release of the Warren Commission Report. The moment the Report was publicly released conjunctive press reports appeared with headlines proclaiming:

- **"Assassin Termed 'Alienated' From Reality"**

- **"British Papers Term Warren Report Honest"**

- **"Secret Service and FBI Receive Criticism"**

On top of this, on the exact same day, Johnson's strategists had the newspapers begin publishing a political series by President Johnson entitled "My Hope for America."

Even if one accepts the conclusions of the Warren Commission, there has never been an adequate explanation as to why Lyndon Johnson was allowed to:

- **create and appoint his own Commission to evaluate a crime in which he was a logical suspect;**

- **permit his Commission to exclude public review of almost all of the criminal evidence until the year 2039; and**

- **require the Commission investigators to report their conclusions directly to him, when he was one of the logical suspects.**

In ancient Greek times there was a mythical giant named Procrustes. According to legend, Procrustes sawed tall people's limbs off and stretched short people out of shape to fit persons of every size into a special bed. From this myth came the word "procrustean" meaning false factual arguments shaped to reach a predetermined conclusion. Like the mythical giant Procrustes, the Warren Commission appears to have chopped and stretched the facts to reach the conclusion that Oswald was a lone assassin and there was no conspiracy.

Could anyone have ever imagined that this would occur in our country? While John F. Kennedy may have received a Presidential funeral, he got far less than a pauper's inquest.

5

Why Political Assassinations Occur

Assassinations of prominent public leaders have occurred in all civilizations throughout history. These types of assassinations usually fit a pattern. For instance, assassinations to advance a political cause or foment a revolution to change a society, by necessity, must involve groups of people banding together to perform the assassination. In such cases, these groups always claim responsibility after the fact in order to rally support. This type of assassination involves a conspiracy with little or no effort to keep the conspiracy secret after the event.

However, when an assassination of a political leader is merely a power grab, the general pattern is different. While a change of political ideals may not be involved and although only one man often benefits, normally a conspiracy still has to exist. This is because it is rare for the person grabbing power to also be the same person who actually kills the leader. Though such a solo act may not be difficult to do, it must be done without public knowledge and with an alibi in order to protect against retribution from the public and the slain leader's supporters. Under these circumstances, a conspiracy with complete secrecy and surprise is necessary to accomplish the act, and ordinarily secrecy must at least be maintained for sometime thereafter in order to provide the new leader with time to maintain control and establish calm.

In the not so rare case, where an assassin acts alone, but not for a proclaimed purpose of advancing a different political ideology or to grab power, there still is usually a simple explanation (i.e. desire to go down in history as a martyr, known mental instability or an irrational desire for publicity). In these cases there is no conspiracy but almost always a motive, for the act is either publicly proclaimed by the assassin or readily apparent. Otherwise, the lone assassin's act served no purpose.

Under these historical assassination patterns, in all but those involving a "power grab", the assassins (or assassin) are quickly known because the motive for the assassination is publicly proclaimed or easily discernible. In fact, this pattern can even be demonstrated by a review of the assassinations and attempted assassinations of American Presidents. To date, there have been a total of six attempted and four successful assassinations of American presidents. Successful assassinations have led to the deaths of Presidents Lincoln, Garfield, McKinley and Kennedy. Unsuccessful attempts were made against Presidents Jackson, Truman, Theodore D. Roosevelt (as an ex-president), Franklin D. Roosevelt (as president-elect), Ford, and Reagan. In all but one of these ten instances the assassins either proclaimed the reason for their actions or it was easily discovered (i.e., enemy of the people, nationalism, fame, love for a movie star, etc.). In all but one case, the American public quickly learned of the motive for the act.

The one exception is the murder of President John F. Kennedy. In the Kennedy case the Warren Commission's findings that Lee Harvey Oswald was a lone assassin without a discernible motive fit neither the general historical pattern of assassinations designed to foment a political change nor the pattern of a lone assassin either seeking publicity or with an obvious motive. While President Kennedy's alleged killer was caught, the man's post-arrest actions and statements were not those of a political assassin of either type (political change or lone assassin). When arrested, Oswald made no confession and disclaimed, rather than claimed, responsibility. The post-arrest searches of his residence and property produced no evidence of any assassination plan nor motive. From arrest until death Oswald proclaimed his innocence. Further, even though the Warren Commission labelled Oswald a lone assassin, he exhibited no known hostility towards President Kennedy and was found by all, including members of the Commission, not to be mentally deranged. Apparently, he was simply a sane killer without a motive, rare in criminal annals, choosing as his first victim the President whom he admired. Reason and common sense should reveal that this scenario is at least questionable.

Unfortunately, Lee Harvey Oswald was eliminated before he could offer any solid help in solving the puzzle of why the President was killed by him or anyone else. His permanent silencing produced an assassination that has always remained a mystery. And, like all unsolved mysteries, various explanations have been offered as a solution. The thousands of articles and books that have been published offering solutions can be classified into seven basic theories relating to the assassination. Each of these classified assassination theories will be analyzed, applying the known facts and examining the benefit that may have been reaped by each suspect group to try to determine both a motive, and of course, opportunity. The basic theories are as follows:

- **The Lone Assassin**

- **The Communist Assassination**

- **The Vietnam Assassination**

- **The Conservative Assassination**

- **The Mob Assassination**

- **The CIA Assassination**

- **The Assassination of Governor Connally**

However, before proceeding further ground rules must be established. Acceptance of the Warren Commission's lone assassination conclusion rules out all possible conspiracy theories. This is because if Oswald acted alone there was no conspiracy. Conversely, if he did not act alone (or perhaps did not even act), then there had to be a conspiracy. And, if there was a conspiracy, then someone in the conspiracy had to have a motive because Oswald had none. As such, the first logical step in reinvestigating the crime involves analyzing the basis for the Warren Commission's conclusion that Oswald acted alone. If the Commission was right, then further investigation of conspiracy will not be necessary.

6

The Commission's Lone Assassin Theory

The principal proponent of the lone assassin theory to explain the murder of President Kennedy has always been the Warren Commission. It was created by an executive order of President Johnson transferring the investigation of President Kennedy's death to the Federal Government, but not to the normal judicial entity handling such matters, at the time controlled by Attorney General Robert Kennedy. The Commission was conceived and created by Johnson and it was required to report directly to him as the new President. Johnson ordered the Commission to be formed on November 29, 1963, only days after the slaying. Ten months later, on September 24, 1964, and immediately prior to the 1964 Presidential election, the Commission reached its conclusions and presented a written report to President Johnson. The report is now commonly known as "The Warren Report". The Warren Report was immediately made public by Johnson. It concluded that:

> **"On the basis of these findings, the Commission has concluded that Lee Harvey Oswald was the assassin of President Kennedy."**

The Warren Commission not only determined that Oswald was a lone assassin but that no conspiracy existed. While the

Commission identified Oswald as the lone assassin, it was unable to find any motive for Oswald to kill the President.

In 1964, when the Commission issued its conclusions, not many Americans believed them. This was partly because the Commission's credibility was questioned when its members began their assignment by refusing to use independent investigators and when it chose to conduct only closed hearings for fear that the public might prematurely reach mistaken conclusions. The final blow to the Commission's credibility came with its decision to seal much of the important evidence from public review until the year 2039.

However, ignoring the issues affecting its credibility, the Warren Commission's conclusion that Oswald was a lone assassin was clearly wrong based upon the publicly known evidence. The Commission's error is based upon a multitude of reasons with each reason being significant enough, by itself, to discredit its final conclusion.

First, the alleged murder weapon, the rifle that Oswald supposedly used, was not mechanically capable of being an assassination weapon. The Commission claimed that Oswald killed Kennedy with a Mannlicher-Carcano rifle. This type of rifle was manufactured in Italy during World War II and was based on a rifle design from the previous century (1891). In the 1960's surplus rifles of this type were sold in bulk quantities for less than $3.00 each. The construction of Mannlicher-Carcano rifles was so poor that the rifles were known to often blow up in the shooter's face. Mannlicher-Carcano rifles were bolt action, meaning that for *each* bullet fired: the bolt lever had to be pushed forward; the bolt handle had to be closed down; the weapon had to be fired; the bolt handle drawn upward; the bolt handle drawn backward; the shell casing ejected; the bolt handle pushed forward; and then the bolt handle pushed downward as another bullet was raised into the chamber. The Mannlicher-Carcano rifle was never considered to be a sharpshooter's weapon (not even in 1891 when it was first made). Rather, it was designed and manufactured en masse for the sole purpose of supplying each Italian Army foot soldier with some type of weapon. Yet, this crude weapon allegedly was capable of precisely killing President Kennedy when fired from a window ledge six stories in the air, at a distance of around 250 feet, at a moving target.

Oswald purchased the weapon by mail for $21.45 (scope and postage included). When the rifle was discovered immediately after the assassination, it was found to be in such a state of disrepair that the Commission's own firearm experts refused to operate the rifle's bolt action during practice sessions for fear of breaking the firing pin and being injured. Even from the Commission's description of the rifle, it would not seem reasonable that Oswald would choose such a weapon if he was serious about intending to assassinate President Kennedy. The alleged choice and use of the Mannlicher-Carcano rifle, one of the poorest made rifles in this century, by itself should have been enough to prove that Oswald, using such a weapon, could not have been a lone assassin, much less an assassin at all.

Further, referring to the Mannlicher-Carcano rifle but concentrating only on the rifle's telescope, the Warren Commission conceded, "The rifle bore a *very inexpensive* . . . sight".[3] Thus, the crude surplus rifle bore a cheap plastic scope that was extremely necessary for zeroing in on distant targets. The scope retailed separately for only $6.17. It magnified images only up to 4 times their actual size and when tested by the Commission, the cheap rifle with its plastic scope created a shooting defect that made all shots go high and to the right, completely missing any target sighted through the scope. While the Warren Commission conceded these indisputable facts, it developed a strange theory that the defective rifle and scope actually helped Oswald obtain greater accuracy. In essence, the Commission claimed that Oswald skillfully compensated for the defects by altering his shooting style to take advantage of the rifle's defects. Logic, evidence, and common sense dictate otherwise.

[3] Emphasis added.

When the Commission gave the defective weapon and scope to world class marksmen to test it for accuracy, none of the top professionals were capable of accurately hitting anything. And, this occurred *after* the Commission let its experts rebuild the rifle scope, correct the rifle's sighting and alignment defects, and then fire it with aid of a professional gun rest. With all of these additional aids and corrections that Oswald did not have, none of the top test marksmen were capable of accurately hitting even a fixed target. The Commission therefore scientifically proved that it was not possible for world class riflemen using the same rifle and scope as Oswald allegedly had used, but rebuilt for their benefit, to accurately hit a fixed target (let alone a moving one). Again, common sense should have told the Commission that Oswald could not possibly have been the appointed assassin.

The Commission also never tried to explain why Oswald, an intelligent ex-Marine, did not merely purchase a quality hunting rifle and scope designed to accurately hit a target, when such a weapon was readily available at any sporting goods store, or for the budget conscious, could have been purchased second hand from any newspaper want ad section. Common sense should have told the Commission that any assassin serious about causing great harm to the President would not have purchased a weapon with the accuracy equivalent to a good B-B gun and costing about as much. This was not rational and Oswald was not an irrational person.

A fourth mystery that detracts from the Commission's conclusion that Oswald was a lone assassin was the Commission's reference to Oswald's attempt to shoot Major General Edwin Walker with the same weapon. It was publicly reported that six months before the assassination, on April 10, 1963, Oswald attempted to shoot Major General Edwin Walker in Texas. At the time of the attempt, Walker was sitting stationary at a desk, and Oswald was reported to have been only 30 to 40 feet away, using a fence as a gun rest. With the target at close range, with no time constraints requiring rapid firing, with a stationary target to shoot at, and with a solid gun rest

. . . Oswald fired and completely missed! The Commission's purpose for including this event in its report was not to emphasize Oswald's failure to hit a target at close range. Rather, the Commission's obvious purpose was to try to show that Oswald was a "nut" who took pot shots at people. However, its reference to this incident also proves that Oswald's weapon or his skill was so poor that just months before the assassination he was incapable of hitting a stationary target from a close distance (or that he never intended to hit Walker in the first place as will be discussed later).

Oswald's known shooting skill or lack thereof, also brings into serious question the Commission's conclusion about Oswald acting alone. The Commission placed great emphasis on Oswald's Marine Corps' certificates for shooting. However, Marine Corps' boot camp shooting labels such as "expert" are mere puffery and are awarded to the bulk of recruits to instill confidence in their own shooting ability in the event of combat.[4] Casting military labels on shooting expertise aside, one of the Commission's marksmen conceded that Oswald finished his military shooting career with a score only 1 point above the minimum qualification level needed to achieve the lowest scaled rating. This put Oswald in the class of a "rather poor shot." A fellow Marine recalled that Oswald regularly got the rifle range "award" for the poorest shoot. At the *very best*, Oswald had only below average skill in firing a rifle accurately.

And yet the Commission concluded that a man who was a "rather poor shot," on the assassination day, using a cheap rifle accurately shot and killed the President at long distance (177 to 266 feet), in a moving limousine, and with only his head and shoulders exposed as the target. All this was done from an alleged position on the sixth floor of the Texas School Book Depository, only seconds after Kennedy's vehicle reappeared from behind blocking tree branches and as it moved

---

[4]However, even Oswald's military labels and rifle range scores demonstrated that at best he had a shooting skill on the very low levels of average.

down the street and away from Oswald. Oswald not only had to look through the trees, sight in on a moving head, but adjust his aim for the weapon's defects, and then fire the bolt action rifle rapidly and accurately.

A fifth item is the report by the House Assassination Committee after reopening the investigations on the executions of President Kennedy and Dr. Martin Luther King in the following decade. The Committee in its segment of re-evaluating JFK's death concluded that a conspiracy existed. Much of this conclusion was based upon a new piece of evidence found in the Dallas Police Department. The new evidence was an audiotape belt that contained a motorcycle policeman's microphone transmissions of the noises occurring at the time of the assassination. The House Committee had the tape scientifically analyzed and to a 95% certainty, the expert tape analyzer determined that the tape contained the sounds of at least 4 (not 3) gunshots. If at least 4 gunshots occurred Lee Harvey Oswald could not possibly have been a lone assassin. This was because the Warren Commission proved that it was impossible for Oswald or any other lone individual to have fired 4 or more shots within the requisite time from Oswald's bolt action rifle. Therefore, if one believed the House Committee's tested results or other substantial physical evidence and eyewitness accounts that demonstrated the existence of 4 or more shots, then Oswald could not have been a lone assassin.

While the Commission went to desperate lengths to "prove that Oswald killed Kennedy with the Mannlicher-Carcano rifle" it in fact proved the contrary. On November 27, 1963 the F.B.I. conducted the initial series of rifle tests with the alleged assassination weapon. As part of the tests the F.B.I. determined that because Kennedy was moving away in the limousine Oswald had at most 5.6 seconds to fire the three shots that allegedly killed him. This time range conclusion was based on observations from Oswald's alleged vantage point on the southwest corner of the 6th floor in the Texas School Book Depository in comparison to films and photographs of the murder. It was established that Oswald's vision of the target was blocked for a time by a large tree. As a result, while the motorcade did travel for almost a full block on Elm Street in front of Oswald, from Oswald's position it was agreed that he had less than 6 full seconds to fire the three shots at the target when it was in view. To prove that this was possible and that Oswald was the lone assassin, the F.B.I. started out by having three master marksmen using Oswald's rifle rapidly fire a series of 3 shots at stationary targets located only 45 feet away. The three experts each fired 3 shots within 9 seconds, 8 seconds and 6 seconds, respectively. In this test none of the marksmen were physically capable of firing the three rounds within the 5.6 second requirement. Also, not surprisingly, all of the marksmen's shots were high and to the right, missing the stationary targets located only 45 feet away.

Because these tests did not support the lone assassin conclusion, the F.B.I. was required to conduct another test on March 16, 1964. However, on this occasion only the best of the three original marksmen was used (Robert Frazier with a previous best time of 6 seconds). In this test Frazier was required to fire a series of 3 shots at a stationary target 300 feet away. On this occasion Frazier's times for each of the 3 shot test series were 5.9 seconds, 6.2 seconds, and 6.5 seconds. Again, the expert failed to match Oswald's alleged time of 5.6 seconds, and again all of the shots were high and to the right of the intended target. Thus, "the best of the best" marksmen still could not help the Commission support the lone assassin theory.

Not giving up, on March 27, 1964 a third test was arranged. This test was conducted by the U.S. Army Ballistic Research Laboratory using three new marksmen again firing at stationary targets. Again, only one of the three experts was capable of firing three shots close to the required time limit. However, continuing its efforts to "prove" the impossible was possible, the Commission allowed the new marksmen to use a gun rest, and to take as much time as they needed to line up their first shot at the stationary target (which Oswald could not do because the Kennedy limousine was emerging from trees). But even with these altered test conditions the marksmen again failed.

Ignoring the three scientific tests which proved that it was impossible for Oswald to have been a lone assassin, the Commission solved the problem on paper rather than on the rifle range. First, the Commission decided to ignore the large oak tree that blocked much of Oswald's view of the motorcade while it was on Elm Street. In doing this, the Commission expanded on paper the time in which Oswald had to fire the 3 shots (from the original maximum of 5.6 seconds based on actual view) to a new time range of 7.1 to 7.9 seconds. This now enabled the Commission to claim that its test results proved it was humanly possible for someone to fire 3 shots in the time that Oswald allegedly had.

The Commission then, rather than accept the test results of the failures to accurately hit the stationary targets, chose instead to rely on the opinion of one of its expert witnesses who claimed that from Oswald's position shooting Kennedy would have been an "easy shot". To bolster this unsupported opinion the Commission then selected extracts from its rifle tests to "prove" that "sometimes" its marksmen with no time constraints were capable of hitting a fixed target at the assumed distance with the rebuilt Mannlicher-Carcano rifle.

The Commission also conducted another test to allegedly prove that its single assassin conclusion was credible. The Commission actually set out to reenact the Kennedy assassination scene in Dallas to "prove" exactly how, and when, Oswald killed President Kennedy. To conduct this test the Commission placed a cameraman in Oswald's presumed location in the southeast corner of the Texas Book Depository with a movie camera attached to a telescopic sight on Oswald's rifle. It then had a Cadillac convertible drive the final stage of the motorcade route with the rifle camera recording the observations through the rifle's sight. To portray even more accuracy, a ground camera also recorded the reenactment from the same location where an eye witness had stood during the assassination taking a home movie of the event. The reenactment route, telescopic sighted movie through Oswald's rifle, and ground camera movie were then compared frame by frame to the actual home movie of the assassination. The Commission was then able to look at the movie taken through the rifle camera in order to determine exactly what Oswald supposedly was able to see during the assassination.

While the Commission's attempt to reenact the assassination was laudable, its execution was skewed. The Commission chose *not* to use the Presidential Lincoln Continental "death vehicle". Instead it used a Cadillac limousine that had been used by trailing Secret Service Agents. It did this despite the fact that there were significant differences between the two vehicles. For example, based on the Continental's design anyone sitting in the Continental would have sat much lower to the ground than in the Cadillac (especially in the rear). Further, the rear passengers in the Continental had a large portion of their upper torso blocked from a rear view by the trunk because they sat lower in the car. For anyone sitting in the Cadillac, because of its rear seat design, much more of the torso and shoulders were exposed. The significance is that when Kennedy was shot sitting in the Continental, he presented a much smaller silhouette than the reenactment model in the Cadillac. As a result, less of the President's head and shoulders were exposed to a bullet from the rear than what the Commission portrayed in its test and the resulting test photographs. Unlike the test, Oswald at best had only a clear shot at Kennedy's head.

In addition to running the reenactment with a model sitting head and shoulders above Kennedy's actual position in the Continental (thereby also changing the calculated angle of fire), the Commission did not include in its reenactment the trailing security car that was following the Presidential limousine by a few feet in the motorcade. During the motorcade the trailing security car held four security men who were standing on elevated running panels on both sides of the car and two agents sitting on top of the rear seats to such a height that they were protruding above the car's windshield. According to rough calculations, if the trailing vehicle was two feet or less behind the Presidential limousine at the exact time of the shots, the security men would have completely blocked Kennedy from any sixth floor rear shot by Oswald.[5] However, this close distance did not happen and it is not critical in evaluating what the Commission actually did.

The point to be learned is that during the actual assassination the agents in the trailing car at least partially shielded Kennedy from an elevated rear attack. Thus, not only did Oswald have to telescopically sight and shoot at President Kennedy as his car emerged from behind tree branches, but he also had to contend with the visual impairment of a close trailing car containing Secret Service Agents who were at least partially obstructing the entire bottom region of his plastic sight. When one looks at any photograph of the Warren Commission's reenactment, it must be remembered that the reenactment is distorted and one must imagine that President Kennedy was actually sitting much lower in his car than shown, and that at the base of the telescope sight were obstructing figures of Secret Service men in the trailing vehicle.

It should also be noted that the Commission's reenactment test used a higher angle of fire than Oswald could have had from the sixth floor. Therefore, both the tree branches and the trailing Secret Service Agents would have hampered his view even more at the time of firing than portrayed in the reenactment.

All of this again shows that the Commission tailored the

---

[5] Kennedy sat in a vehicle whose sides were approximately 34″ off the ground. Initially his shoulders were approximately 2″–3″ exposed as well as his head by 10″–12″. Maximum height of the exposed President was 49″. The Security Agents at 6′ tall stood 12″–14″ off the pavement on the running boards. With the limousine trunk extending less than 5′ and the Agents standing less than 6′ from the front of the Cadillac all shots from a 24 degree angle (the angle attributed to Oswald's sixth floor vantage point) and below would have been blocked at a trailing car distance of 24″ or less.

known facts to fit its theories. It concluded that its own photographic evidence of the actual sniper's nest, which showed the height and location of the boxes used for the gun rest, was wrong and had to be "corrected" for its reenactment (Commission Exhibit No. 1301). For its reenactment, it then changed the known height of the gun rest to a higher point which most certainly also changed the angle of fire significantly enough to eliminate more of the blocking tree branches.

While the Warren Commission probably spent tens of thousands of dollars and hundreds of man hours on its reenactment, the only principle that it proved was that educated men are not always wise men. This is because it is clear that the Commission with all of its experts failed to use common sense. No one disputes that the actual location of the assassination occurred beyond the Texas School Book Depository, and therefore beyond Oswald's alleged assassination post. Thus, the Presidential limousine traveled for an entire block down Houston Street all the while facing Oswald's alleged sniper post. No shots were fired during this period. And, as the limousine was at its slowest point, making a slow left turn onto Elm Street . . . directly in front of the alleged sniper post . . . no shots were fired. Rather, Oswald as an assassin desiring to kill the President, supposedly passed up all opportunities of shorter range shots at his clear unimpeded target in favor of waiting for the target to get further down the street, away from him, and to attempt his first shot as Kennedy's figure in the limousine blindly emerged from blocking trees and in front of blocking Secret Service Agents.

This makes absolutely no sense. But these are the absolute undisputed facts. The photograph and diagram of the assassination scene depicted as Diagram 6:1 (in the photo section) clearly shows that the actual assassination firing pattern in relation to Oswald's alleged 6th floor position is ludicrous.

Perhaps the most compelling reason why Oswald was not a lone assassin was his lack of a motive. Oswald understood the American political system and realized that the death of John F. Kennedy would not change anything since Johnson, being of the same political party, would merely replace him. Oswald stated this to his captors after his arrest. And, there was also no evidence that Oswald wanted any political change at all, much less from Kennedy to Johnson. Before his arrest, Oswald publicly proclaimed on numerous occasions his great admiration for President Kennedy. He was especially pleased with the progress Kennedy had been making to achieve an end to the Cold War and his position on civil rights.

From the time of his arrest until his death, Lee Harvey Oswald spent much of his remaining life being interrogated, repeatedly denying his guilt and strongly proclaiming his innocence. In spite of this, the Warren Commission "gave little weight to Oswald's denials of guilt." It completely ignored Oswald's claims such as:

> *"I am a patsy."*

> *   *   *   *

> *"I am not a malcontent; nothing irritated me about the President."*

> *   *   *   *

> *"I have nothing against President John F. Kennedy. . . ."*

Can any reasonable person truly believe that Oswald, without any motive, acted alone, using a cheap rifle with a plastic telescopic sight to kill the President, when skilled marksmen using the same weapon under ideal conditions could not even accurately hit a stationary target? If there is at least a lingering doubt, then "Pandora's Box" is opened and the only alternative is to consider a conspiracy theory of some type.

7

Analysis of Popular Assassination Theories

Numerous books, magazine articles, newspaper accounts, and even radio and television discussions rejecting the Warren Commission's lone assassination conclusion and advancing various conspiracy theories as an explanation for the Kennedy murder have been offered. They all basically boil down to six different assassination theories with each involving a different responsible group or different objective. However, when each of the theories is examined in the context of the undisputed facts presently known, few actually offer a reasonable explanation for the assassination.

This chapter will briefly discuss each of these theories and examine why it is or is not a reasonable explanation.

THE COMMUNIST ASSASSINATION THEORY

If there ever was support for the adage "Don't jump to conclusions," the Communist assassination theory is the perfect example. The theory is simple, our Communist enemies killed President Kennedy. The theory is supported by some evidence such as: Oswald leaving America to live in Russia; returning to the United States and creating a public incident in New Orleans over support for Castro; and, then just months before his death, causing a disturbance in the Cuban Embassy in Mexico City. This theory easily allowed Americans to find a motive for the murder: the Communists hate us; Oswald was a communist; Oswald did it; therefore, Communists were involved in JFK's death. But, the Communist assassination theory, while elementary and easy to accept, lacks merit. It is based on the emotions of suspicion, hate and fear. Although the theory had to be the creation of a political hack, it was, for a long time in the early 1960's, one of the most popular accepted conspiracy theories.

One of the strongest proponents of the Communist assassination theory was Lyndon B. Johnson. As the succeeding President, Johnson as a "man in the know" had off the record discussions with the press advancing this theory knowing full well that rumors about his discussions would publicly surface. Johnson claimed to the press that Castro probably killed Kennedy in retribution "because Kennedy had been trying to kill Castro."

In order to properly evaluate Johnson's private claim that the assassination involved the Communists, one first has to divide communists into three separate factions: the "Russians"; the Cubans; and, the domestic Communists. Added to this division must be a short review of Lee Harvey Oswald's past—he never claimed to be a "Communist", rather he claimed to be a "Socialist". In fact, Oswald spent a great part of his short adult life (even on the day of his death) repeatedly attempting to explain to whomever would listen that he was not a Communist, but rather a Socialist. And, while Oswald left the United States to experience life in Communist Russia, he quickly became disenchanted with the Communist system and tried to return to America, finally accomplishing his return in 1962.

The "Russian" Communists

Before 1963 the United States and the Soviets were engaged in a "cold war". The Berlin wall had been built, the U.S. had stopped Soviet-made warheads from entering Cuba (the Cuban Missile Crisis), the nuclear arms race was increasing, Americans in fear of war were storing canned foods in converted basement "fallout shelters", and Khrushchev, the leader of the USSR, after making threats had taken off his shoe and pounded it on the table before the United Nations for emphasis. However, by 1963 the Cold War was ending. Both sides began to develop a working relationship and East-West trade was opening up. By the Spring of 1963 Great Britain, which had barred imports of Soviet oil, was considering lifting the embargo. Also, by 1963 the West Germans, who had their major city divided by the Berlin wall, were proposing to sell the Soviets 163,000 tons of badly needed steel pipe.

Beginning in 1963, America, under the leadership of President Kennedy, initiated a "pause in the Cold War" with the Soviets and was preparing for a "time for change." For the first time ever the leaders of the two major world powers established a direct "hot-line" between the White House and the Kremlin. The leaders were not only talking but had instant access to each other. By the summer of 1963 the long hoped for Nuclear Test Ban Treaty was signed by the superpowers. The treaty was the first in history between the two strongest countries in the world reaching an accord relating to weapons. The treaty was overwhelmingly ratified by a euphoric U.S. Senate less than 60 days before the President's death.

While President Kennedy had initially been criticized by the media for his peace overtures, his international successes were so monumental that even his original critics reversed themselves and admitted their error. And, by the summer of 1963 when the President made a European trip to promote the new relationship with the Kremlin, the Soviets as a gesture of good faith stopped jamming the radio free broadcasts into the USSR. They allowed a full printing of Kennedy's speech in Russian papers. In the fall of 1963, Kennedy and Khrushchev began to exchange secret letters on important subjects. When John F. Kennedy flew into Dallas on November 22, 1963, some Dallas conservatives who were friends of LBJ, actually objected to Kennedy's peace acts to the extent that they "greeted" him with handbills and a full page Dallas newspaper ad labeling him as a communist liberal who was "wanted for treason".

From this factual standpoint it is hard to rationalize why any "Russian" communist wanted Kennedy killed. An acceptable working relationship had finally developed between the leaders of the two countries. At last the Soviet Union was obtaining imported goods that had not been available because of embargoes. In fact, from the USSR's standpoint Khrushchev saw Kennedy as a "weak leader who could be pushed around." For the Soviets to risk killing America's leader under these circumstances would have been foolhardy. After the slaying when facts about Oswald's stay in Russia surfaced, the Kremlin not only denied any involvement with the assassination, but brought forth additional facts to prove that they had tried to kick Oswald out of Russia.

Proof of innocence is further confirmed by all subsequent events. Following the assassination the Soviets did nothing! No one was attacked, our shores were not invaded and missile shipments into Cuba did not resume. The Soviet Union did absolutely nothing to anyone, anywhere. In all likelihood, they were as frightened as we were, and their inaction only makes sense if they were innocent.

Surely, if the Russian communists had wanted to murder Jack Kennedy they would not have used a man (Oswald) who had direct ties to their country (and they also would have used a man who owned a better rifle and could shoot better). Therefore, the Russian Communists did not kill our President, who himself was labeled as a communist and who had been helping the Soviet economy.

The Cuban Communists

By 1963 Fidel Castro's revolutionary forces had controlled and ruled Cuba for several years. However, because of its communist form of government Cuba was the subject of trade embargoes by most of the other North and South American countries. As a result of such embargoes, the loss of foreign business interests, the fleeing of the wealthy and educated Cubans to other lands, and the Cuban economy destroyed from years of civil war—the island was barren. Cuba's only ally at the time was the Soviet Union.

The Soviet Union supplied Cuba with significant economic aid including food and weapons. It trained Cuba's soldiers and educated Cuba's military elite in its own military schools. In 1961, 1962, and more importantly in 1963, Cuba was a Soviet satellite completely dependent on its eastern ally. Cuba obeyed the USSR with the Kremlin directly dictating orders to Castro. Castro's Cuba was so dependent upon the Soviets that even the issuance of visitation visas to foreigners to visit Cuba was subject to Soviet review and approval.

While it is true that Castro despised America and its free market democratic system, if one ignores the subjective evaluations as to the righteousness of one country's political system over another, Fidel Castro actually had plenty to complain about. He believed it was American business and Cuban elitists who initially impoverished the Cuban people. And it was American aid and American arms that helped oppose his revolution. Later, after Castro's successful revolution, it was American influence that caused the establishment of trade embargoes against Cuba which drastically harmed the economy. Worse yet, it was American backed Cuban exiles who re-stormed Cuba in 1961 to try to recapture Cuba in the infamous Bay of Pigs Invasion. Therefore, it was perfectly natural for Castro to become upset when he discovered that the CIA was repeatedly trying to kill him. If one stood in Castro's shoes it would be easy to see why he hated America. However, there are at least *four* excellent reasons which explain why Castro and his countrymen were innocent of murdering our President.

One, since Cuba at the time was a totally dependent pawn of the Soviet Union, for Fidel Castro to organize an assassination attempt of President John Kennedy, he would have needed Soviet approval. For reasons set forth above, Soviet approval in 1963 of a Cuban retribution assassination of Kennedy would not have been allowed. It would have jeopardized the Soviet Union's newly acquired ability to purchase free world goods. Since the economic survival of the Soviet Union would have been at risk, it is not reasonable to believe that the Kremlin would have permitted the act.

Two, if Castro had acted on his own without Soviet consent he would have risked destruction from either, or both, superpowers. If the Kremlin had discovered Castro's plan, it would have probably "eliminated" Castro and may have stopped being Cuba's benefactor. This would have destroyed Castro's Cuba within weeks. And, of course, if America located only 70 miles from Cuba's shores ever unraveled such a Cuban assassination involvement, the entire island nation would have been destroyed by U.S. military action. While many people have disagreed with Castro and his principles, no one has ever claimed that he was a mad dictator. Rather, in spite of extreme economic difficulties, most political scientists have marveled at how shrewd Castro has been enabling him to stay in power for over three decades. There is no doubt that Fidel Castro was smart enough to realize that his problems with the U.S. were his own problems which he would have to endure. If Kennedy was not a problem to Castro's Soviet benefactors, then Castro's problems with America and its leaders had to be ignored to maintain continued Soviet aid to the island.

The third basic reason to conclude that Castro's Cuba was not involved in the assassination was Oswald's direct contacts with Cuba. While this may initially appear to be a peculiar reason, it should be noted that Lee Harvey Oswald, until only a few months of his death, demonstrated no significant interest in Cuba. However, what is known is that in the summer of

1963, Oswald began a brief *unilateral* association with Cuba which created public notoriety. Interestingly, after this brief episode of public attention connecting Oswald to Cuba—Oswald completely stopped his public campaign. From beginning to end this short period of frenzied pro-Castro activities lasted only 12 days (8/9/63–8/21/63). Then Oswald stopped! Oswald came out of nowhere and for a brief moment created a substantial amount of publicity for his apparent Cuban connection.

While it is true that Oswald later appeared on September 27, 1963 at both the Cuban and Russian Embassies in Mexico City to contact communist officials—these actions were also publicly focused for attention and again one sided. In fact, the Communist officials at both embassies refused to have anything to do with him. When he reappeared back at the Cuban Embassy to create another public disturbance, the Cuban counsel flatly told Oswald that it was his type who was harming the Cuban Revolution. These publicity stunts "created a public record" of an Oswald-Cuban connection. But it is extremely doubtful that if Castro had intended to kill Kennedy he would have used a man like Oswald who had deliberately and publicly created a known and traceable connection with Cuba only months before the assassination.

A fourth reason for Cuba's lack of involvement are President Lyndon Johnson's subsequent acts. Although he made allegations of Cuba's involvement in the assassination to the press, he continued using the CIA to try to kill Castro. Johnson either was so brave that he had no concern for another retribution killing by Castro, or he knew that his finger-pointing claim against Castro was untrue and he was in no danger at all.

The Domestic Communists

Since ultra conservative Americans in 1963 branded President John F. Kennedy not only as a liberal but also as a communist, the American communists, as a tiny minority political group, would have had no reason to want to see him dead. Further, following the purge of domestic Communists after McCarthyism in the 1950's, the government not only kept close tabs on them, but regularly infiltrated their organizations. Aside from a lack of motive to kill Kennedy, any domestic communist plan to kill Kennedy probably would have been known within hours of its formation. No evidence has ever surfaced even tangentially linking any domestic Communist group to the murder.

THE VIETNAM ASSASSINATION THEORY

Lyndon Johnson was excellent at pointing fingers when it came to blaming someone else for the slaying of President John F. Kennedy. When Johnson's Communist assassination theory (i.e. "it was Castro") began falling apart, Johnson turned his finger of blame to Vietnam with another assassination theory. However, not one shred of evidence has ever surfaced to support this Johnson claim. In fact, the only support for the Vietnam assassination theory came from Johnson. Again as the president and as "a man in the know", LBJ, in another "off the record" discussion with the press blamed South Vietnam rather than Castro. He stated that Kennedy's murder may well have been "some kind of terrible retribution" by the South Vietnamese. However, by the time LBJ began floating these rumors, his credibility had already been seriously diminished, and few journalists ever accepted this theory as anything other than decoy bait.

It is true that on November 1, 1963, President Diem of South Vietnam was assassinated. His murder, only 21 days before John F. Kennedy's death, was widely believed to be the result of American CIA activity, and many also believed Kennedy may have allowed it to occur. However, other than these known facts Johnson's theory has never had any rational or factual basis.

For one thing, LBJ's theory would have had the South Vietnamese burying their leader, planning, and then executing a perfect retribution assassination half way around the world in less than 21 days (11/1/63–11/22/63). It also assumes the South Vietnamese managed to discover that the CIA caused Diem's assassination, and link this death to President Kennedy, all within a few days enabling them sufficient time to plan the retribution killing.

When one examines the history of overthrows of South Vietnam's leaders the claim becomes even more preposterous. By 1963, South Vietnam had been at war with North Vietnam for over ten years. Within that time span eight South Vietnamese leaders had been overthrown, killed or deposed. Because of high rate of leadership turnover, and knowledge that President Diem had only possessed power for a short period, why would the Vietnamese have cared enough about one more turnover to the extent that they would kill an American President? The answer is that they did not.

From a common sense standpoint this assassination theory made neither economic nor political sense for South Vietnam. By November of 1963 with France withdrawing, South Vietnam's only hope of continued assistance for its war effort was America. If a retribution assassination of President Kennedy had been attempted, whether it failed or succeeded, any hint of Vietnamese involvement would have stopped America's support for South Vietnam. Equally as important, while Kennedy never hawkishly supported the war and kept American troop involvement small, there were no public statements by Johnson, prior to the assassination, of support for Vietnam. Vietnam had little to gain and much to lose from an attempted assassination.

THE CONSERVATIVE ASSASSINATION THEORY

After the emotionalism and fear following the assassination subsided, and after the Communists did not attack, and South

Vietnamese involvement was dismissed, the public started to focus on such theories as: *the Conservatives did it; it had to be a Mob Hit; or finally, it was a CIA plot*. While all of these suggestions have more credibility than the Communist or the South Vietnamese conspiracies, none of these are clearly credible explanations for the assassination, either.

The Conservative Assassination Theory, depending on the proponent, blamed different conservative groups who were singled out because they may have had an interest in wanting to see President Kennedy dead.

One group of conservatives that may have had a strong motive to kill President Kennedy were the anti-Castro Cuban exiles living in the United States. Large numbers of Cuban's fled to the United States during and after Castro's revolution. While residing outside of Cuba, their goal was to retake it from Castro and in the early 1960's several unsuccessful counter-revolutionary attempts of this sort were made. The United States eventually became involved.

In April of 1961 the infamous Bay of Pigs Invasion was attempted. After months of CIA training in Guatemala, U.S. backed Cuban exiles landed on the beaches of Cuba off the Bay of Pigs to initiate a counterrevolution. It failed. The U.S. backed Cuban exiles became bogged down on the beaches off the southern coast of Cuba in the Bay of Pigs. To make matters worse, although President Kennedy's advisors had originally promised full military support for the invaders when they hit the beaches, Kennedy called off the support when it became clear that the invasion was being turned into an international incident of American aggression. This left the attackers stranded on the beaches unable to move forward and nowhere to retreat. Eventually 114 Cuban exiles were killed and about 1,189 were captured.

Kennedy's abandonment of the Bay of Pigs Invasion in the midst of battle resulted in needless loss of lives. It certainly supplied a basis for a revenge motive in any assassination attempt. But this ''revenge'' motive is not so clear cut when one examines Kennedy's subsequent significant amends attempting to help the anti-Castro exiles. First, he accepted sole responsibility for America's part in the failed invasion. Then, which most historians who advance the Cuban exile assassination theory ignore, Kennedy bought his way back into the hearts of this conservative group. He did it by paying a huge ransom to Castro for the return of the captured Cuban exiles. On December 22, 1962 Kennedy gave $50 million in food and money to Castro in exchange for the return of the 1200 captured exile troops. Certainly after this the anti-Castro forces faith in Kennedy was partially restored and he was again believed to be a strong supporter of their cause.

Further fortifying his ties to this group were the continued CIA backed attempts to eliminate Castro, and Kennedy's decisive action taken during the Cuban Missile Crisis in October of 1962 when he faced down the Kremlin and prevented fortification of the Cuban island with nuclear military hardware (the Cuban Missile Crisis). While President Kennedy could have been a "revenge" target for this conservative group at anytime between April 16th, 1961 to October 1962 (failure of the Bay of Pigs Invasion until The Cuban Missile Crisis), his actions thereafter restored him as a hero and he no longer would have remained an assassination target for this anti-Castro group.

Another assassination theory involving conservatives is the claim that a group of wealthy oil men trying to protect their investments killed the President. This conservative theory centered upon a 1962 Congressional bill proposed by Kennedy to eliminate (or reduce) federal oil depletion allowances. The elimination of the oil depletion allowance would have increased federal tax revenues by millions while reducing oil profits by the same amount. Because of this proposed 1962 bill, it has been speculated by some that the oil men killed Kennedy to prevent losing millions. If all this were true, it may have supplied a motive for the assassination. But it is pure fiction.

The oil men knew that Congress, not the President, passes the laws and that killing a President to stop the enactment of

WELCOME MR. KENNEDY

TO DALLAS...

...A CITY so disgraced by a recent Liberal smear attempt that its citizens have just elected two more Conservative Americans to public office.

...A CITY that is an economic "boom town," not because of Federal handouts, but through conservative economic and business practices.

...A CITY that will continue to grow and prosper despite efforts by you and your administration to penalize it for its non-conformity to "New Frontierism."

...A CITY that rejected your philosophy and policies in 1960 and will do so again in 1964—even more emphatically than before.

MR. KENNEDY, despite contentions on the part of your administration, the State Department, the Mayor of Dallas, the Dallas City Council, and members of your party, we free-thinking and America-thinking citizens of Dallas still have, through a Constitution largely ignored by you, the right to address our grievances, to question you, to disagree with you, and to criticize you.

In asserting this constitutional right, we wish to ask you publicly the following questions—indeed, questions of paramount importance and interest to all free peoples everywhere—which we trust you will answer ... in public, without sophistry. These questions are:

WHY is Latin America turning either anti-American or Communistic, or both, despite increased U.S. foreign aid, State Department policy, and your own Ivy-Tower pronouncements?

WHY do you say we have built a "wall of freedom" around Cuba when there is no freedom in Cuba today? Because of your policy, thousands of Cubans have been imprisoned, are starving and being persecuted—with thousands already murdered and thousands more awaiting execution, and, in addition, the entire population of almost 7,000,000 Cubans are living in slavery.

WHY have you approved the sale of wheat and corn to our enemies when you knew the Communist soldiers "travel on their stomachs" just as ours do? Communist soldiers are daily wounding and or killing American soldiers in South Viet Nam.

WHY did you host, salute and entertain Tito — Moscow's Trojan Horse — just a short time after our sworn enemy, Khrushchev, embraced the Yugoslav dictator as a great hero and leader of Communism?

WHY have you urged greater aid, comfort, recognition, and understanding for Yugoslavia, Poland, Hungary, and other Communist countries, while turning your back on the pleas of Hungarian, East German, Cuban and other anti-Communist freedom fighters?

WHY did Cambodia kick the U.S. out of its country after we poured nearly 400 Million Dollars of aid into its ultra-leftist government?

WHY has Gus Hall, head of the U.S. Communist Party praised almost every one of your policies and announced that the party will endorse and support your re-election in 1964?

WHY have you banned the showing at U.S. military bases of the film "Operation Abolition"—the movie by the House Committee on Un-American Activities exposing Communism in America?

WHY have you ordered or permitted your brother Bobby, the Attorney General, to go soft on Communists, fellow-travelers, and ultra-leftists in America, while permitting him to persecute loyal Americans who criticize you, your administration, and your leadership?

WHY are you in favor of the U.S. continuing to give economic aid to Argentina, in spite of that fact that Argentina has just seized almost 400 Million Dollars of American private property?

WHY has the Foreign Policy of the United States degenerated to the point that the C.I.A. is arranging coups and having staunch Anti-Communist Allies of the U.S. bloodily exterminated?

WHY have you scrapped the Monroe Doctrine in favor of the "Spirit of Moscow"?

MR. KENNEDY, as citizens of these United States of America, we DEMAND answers to these questions, and we want them NOW.

THE AMERICAN FACT-FINDING COMMITTEE

"An unaffiliated and non-partisan group of citizens who seek truth"

BERNARD WEISSMAN,
Chairman

P.O. Box 1792—Dallas 21, Texas

COMMISSION EXHIBIT NO. 1031

A handbill "welcoming" President Kennedy to Dallas. It was part of a campaign to label President Kennedy as a communist and a traitor. Lyndon Johnson's friends were involved with the production of some of this material.

any law was pointless. Further and more importantly, while the bill was initially proposed by Kennedy, it was soundly defeated in Congress in 1962 and was never raised again. After 1962, there was no economic motive for any oil men to kill the President over an oil bill or oil investments, and this theory therefore makes no common sense.

A third group of conservatives theorized by some as conspirators in a plot to kill President Kennedy involved wealthy ultraconservatives who did not like Kennedy's liberal political policies. The motive advanced to blame these ultra right wingers for the killing was their goal to advance conservative causes. Considering that Kennedy was an eastern liberal advancing federal intervention as a solution to most national problems, had opened international channels of communication with the communists, and was publicly denounced by many conservatives as being not merely a liberal but a "communist", the theory has some credence. But the actual time of the assassination does not logically fit the theory because Kennedy's death in 1963 was too early prior to the 1964 Presidential election to have maximum effect on the outcome, and in November 1963 the Democrats were in enough trouble on their own.

In the fall of 1963, the press was having a field day with a scandal involving Vice President Johnson's good friend, Bobby Baker. Rumors swirled that the Baker scandal would go much deeper to eventually involve Johnson. Therefore, by just waiting, Johnson would have most probably been eliminated from any 1964 presidential ticket, and the scandal would have tarnished the entire Kennedy administration just as the 1964 presidential campaign was beginning. By the fall of 1963, Kennedy who had barely beaten his Republican rival in 1960 was losing some public support. With the addition of any scandal involving members of his administration, support would surely erode even further. By simply waiting and adding fuel to the blazing political scandals, Kennedy could have been politically destroyed by the spring of 1964.

Adding validity to this analysis, all one has to do is examine the news accounts and editorials after the assassination.

Within days of the assassination almost every major newspaper published political predictions that the assassination of President Kennedy would seriously harm Republican senator Barry Goldwater's chances in the 1964 election.

With these historical facts in mind, if these conservative individuals were serious about murdering Kennedy as the best way to advance their cause of conservative change, an assassination in late spring of 1964 or even later would have been much more effective. President Kennedy, the obvious 1964 presidential candidate of the Democrats, would have been dead and the Democrats would have had to go to their National Convention in complete confusion and without a top contender. At best, they would only have had a few months to publicly promote another candidate before the National election. More importantly, if the assassination was linked to Oswald as a communist, Republican Senator Goldwater, the champion of the conservatives, would have been able to ride the tide of anti-communism right into office without fear of a sympathetic backlash from the voters.

In one best selling assassination book, the conservative assassination theory was taken to the peak of absurdity. The authors grouped almost every possible conservative faction into one conspiratorial band which they called the "Secret Team". This multi-factioned group of various conservatives allegedly consisted of: ultra right wingers; wealthy conservatives; CIA controlled Cuban exiles; and organized crime members. The authors claimed that everyone worked together to kill President Kennedy, trying to stop him from de-escalating America's involvement in Vietnam.

The flaws in this "Secret Team" conspiracy theory begin with the fact that not all of the separate conservative groups harbored hostility against Kennedy at the time of the assassination as discussed earlier in this chapter. Therefore, not all of these groups in the "Secret Team" possessed a motive at the time.

More importantly, and as discussed earlier in relation to The Vietnam Assassination Theory, the Vietnam war was *not*

It's a Brand New Ball Game Now

The Albuquerque Tribune
November 23, 1963

Sen. Goldwater Chances Fading

By JACK STEELE
Scripps-Howard Staff Writer

WASHINGTON, Nov. 23 — Sen. Barry M. Goldwater's chances of winning the GOP nomination next year may have died with the assassin's bullet which struck down President Kennedy yesterday in Dallas.

This was the initial assessment made today by many of Washington's top politicians—Republicans and Democrats alike—of the impact of JFK's death on the 1964 presidential election, now less than a year away.

Leaders of both parties, in their shock and grief over the nation's tragedy, declined to comment publicly on its possible political repercussions.

But they agreed privately that it will force both parties to rewrite their scripts for the 1964 election — and that Goldwater is likely to end up with a lesser role, if any at all.

New Ball Game

One Democratic senator, surveying the wreckage of 1964 cam___ ___ ___

political wounds of Democrats in his native South.

Such moves would cut deeply into the appeal Sen. Goldwater has had for Republicans in his role of "Mr. Conservative."

Goldwater's basic campaign strategy for 1964 has been for the GOP — with himself as nominee — to sweep the South, Midwest and R o c k y Mountain area while conceding to JFK the populous, urban states of the Northeast and Far West.

With Johnson as the Democratic nominee, this G o l d water strategy no longer is likely to entrance the GOP.

Republican leaders now are expected to look for a more liberal or middle - of - the - road candidate who w o u l d have a better chance against Johnson than against Kennedy in the states with big electoral votes such as New York, Pennsylvania, Michigan and even Massachusetts.

Hits Extremists

Some political leaders here also predicted the assassina___

Louisiana and some o t h e r states will be forgotten now," one southern senator said. "These things were a i m e d chiefly at the Kennedys."

Democrats voiced differing opinions as to whether Johnson might drop Atty. Gen. Robert F. Kennedy from the cabinet.

Some contended that Bobby's days are numbered in the new administration, recalling that he had opposed his brother's decision to make Johnson his running - mate in 1960. Others said they expected the President would urge the attorney general to stay on as a move for party unity.

Most Democrats said they were c o n f i d e n t President Johnson would tap a Northern liberal for his 1964 running - mate. They mentioned Sen. Hubert H u m p h r e y (Minn.), now Senate w h i p, as the most likely.

Johnson a n d Humphrey worked together in 1960 in an effort to block Kennedy from the nomination. After Humphrey lost in the primaries, ___ carried ___ ___ to a significant issue in 1963. If this conservative combination had truly wanted to escalate the Vietnam War, their goal would have been better served if Kennedy was killed at a time when conservative presidential contender, Senator Barry Goldwater, could have best benefitted. The point of assassination timing again is a consideration. If President Kennedy was killed to advance the war in Vietnam, then he should have been killed in mid-1964, when Goldwater as a perceived war candidate could have benefitted. Obviously, this did not occur. And finally, no serious explanation has ever been offered as how each group in the conservative "Secret Team" (i.e. Cuban exiles, organized crime members and wealthy conservatives) could have possibly benefitted from an escalation of the war in Vietnam.

The realistic conclusion is that none of the conservative groups conspired together to kill President Kennedy. They either did not possess a motive at the time of the murder or the date of the actual assassination was inappropriate to meet their goals. However, this conclusion does not necessarily absolve all conservatives, all oilmen, nor all wealthy businessmen from being involved in President Kennedy's murder. Some may have been involved but their motives did not relate to: advancing conservative goals; saving on taxes; or escalating the war in Vietnam. Rather, if this occurred their motives had to have related to advancing some other cause or some other potential presidential candidates (other than Senator Goldwater) because the timing of the November 1963 assassination had to have been important to serve their purpose. While anti-Kennedy conservative individuals can not be ignored, their involvement must have related to a different assassination concept.

THE MOB ASSASSINATION THEORY

Another of the assassination theories advanced to date has been the Mob Assassination Theory. One of the most recent proponents advancing the Mafia plot has been author David E. Schiem (*"Contract on America: The Mafia Murder of President John F. Kennedy"*). However, Schiem's basic claim has been advanced by others as far back as the late 1960's. In all of these claims of a Mob conspiracy, the same basic evidence has been used in an attempt to "blame-it-on-the-Mob."

Although claims have been made that the assassination by the Mob was carried out in retaliation for its loss of profitable gambling operations in Cuba, there is no evidence to support such claims and in any event the loss occurred prior to Kennedy even taking office. The other leg of the Mob Assassination Theory is that it was based upon anger brought on by Robert Kennedy's personal crusade, as U.S. Attorney General, against organized crime, especially in the area of union activities. During Bobby Kennedy's tenure his staff secured indictments against 116 underworld figures. He also conducted crusades to indict and convict teamster Jimmy Hoffa and New Orleans criminal figure Carlos Marcello. In 1961, Robert Kennedy had Marcello deported to Guatemala while having the FBI keep constant surveillance on Hoffa. Therefore, at the time of President Kennedy's murder, both Hoffa and Marcello, as well as other underworld figures probably wanted Robert Kennedy dead. Investigators who follow this theory then transfer the underworld hate against U.S. Attorney General Robert Kennedy, to his brother, President John Kennedy, to explain the murder (others also directly link Kennedy to a "double cross" against the Mob).

But the Mob does not work this way. As most Americans now know, for the Mafia to undertake a "hit" of such importance, approval must be obtained from the full Mafia commission which includes organized crime families throughout the United States. In 1963, the nationwide crime syndicate was controlled by several families located in the east, midwest and west. A recognized member of the commission was Sam Giancana, the well known Chicago Mafia boss. For a "hit" to have been made against the President, Sam Giancana, among other members, would have had to consent. Independent action by minor underlings such as Marcello would not have been allowed; and in the case of Hoffa (who was not part of any organized crime family) action on his part would have been independent of the Mob. Recent evidence revealing Kennedy's relationship to the Mafia is such that the heads of this criminal association would never have sanctioned a "hit".

Ignoring claims tying Kennedy's father to the Mob, by 1960 the Mafia began to cultivate a relationship with John F. Kennedy, the politician, correctly spotting him as a rising star. When Kennedy entered the West Virginia Democratic Presidential Primary in 1960, organized crime jumped in and was the factor that enabled him to win the primary. He knew it, and counted on it. Kennedy continued to court the criminal element which eventually helped him capture the 1960 Democratic nomination for President. Even his victory in the November 1960 presidential election was the work of the Mob. In a vote fixing scandal that reached national proportions, Kennedy's Presidential "victory" came from underworld vote fixing in Chicago, snatching victory from defeat. The Chicago victory was the direct result of the work of Sam Giancana of Chicago. In at least 1960, President John F. Kennedy and his politically appointed brother, owed the Mob.

No one knows whether John F. Kennedy rewarded his underworld supporters for helping him obtain the presidency, but it is known that the relationship continued. Through the CIA, Kennedy involved the Mafia in assassination plots against Fidel Castro. These joint efforts were intended to help both America and the Mob. Kennedy also shared other interests with the underworld. Mobster Sam Giancana's girlfriend, Judith Exner, not only acted as a courier for messages between Kennedy and Giancana, but was also one of JFK's mistresses. The sexual relationship between Kennedy and Miss Exner ended in 1962 (on the advice of F.B.I. Director J. Edgar Hoover) but JFK's contacts with Giancana and others probably continued. Even Bobby Kennedy, as Attorney General, used Mafia members to carry out important matters for the Justice Department and used Mafia members after the assassination of his brother, which is inconsistent with any belief on his part that the Mafia was even suspected of being involved in his brother's assassination. Bobby's contacts, and those long standing contacts of his father, Joe, would certainly have given them information if there was any.

That the top leaders of the Mafia had no reason to quarrel with Bobby or Jack can also be seen by what Bobby Kennedy actually did about organized crime. While the Attorney General talked tough about organized crime and indictments were issued, he never went after the "big guys" (this did not really begin until the 1980's when Ralph Guiliani, the United States Attorney in New York and others, proceeded against Mafia chieftains under federal racketeering acts). In fact, in one of the known instances where Robert Kennedy was considering prosecuting a top boss, he was told to stop because the boss was "untouchable" due to his contacts with the CIA and involvement in the Bay of Pigs invasion. Whether selective enforcement was the order of the day and Mafia prosecutions were only against the small timers and Mob trouble makers, is unknown. What is known is that the Mafia was close to the President, his brother, and even to his movie star brother-in-law.[6]

The Mafia had a relationship with the Kennedys and enough information on the President that they had no need to kill him to control his administration. The President, his brother, and his entire administration could have been destroyed by one Mafia leak to the press about: the corruption in the West Virginia primary; the Chicago vote fraud in the 1960 Presidential election; Mafia ties to the White House; Mafia connected political assassination plots against Castro; the President's eye for women; the President's written contacts with Sam Giancana; the President's adulterous affair with a Mafia princess; Bobby's use of the Mafia to carry out illegal

[6]Peter Lawford

activities; or perhaps other matters not publicly known even today.

Because of what the Mafia knew, the President was a perfect blackmail subject, and the underworld does not kill those it can control. If the Mafia had really wanted to stop Bobby Kennedy's criminal prosecutions, all it had to do was have its Mafia wiretappers get "caught" on one of the illegal wiretap jobs ordered by Bobby. In any case, the Mafia could control Bobby, and there was no need to kill the President.

While some underworld characters can be indirectly linked to the Kennedy assassination, these men were not professional "hit men" and were at best "nickel and dime" players in the overall crime syndicate. From what is known of the Mafia it does not use small time criminals for a big "hit" (the shooter flies in and out and none of the local boys even know), and it is illogical to assume they broke the pattern in this case.

For all of these reasons, the Mafia assassination theory is not logical, and, the link of small time hoods to any conspiracy was more likely someone trying to create a false tie to implicate the Mob, or someone who was simply using the small time hoods as "free lancers" to help in a non-Mob connected assassination.

A CIA PLOT

In recent years public fascination with the Mob assassination theory has given way to a new, and perhaps more interesting theory, a CIA plot (Central Intelligence Agency) to kill President Kennedy. Ricky Don White of Medville, Texas, recently grabbed the public's attention with the claim that his father, Roscoe White, as a Dallas police officer, was one of three CIA operatives ordered to kill Kennedy. Many of White's claims were based on his father's diary of the events which has now allegedly disappeared. But White's claim is not new since the same theory was originally advanced in the 1960's by a New Orleans businessman.

Blaming the CIA for the assassination is similar to blaming the Mob. Most Americans do not understand the workings of either organization. All they know is that both secretly deal in murder, mystery, and intrigue. If some major crime, such as the murder of a President or the disappearance of Jimmy Hoffa can not be explained or is not understood because there is no apparent motive, the public often passes it off as the work of the Mob or the CIA, particularly if there is any hint of Mob or CIA connection. And a CIA connection to the Kennedy assassination appears to have some validity.

Some individuals in the CIA may have had a motive for assassinating President Kennedy. This would have stemmed from the botched Bay of Pigs Invasion. Kennedy blamed the CIA's poorly made plans for the international embarrassment. As a result, he "cleaned house" and one of the most important characters to "resign" was CIA Director Allan Dulles (later appointed by Johnson to the Warren Commission) and General Cabella (the brother of the Dallas Mayor). Some have speculated that those who remained at the CIA decided to execute Kennedy in retribution for his termination of the invasion leaving the attackers stranded on the beach, and then blaming the Agency for the fiasco.

This theory raises the most fundamental question why a professional organization would use Oswald, with a cheap rifle, to kill Kennedy. This simply is not rational.

The CIA assassination theory also has other flaws. Under Federal law the CIA reported directly to the President, and, therefore, the theory must assume that the organization that killed the President reported directly to him. It is conceivable that the Agency, or any agency head not loyal to the President, could have done it; but it is more difficult to believe that after Kennedy replaced Allan Dulles in 1962 with a CIA director loyal to himself, an assassination from within the CIA could have occurred. It would have meant that Kennedy's own new director either was involved or completely ignorant of the existence of a conspiracy occurring within his own organization. And, while it is true that some CIA employees were upset with Kennedy's post Bay of Pigs "cleaning house" at the CIA, the truth is that the disgruntled employees were eliminated from the Agency.

The final question as to possible CIA involvement is who would have benefitted within the CIA so as to order it? Neither the new director nor anyone else in the Agency would have obtained any personal gain from the assassination, and a killing to merely further general CIA goals is questionable. Kennedy's liberal detente policy towards the Russians and steps to end the cold war may have been contrary to what some CIA employees wanted, but he did not stop using the Agency around the world. In fact, just before his death and presumably with his knowledge, the CIA murdered South Vietnam's President causing a power change in that country, and the Agency was considering plans for another attempt to assassinate Fidel Castro.

The fact that the CIA did not plan and carry out the assassination does not rule out CIA involvement completely. The CIA may have acquired knowledge as to the identity of the real assassins after the murder but, for National Security reasons, failed to disclose it. This subsequent knowledge and silence would explain the rumors that have persisted for years that the CIA knew more about the assassination than it initially admitted. Along similar lines, it is also possible that private third parties killed Kennedy using independent professional assassins who were sometimes used by the CIA, thereby making a CIA connection appear to exist. This concept is extremely important if one attempts to harmonize Ricky Don White's claim of his father's CIA involvement with those of others. White, as part of his claim, stated that his father was a CIA operative along with another man known as "Saul". A similar claim was made almost 20 years ago by Hugh McDonald, Chief of Detectives of the Los Angeles County Sheriff's Department, who claimed that he had met and spoken with "Saul." McDonald claimed he learned that Saul, operating independent of any organization, was hired by certain private American citizens to execute Kennedy in Dallas.

The only major difference between the claims of White and McDonald is that Chief McDonald was allegedly told by Saul that the contract to hit Kennedy was a private hit paid for by people who wanted Johnson to be President, while White believed that his father and Saul participated in Kennedy's murder presumably as possible CIA agents.

McDonald's personal manhunt to confront the professional killer, Saul, has been chronicled in the book *Appointment in Dallas: The Final Solution*. The essence of the book is that John F. Kennedy was assassinated by one or more professional assassins hired by a private group who preferred to have Johnson as President, and that Lee Harvey Oswald was set up as a patsy to take the fall. This private group was able to supply the professional hit men with government documents giving them the minute by minute activities for the President, on the day of his killing.

McDonald's report of what Saul told him appears to fit the facts. The killer was allegedly contacted in May of 1963 for a meeting in Haiti to discuss a private arranged hit of President Kennedy (the first meeting setting up the Texas trip was within the same time frame). The killer was told the basic details of the "hit" and that it had to occur before the end of 1963. He also was told that everything else would be taken care of and that they even had a patsy (Oswald) who would be firing a shot near the President under the mistaken belief that it would scare the President into using more security on future trips.[7] What the killer claimed he was told is consistent in time with the move to dump Johnson from the 1964 Democratic ticket (the hit had to be before he was publicly dumped) and was also consistent with Oswald's publicity antics creating a record of his actions which made him the perfect patsy. The problem with McDonald's claims are that they are unverifiable and Saul has never been found. However, Saul's photo-

---

[7]The Secret Service was concerned with President Kenndy's practice of "breaking off" from his security. Just before his murder he did this in New York City to the concern of his staff.

graph is included in the Warren Commission Report as Exhibit 237. According to McDonald, the Warren Commission acted as if it did not realize the significance of the exhibit.

Without further proof, Chief McDonald's claims of what Saul said are subject to doubt. But his credibility has always been considered impeccable. McDonald was not just an ordinary cop. He spent eight years as second in command of our nation's largest military intelligence school. He was involved with military intelligence for the U.S. Army and had strong ties to the CIA's top brass as well as to the FBI. He was the author of three standard police text books and the inventor of a criminal identification kit used worldwide.

The theory of a direct CIA plan to kill Kennedy, with at best only a secondary motive and without any solid links to the actual assassination, is certainly dubious as the explanation for the murder. Less questionable is the possibility that some third party or group used ex-CIA employees or independent professional assassins to kill JFK. While this possibility of ex-CIA assassins does bear on the "mechanics" of the crime and who did it, it fails to address or explain who the third party or group was—the actual planner. For this reason, identifying the hit man as CIA or non-CIA is of no assistance in identifying the person who set the plan in motion in the first place, and therefore, this theory must be ignored if real truth is the goal.

GOVERNOR CONNALLY AS THE INTENDED TARGET THEORY

Another assassination theory has recently developed which does not necessarily involve a conspiracy. The theory made the cover of *Time* magazine and is part of a book written by James Reston, Jr. entitled *The Lone Star: The Life of John Connally*. Reston's theory is that Oswald had no intention to kill President Kennedy, rather Governor John Connally was his target. The initial basis for Reston's claim is that before the murder Oswald undeniably had contacts with Connally. From this foundation, the theory proceeds to the conclusion that Oswald blamed Connally as the Secretary of the Navy for his military discharge status downgrade. To the theory's credit, it is true that Oswald had communicated with Connally (when he was the Ex-Secretary of the Navy) in hopes that Connally would get the military to reverse its decision. It was also true that Oswald was upset with his military downgrade after his discharge. Combining these facts with evidence of Oswald's repeated positive statements about President Kennedy ("JFK deserved to be President . . . He will be the greatest President in history"), the conclusion drawn by Reston is that Connally was the intended target and Oswald missed and accidentally killed Kennedy.

Both facts and common sense reveal that any theory that Governor John Connally was the actual assassination target is a fantasy. Regardless whether Oswald was shooting at Kennedy or Connally, as an ex-marine he choose the wrong weapon. He could not have hit either man with the cheap Mannlicher-Carcano rifle. Further, an attempt to kill Governor Connally at that time and location made no sense at all. Why would anyone who wanted to kill Connally wait until he was in a Presidential motorcade? As the governor of Texas, Connally, as most governors on all but the assassination day, had only limited security protection. Before November 22, 1963, Oswald had the opportunity to kill Governor Connally at almost any time before he was within Presidential security. Connally had his permanent residence in Oswald's home town of Forth Worth, Texas, and Oswald could have killed him there any time. Lastly, if one compares the location of Governor Connally, when he was shot, to the alleged sniper post (6th floor Book Depository) it becomes clear that the theory is meritless. This is because the theory is premised upon Oswald passing up all clear shots at Governor Connally in order to shoot through President Kennedy in an attempt to strike his target.

Reston's theory, premised on the belief that Oswald chose

the worst possible day to try to kill the governor, missed and killed Kennedy by mistake, is simply not believable.

CONCLUSION

The Warren Commission had only one of two choices as to how Kennedy's assassination was accomplished: A lone assassin or a conspiracy. It also had only three basic choices in determining the motive for the killing:

- **a true political assassination—to start a revolution, precede a military attack, advance a political cause, or kill a leader identified as an enemy;**

- **a power grab by someone without any intent to change the political structure; or**

- **a mentally deranged or publicity seeking martyr.**

As discussed earlier, the evidence does not fully support the Warren Commission's sole assassin theory, which leads to the only other possible alternative, a conspiracy. As such, it appears probable that a conspiracy of some sort had to have existed.

Taking this subject a step further, it should be noted that the Warren Commission did not make a choice as to motive because it miraculously concluded that Oswald was an assassin without a determinable motive. However, since there was no military attack or any other attempted political change coming from within or outside the U.S. following the assassination, the assassination does not fit the pattern of a true political assassination. And because Oswald, the only identified assassin, was acknowledged by all not to be mentally deranged (but in fact quite intelligent) and since he did not have any known motive, he did not fit the motive pattern of a mentally deranged or publicity seeking martyr. This leaves only one remaining logical alternative, a possible power grab since there was an obvious transfer of power from Kennedy to Johnson.

Consistent with this, as just discussed, is the fact that none of the conspiracy assassination theories advanced to date have offered a rational explanation as to why any of the identified conspiracy groups could have benefitted enough from a transfer of presidential power from Kennedy to Johnson to cause them to plot Kennedy's assassination. There must be another explanation.

8

Right Hand Man Assassinations

To this point the majority of the various Kennedy assassination theories have been briefly discussed. Some are totally without merit, while others appear to be at least plausible. And still others have some credibility based upon one's view of the accompanying evidence. However, one final assassination theory that has not yet been directly addressed in depth in this book is the Right Hand Man Concept.

Assassinations by a subordinate to seize power are as old as civilization and have occurred repeatedly throughout history. They are usually the result of the jealous greed and the power desires of a leader's subordinates. These lesser men sometimes, out of desperation, try to obtain a leader's position illegitimately. To believe that this could not or will not ever happen in America is to ignore politics, to ignore human nature, and to ignore history.

Loyalty and politics is an oxymoron because neither politicians nor their supporters get involved in the political game to lose. Therefore, true loyalty to one person, or to one ideal, is rare. Politicians switch positions on an issue or even change their party allegiance entirely to obtain or retain the support of their followers. Further, since most human beings enjoy the benefits of power, every politician, being only human, wants to attain the most powerful position that he can possess.

Political power increases as higher offices are attained and historical immortality is sometimes awarded to those who hold the highest positions. This is why citizens run for local council seats, local councilmen run for mayor, mayors run for governor, governors run for the U.S. Senate, and senators try to obtain the power of the Presidency. In this order of ascension, those in secondary positions can be classified as right hand men lusting for the power of a superior office or they would not have gotten into the business of politics to begin with.

Lust for recognition is not confined to politics but is part of human nature. Whether the business is acting, sports, or politics, every person who is waiting in the wings as a backup has dreams of replacing the present star and shining in his own light. Most people as subordinates will patiently wait, hope, and pray for their turn without doing anything improper to hasten their chance. But because the power over people is greater in politics where the stakes are high, the temptation is sometimes greater to engage in "dirty tricks". For this reason, in politics, depending upon a person's moral character, the question is not what if, but rather, when and whether, a power ascent of some sort can be accomplished without repercussions. If the answer to the latter questions are a probable yes, then an act may be attempted to bring this about. History is replete with instances of a right hand man attempting to grab political power.

In this chapter the history of right hand man assassinations is briefly discussed. The reader should note that while a number of these acts are highlighted, for brevity's sake many other right hand man assassinations have been excluded. The point is that this is *not* an uncommon occurrence. Even the most civilized societies in their time had their share of right hand man assassinations.

The most famous right hand man assassination occurred over 2,000 years ago. Yet, from that day forward almost every person who has ever lived has known or heard something about it. It involved the assassination of Roman leader

Julius Caesar who was killed by members of the Roman Senate as he entered the forum to address them. The assassination plot had been long in the making with high ranking Roman Senators as well as Caesar's "friends" involved in the assassination plot's intimate details. For instance, Decimus Brutus scheduled festive games in a forum adjacent to the Roman Senate Hall which was to be the site of the assassination. The purported purpose of the gladiatorial games was to celebrate Caesar's visit. However the real intent was to keep the crowds distracted and pacified while Caesar was executed.

Ironically, Caesar's trip and assassination closely parallels the assassination of President John F. Kennedy. Both men were warned by aides not to make the trip and both were eventually talked into making the journey. In Julius Caesar's case when he was contemplating not appearing and not addressing the Roman Senate, it was Decimus Brutus the conspiratorial planner of the adjacent gladiatorial games, who visited Caesar and chided him into attending by saying "Caesar, ignore the rumors and do the business that deserves the attention of Caesar." As a result, Caesar marched into the Hall of Pompeius and was repeatedly stabbed to death by the group of conspirators. As Caesar was repeatedly being stabbed he shouted out the immortal words "Et Tu Brutae"[8] when his own loyal friend Brutus plunged a dagger into his side.

After the death of Caesar came the right hand man assassinations of other Roman leaders. In 54 B.C. Roman leader Claudius was assassinated by his second wife Agrippina. She did this to provide easy access for her son Nero's rise to power. Unfortunately for Agrippina her efforts were not rewarded. Upon Claudius' death, Nero, the stepson of Claudius, poisoned Claudius' real son to end any potential leadership disputes. And to clean up all remaining loose ends, Nero then had an assassin kill his conspiring mother (Agrip-

[8] And you too, Brutus!

pina). However, Nero's malevolent acts did not establish his place in history as much as his subsequent act, as the Emperor who played his fiddle while Rome burned.

Other bloody right hand man assassinations followed Nero's act. Roman ruler Caracella was stabbed to death by his centurion guards as he relieved himself. Members of Caracella's Court were the primary assassination suspects in this power move. After this right hand man murder, others came in close succession. Roman emperor Elagabalus was assassinated by his special troops. It was eventually discovered that the Emperor's aunt had bribed the troops to commit the murder so her son Severus Alexander could take power. However, in Severus' case his reign was quickly ended when his own right hand man Maximinus slit his throat to seize power for himself. And even Maximinus' rule was short lived since he was later lynched by his own troops.

Right hand man assassinations have never been exclusive to the Romans. For instance, a review of the book of Kings in the Bible demonstrates that even in one of the world's oldest books the historic existence of assassinations as a way to power was mentioned. At one time Elah, the son of Basha, ruled over Israel. However, he was killed by his right hand man Zimri who commanded Elah's chariots. And Zimri, to prevent retribution, then proceeded to execute the remainder of Elah's friends and relatives. While Zimri did not live long after his assassination of Elah, his act made it one of the earliest recorded right hand man assassinations.

To trace the viability of the right hand man concept even further all one has to do is pick any country, since at some point in time a right hand man coup probably occurred. For example:

AUSTRIA: In the Merouingian Kingdom, geographically located in the area of the present day Austria and Germany, Grimoald, the prime minister of the Frankish Kingdom of Austrasia, unsuccessfully attempted to grab power. The failed coup resulted in his beheading.

GERMANY: On July 20, 1944 an assassination attempt was made against German Fuehrer, Adolph Hitler. Count von Stauffenberg and other German officers planted a briefcase bomb at a conference attended by Hitler. Contrary to some historian's claims, the conspirators did *not* have the altruistic goal of deposing a despot, but instead despised Hilter for his popularity and had plans to divide his power among old line German military aristocracy.

HAITI: In 1806 Haitian Emperor Jean-Jacques Dessalines was assassinated by his leading general Henri Christophe. Christophe then took control of the tiny Caribbean country.

IRAN: Ruler Abbasid Caliph Al-Hadi was found dead in 786 B.C. His younger brother succeeded him amidst rumors of foul play, including suffocation, since Al-Hadi's wife and his officials preferred the younger ruler. And, in an act resembling the post Kennedy assassination events, when the younger brother obtained power, he handled the investigation and then by decree officially ordered an end to all of the assassination rumors.

INDIA: Around 1605 Akbar, the greatest of the Moghul rulers, was murdered by poison by someone close within his household. At the time of his death he ruled two thirds of the subcontinent of eastern Asia. Unfortunately, the list of suspects wanting his power was so numerous that the crime was never attributed to one specific right hand man.

JAPAN: Japanese Emperor Iruka was assassinated by Prince Nakano. This occurred in 645 B.C. while the Emperor was in a crowded hall.

RUSSIA: Russian Czar Paul I was killed by his own troops in a bedchamber military murder in 1801. The Czar's troops, as part of their plan, then replaced Paul with his young son Alexander.

SWEDEN: King Gustavus III was murdered at a masquerade ball by his own troops in 1792. Gustavus was gunned down as part of a conspiracy plan by a group of his own military officers and officials.

TURKEY: Turkish Sultan Osman II was deposed from his throne by the conspiratorial acts of his own men. Osman's bodyguards strangled him to take his power.

ZULU: The African Zulu tribe chief Shaka was assassinated in 1828 by his step brother. Chief Shaka's tribe controlled the southeastern quarter of the African continent making him the most powerful leader in Africa. Originally, Shaka ascended to power by killing his own father and he managed to retain the power despite narrowly escaping other attempts on his life.

In fact, at almost the exact time of President Kennedy's death and only a few miles off U.S. shores in Cuba, Fidel Castro was a target of a right hand man assassination attempt by Dr. Rolando Cubella Secades of Cuba.[9]

While this was Cubella's original intent, after Kennedy's murder, the Cubella assassination attempt on Castro did go forward. And it was not until after JFK's death that Castro

[9] As a side note, this right hand man attempt gained national attention in the United States because of alleged CIA involvement and suggested links to the Kennedy assassination. Dr. Cubella was one of Castro's originally loyal Cuban Revolution guerillas. Because of his original loyalty to Castro, he was rewarded with an Envoyship and thereafter maintained a strong personal relationship with Castro. However, Cubella wanted Fidel Castro killed and wanted his power. And it was Cubella who coincidentally secretly met with the CIA on the day President Kennedy was killed to plan such a murder. Because of this meeting a few have theorized that Castro had Kennedy killed, since as the theory goes, Castro was using Cubella to "test" Kennedy and the CIA to determine whether they would continue to try to kill him despite his demand that they stop. However, those who have advanced this theory have not told the public the full details of the Cubella right hand man attempt which is discussed above.

discovered this right hand man plot and Cubella was arrested. He was tried for conspiracy and treason, and testified in open court that, as one of Castro's right hand men, he intended to kill Castro to grab some of his power expecting to receive an even higher post in the next regime.

Assassinations of world leaders have occurred countless times. Right hand man assassinations have been the motive for scores of these. Therefore, when a leader is mysteriously assassinated, the thought that naturally comes to mind is whether the leader's right hand men were responsible and, of course, of all right hand men, the actual successor would always be a prime suspect.

In President Kennedy's case, his right hand man was Lyndon Baines Johnson. Since none of the other assassination theories considered and discussed to date have proven to be completely viable, the remainder of this book will examine the evidence of a right hand man theory in the assassination of President John F. Kennedy.

Some Americans may believe and argue that a crime of this nature could not happen in the United States, a nation that leads the world in per capita murders and violent crimes, but such arguments will be left to American philosophers. At this stage, before any evaluation of the known facts is made, all that is required is an open mind to at least agree that:

1. Throughout history right hand man assassinations have been commonplace; and

2. It is at least possible to think that such an act could occur in the United States of America.

9

Principles of Criminal Investigations

After a crime has been committed, the first principle in any criminal investigation is to evaluate the crime scene for clues. Once this has been accomplished the next phase of every criminal investigation focuses upon the persons who may have committed the crime. This not only involves attempting to physically link the evidence to particular suspects, but it is also strongly based upon logical deduction (i.e. common sense). Logical deduction in a criminal case requires an examination of each criminal suspect in relation to three factors of the crime: character, motive, and opportunity. A proper evaluation of each criminal suspect then results in a separation of the suspects into one of two categories known as "Prime Suspects" and "Suspects". As more evidence is acquired and as additional deduction occurs, the suspects are then moved from one category to the other. Hopefully, this eventually results in one prime suspect who is deemed to be the probable culprit and is then normally charged with the crime.

In this case, so far as is known and publicly reported, the Warren Commission only performed its criminal investigation as to one suspect, Lee Harvey Oswald. It failed to examine the criminal potential of any other suspects. By investigating only one suspect, the Commission failed to fully investigate the assassination of a world leader.

Fortunately, the Commission's error has been partially rectified by the subsequent investigations of others who, for the past decades, have performed their own criminal investigations on other potential subjects (i.e. Mafia, ultra conservatives, communists, etc).

To fully correct the Warren Commission's omission and to complete a criminal investigation that should have been conducted almost 30 years ago, the next sections of this book will be devoted to the criminal investigation of the one remaining assassination suspect, Lyndon B. Johnson. This will include a brief look at the character traits of President Kennedy's right hand man which may offer some initial insight into his disposition to commit a criminal act. This will then be followed by an evaluation of this suspect's motives. If it is then found that John Kennedy's subordinate had a predisposing character to commit a crime as well as a motive, the criminal investigation will be continued. A determination then will be made as to whether this right hand man had an actual opportunity to commit the murder. The criminal investigation of Lyndon B. Johnson is therefore divided into the sequence that the Warren Commission should have followed:

SECTION II: THE CHARACTER OF LBJ

SECTION III: LBJ'S MOTIVES

SECTION IV: LBJ'S OPPORTUNITY

SECTION 2

The Character of LBJ

10

Character Evidence in Criminal Investigations

All forms of life usually repeat certain acts over the course of life. Birds fly south in the winter. When frightened, cats straighten their hair. And most mammals in response to stress raise their heart rate and release adrenaline. When these types of responses are applied to a person's personality, they are known as a person's character or disposition, revealing the person's known and usual action in a given situation. While evidence as to a person's character or disposition to act does not conclusively establish that on a specific occasion he acted in conformance to his character (sometimes people act "out of character"), it does supply a useful aid in determining the initial likelihood of whether the person could have performed the act in question.

In fact, the legal system has not only accepted the concept of habits and traits as a means of predicting behavior so as to permit witnesses to testify about what they personally know about an accused, but it has expanded the subject. Courts now allow evidence of the person's prior bad acts, and even evidence relating to his reputation to be used. Admissible character evidence involves the particular traits of the person in question, including among others things the traits of aggression, passivity, and untruthfulness. Evidence of prior bad acts that is admissible can relate to specific past wrongful conduct of the individual, including other crimes beyond the one at issue in the case. Both character evidence as well as prior bad acts evidence can be proven in court with either reputation or opinion evidence. The basic presumption in law for permitting such evidence to be considered by the court in determining guilt or innocence of an accused is that normally a saint does not become a sinner, nor a sinner a saint.

The point of this discussion is to acquaint the reader with the fact that character, prior acts and reputation evidence relating to an accused is recognized as useful information by American courts under the right circumstances. In fact, such evidence is almost always considered "logically relevant" since it has the tendency of making the existence of a fact at issue, the guilt or innocence of the accused, more or less probable than without it.[10] However, normally such evidence only establishes a few broad traits of a person clearly repeated over time.

With this as a backdrop, these evidentiary tools will be used to investigate the character and reputation of President Kennedy's right hand man, Lyndon Johnson. This will provide the reader with an opportunity to decide whether LBJ was the type of man who could possibly commit one of America's most atrocious crimes. Fortunately, since Johnson was a life long politician with decades of public exposure, his character and reputation is not difficult to trace. But before the character investigation even begins, Johnson's political campaign claims of being a "gentle person" only interested in the "little things" can be dismissed as being absolute lies.

As an initial overview of Lyndon Johnson's character, it can be said that some people viewed Johnson as "a man who would stoop to commit any type of act and who managed to combine the worst elements of mankind's traits into his

---

[10] While such evidence is almost always considered to be "logically relevant" in a Court of law, the actual admission of it is often limited to specific circumstances and otherwise excluded under other evidentiary rules of law in order to protect the rights of a defendant or an accused.

personality.'' Others who reported on his political career considered him to be a ''total opportunist, devoted only to profit and personal gain.'' And still others, including a fellow U.S. Senator, felt that Johnson was the ''phoniest individual who ever came around.'' These opinion statements could be considered as only jealous comments by a few enemies if they had not been regularly repeated by hundreds of different people throughout Johnson's career. In fact, Lyndon Johnson's grandmother pulled no punches about her own negative feelings for him. Repeatedly she declared that LBJ was going to wind up in jail—''just mark my words.'' Even though Johnson missed the penitentiary for the presidency his grandmother's prophecy still came very close to the mark. While he was never indicted nor convicted of a crime, Johnson led a political life that was constantly embroiled in scandals and a number of his cohorts, who were less politically connected, ended up being convicted of crimes and jailed.

To obtain a correct initial perception of Lyndon B. Johnson's character the concepts of good, moral, and decent must be erased from the mind. A clean slate must be used and filled with only one word, a word that was Johnson's favorite description of his colleagues and his feeling as to their expendability to him: ''PISS-ANTS''[11]

---

[11]The exact meaning of Mr. Johnson's word is unclear to this author. It is presumed that he meant that everyone else in the world were little worker ants, who while performing jobs, could easily be eliminated by the act of urinating with little consequence or conscience to him.

11 _____

LBJ's Violations of Moral Rules

One important method used to judge an individual's character is to evaluate the person's attitude towards the rules of morality relating to personal conduct. Although violations of the rules of morality will not result in a criminal conviction, it still provides a clue as to a person's basic nature and capacity for good or evil.

In Lyndon Johnson's case it can be positively stated that he went to church. In fact, on any given Sunday Johnson was often seen in more than one church. But, this is the only positive thing that can be said about his religious practices. From boyhood on Johnson refused to take to Christianity and in the words of a friend "LBJ never had a religion." Johnson went to church and attended multiple church services because that was where the voters were on Sunday. One Washington religious leader publicly proclaimed that LBJ was a man "whose public house was splendid in appearance . . . but whose entire foundation was rotted by termites." While others stayed for post-service coffee, Johnson would race away at high speed to another church full of voters. And, while Johnson's press agents attempted to impress the public by disclosing Johnson's religious generosity, such as his "gift" of an automobile to a poor minister, they couldn't hide the truth forever. It later was discovered that his wonderful "gift" of an automobile was actually a gift of U.S. government property!

Perhaps the best example of his attitude toward and failure to understand religion was his meeting with the Catholic Pope in Rome. When Johnson was granted an audience, he decided to offer the Pope a gift that he thought was suitable for the historic occasion. However, the gift was probably one of the most unusual that any Pope had ever received, since Johnson presented the Pope with a bust of himself—a mini LBJ.

These antics pale in comparison to Johnson's wilful and perverse violations of moral rules. Johnson spent 30 years violating the Seventh Commandment by committing numerous acts of adultery.

To trace Lyndon Johnson's career as an adulterer merely requires a review of his political career. As a young man in school Johnson used to dig into his pants and pull out his penis. With a few shakes and twirls he would declare "Jumbo's going to get a workout tonight . . . I wonder who I'll fuck tonight." Tragically, Johnson's youthful crudeness did not diminish with age nor political stature. As an esteemed political statesman, Lyndon B. Johnson would approach attractive female government employees and ask them point blank whether they would "shuck their britches."

Johnson's first known adulterous affair began in 1938. He had been married only four years at the time. It occurred with a beautiful woman named Alice Glass who was the common law wife of newspaper magnate Charles Marsh. She was also the mother of his children. This made the affair one of extreme danger since Charles Marsh was one of Johnson's foremost political and economic supporters. Marsh repeatedly advanced Johnson's career by not only supplying him with political advice, but also by running pro-Johnson articles and editorials in his newspapers. Marsh's support of Johnson was so deep that he created a land deal for Johnson allowing him to reap a huge profit and making him financially secure. And, while Marsh was making Johnson wealthy and politically successful, LBJ was secretly making love to Alice. To third party observers, like Alice's sister, the actions of LBJ in this relationship were despicable. When in Marsh's presence, Johnson would fawn over Marsh and accept significant favors, but the moment Marsh would leave town Johnson would sneak over to Marsh's estate to seduce Alice. This first affair continued for over 20 years.

Johnson, while still carrying on a relationship with Alice Glass, expanded his known sexual misadventures. In 1948 he met a 23 year old Texan named Madeline Brown and established a second affair that also continued for over 20 more years. Recently, Ms. Brown revealed that her affair with Johnson produced an illegitimate son and that Johnson supported her for decades. This included giving her a home, a live-in maid, and a regular allowance.

In addition to Glass and Brown, Lyndon Johnson entered the halls of history with another known affair. He had a sexual encounter with Dr. Doris Kerns, who became an associate professor of history at Harvard University. The uniqueness of the Johnson-Kerns relationship was that it was the only known affair where Johnson actually proposed marriage to his mistress. What LBJ expected to do with Lady Bird is unknown. However, Johnson's former press aide, when informed of the matter, in typical Johnson administration fashion, did not deny the affair nor the wedding proposal. Rather, the press aide commented that what Dr. Kerns "heard [from Johnson] was probably accurate, but she did not understand what Johnson really meant." In real world terms this meant that Lyndon Johnson lied to Dr. Kerns, loved her, and then left her.

Lyndon B. Johnson had an excessive thirst for sex and a willingness to repeatedly commit adultery. But as a credit to him, he committed most of these immoral activities behind closed doors. Unfortunately, his discretion in adultery was not followed in the area of alcohol abuse. Johnson's public drunkenness raised alcohol abuse to an art form. And his proficiency in this activity reveals his true character as a man, a politician, and as an immoralist.

Johnson's first recorded abuse of alcohol was as a relatively young man. In this first instance, he not only got drunk but destroyed his father's car while returning from a trip to a local bootlegger. This occurred before the start of his political career but the way he effectively handled the incident supplies insight into his later ability to handle potentially damaging incidents. After destroying his father's car he decided that he did not want to be reprimanded. Therefore, he just abandoned the car on the roadway, ran away, and refused to come home. The strategy worked and Johnson negotiated an agreement with his parents that in exchange for his return home he would not be punished for his alcohol abuse, the trip to the bootleggers, nor the destruction of the family car. This may have been Johnson's first occasion to learn that he had the ability to cover things up and to turn the tables on disaster.

It is truly amazing that Lyndon B. Johnson was able to successfully stay in political office for over 35 years in spite of his public displays of drunkenness. It has been confirmed that during his Presidency, LBJ consumed more alcohol than the three preceding presidents combined. While his favorite drinks were made by combining bottles of Cutty Sark with water, LBJ was also known to regularly handle "traveling beers". These "traveling beers" fit perfectly into his hand as he raced down the road in his Lincoln Continental convertible drinking his beer and roaring past his constituents on the public highways. However, though Johnson had the capacity to drink heavily, it has long been rumored that Johnson's capacity for exceeding even his excessive drinking limits necessitated a permanent "sober up room" in a local hospital.

Johnson normally drank when he was feeling good, but alcohol did not make him a happy drunk. When drunk, LBJ would swear and belittle friends and constituents in public. While a true friend might tolerate drunken obscenities, ordinarily the American public would not be as tolerant. However, because of Johnson's strong political power, his drunkenness was tolerated by his constituents. In fact, when political dinners conflicted with Johnson's drinking schedule, the drinking would take priority and the paying dinner guests were forced to wait hours for his arrival. And when he would eventually appear (sometimes up to two hours late), Johnson, in a state of inebriation, would often step to the speaker's platform and begin his speech with a barrage of obscenities and insults at everyone present.

While Americans today may think that this is hard to believe, these are all matters of public record. What is unknown is the extent of Johnson's drinking at home. Lady Bird has never publicly commented on his private drinking excesses nor has she ever disclosed whether, in drunken rages, he would verbally abuse her as he did his friends and voters. However, in spite of her silence, her husband's binging tendencies and drunken belligerence obviously concerned her greatly because she urged LBJ to continue with his political career. In a note asking him not to retire from public office she stated he should continue since "you may drink too much—for lack of a higher calling." Even Lady Bird was aware that Lyndon Johnson's life-style of alcohol abuse bore proof to the adage that the only thing worse than a politician drunk with power is a drunken politician with power.

From a moral standpoint Johnson had no use for religion except for the political benefits that it bestowed upon him. He had no use for the sanctity of marriage except for the voting benefits it offered to him as a "married man." And, his desire for alcohol, just like with sex, was excessive. In short, moral rules relating to his personal conduct had no effect on stopping him from getting what he wanted.

12 _____

Political Victories
by Illusion

How did a man like Lyndon Baines Johnson ever get elected to anything? The simple answer is that even though Lyndon Johnson was not a nice fellow, he was a master of the political game. And, as a political master he was capable of stealing elections. Johnson learned very early in his career that it did not matter how the game was played as long as he won. While many American's mistakenly believe that the name "Landslide Lyndon" was given to Johnson as a result of his strong political victory over Senator Barry Goldwater in the 1964 presidential election, quite the opposite was true. The "Landslide Lyndon" tag was given to Johnson during the 1940's as a result of Johnson's alleged Senatorial "victory" in Texas by only 87 votes (out of almost one million votes cast). Johnson's opponent not only claimed that illegal ballot box-stuffing occurred but carried his protest of the illegalities all the way to the Supreme Court.

Lyndon Johnson was "an opportunist whose mastery of pure politics is devoted . . . to personal ambition." Those were the descriptive words of a *Wall Street Journal* Washington Bureau Chief after years of following Johnson's political career. These words and others like them were viewed by Johnson as compliments. LBJ was proud of his political dirty tricks and made jokes of his stolen elections. One joke that

Johnson repeatedly told was of a crying little Mexican boy who believed that his deceased father had returned from the dead but had failed to visit the boy. As the joke continues, the boy was reminded of his father's death and the unlikelihood of his father's ability to return from the dead. However in response the Mexican boy replied, "But he was here, I know it for sure, cuz just last Saturday he voted for Lyndon Johnson!"

Johnson had more than just the dead vote for him. Those alive often voted for him several times in the same election. This was the first political strategy that Johnson learned and he used it effectively to win his first election. Johnson stole a college election even though he was extremely unpopular. Even 40 years after the fact he reminisced proudly about his first stolen election by calling his college election victory a "pretty vicious operation" and his first real "Hitlerized operation". The "vicious" "Hitlerized operation" consisted of Johnson and a small group of students banding together to vote repeatedly for Johnson. They accomplished their multiple voting by running in and out of each classroom so they could vote several times for LBJ. Johnson's success using this tactic depended upon exquisite timing. It required the voting in some classrooms to be stalled, and voting in other classrooms be rushed, so the same small group of Johnson supporters could vote in each classroom. This first election "victory" demonstrated to Johnson at an early age that with a small group of dedicated supporters and by perfect planning, he could attain power in spite of the wishes of the majority.

When Johnson entered the real world of politics he also learned that money and influence could pull the political lever, buy a campaign, or steal a state. In 1937, Johnson entered his first congressional race in Texas. It soon became one of the most expensive congressional campaigns in Texas history. And by 1948, when he launched his first campaign to become a U.S. Senator, LBJ's influence got him a campaign helicopter equipped with loudspeakers supplied by a wealthy Texas oil man. When LBJ came down from the clouds and took to the streets, he used his campaign manager to forcefully solidify the voters (his tough campaign manager was not only a convicted murderer, but also heavily involved in the Ku Klux Klan).

With all of this money and campaign help, Johnson still did not win in the 1948 race for U.S. Senator. His opponent won the run-off election after all of the returns were counted. But Johnson arranged a "recanvasing" more than 5 days after the election resulting in a "correction" and the "correction" made Johnson the victor by less than 100 votes. A political fight erupted with Johnson's opponent, who knew full well that Johnson had stuffed the ballot boxes during the recanvasing. When attempts were made to view the ballots to determine the authenticity of the "correction", the ballot boxes were found to be empty. The excuse supplied was that a janitor had mistakenly burned all of the ballots. But Johnson's opponent was still not deterred. The opponent then demanded to look at the poll taxes and voting records in the counties where the "recanvasing" vote fraud was the worst. Typically Johnson, none of these items were available either. The excuse supplied on this occasion was that materials had been thrown away during "house cleaning". After this fraud even the Governor of Texas, agreeing with Johnson's grandmother, said that if the people of Texas had done their jobs "Lyndon Johnson would be in the penitentiary instead of the United States Senate."

One of the best known loss of records scandals which involved Johnson also involved one of his staunch supporters, the Brown & Root Company. It began in the late 1940's and ended in the 1950's. At the time, the Federal Corrupt Practices Act prohibited political contributions by corporations and limited individual contributions to a maximum $5,000 limit. However, the Brown & Root Company circumvented the law by arranging to have their business associates, subcontractors, employees, and even legal counsel each make the same $5,000 maximum contribution to Johnson's campaigns. When the Internal Revenue Service began tracking the suspicious contributions it noticed that the exact amount contributed by these groups and individuals to Johnson's campaigns matched a "bonus" paid to them by the Brown & Root Company. Thus, Brown & Root conveniently paid Johnson's contributors a bonus and each contributor then decided to use it entirely to support Johnson. When the IRS investigation got too serious the investigation was "stopped" by order of President Roosevelt. In the 1950's when another I.R.S. investigation on the same subject began (with FDR gone) the matter had to be abandoned when it was discovered that the evidence the I.R.S. needed to support its claim had been "accidentally" taken from a fireproof storage warehouse and put into a shanty which then burned completely to the ground.

However, even without an I.R.S. determination that the Brown & Root Company illegally supported Johnson, it cannot be denied that Johnson had a relationship with his supporters of trading political help and money for political favors. For instance, most Americans have heard of the NASA Space Center located in Texas. Why it was built in Texas rather than in Florida where billions of dollars had already had been spent developing the nation's space center, is another corrupt story. Further, why the Texas Space Center was built in a desolate desert area 22 miles from Houston is still another chapter on corrupt practices, political pressure, and probably payola. The NASA Space Center was built on a Texas wasteland because Johnson was the head of the Space Council for a period of time. The Space Center was built on Texas wasteland "donated" to the center by a large oil company which was permitted to retain all of the surrounding land. The result of the "donation" was that the oil company built a large industrial park next to the Space Center and increased the value of its 50,000 surrounding acres by at least seven times its original value. To make matters worse, the company chosen to build the Space Center was none other than the Brown & Root Company which was awarded the 90 million dollar federal government construction contract on a cost "plus" basis.

In the 1960 Presidential race Johnson again used his corrupt political power to: almost steal the Democratic Presidential nomination from his rival John Kennedy; secure the position as the Vice Presidential candidate with Kennedy; and, to help steal the 1960 Presidential election for the Kennedy-Johnson ticket. Further, to guarantee that LBJ would still have a political position regardless of the outcome of the 1960 presidential election, Johnson had a special law passed in Texas giving him a "win-win" election position. Johnson got the Texas legislature to pass a special law allowing him to run on the Texas election ballot as both a U.S. Senate candidate and as Kennedy's Vice-Presidential candidate. If the Kennedy-Johnson ticket lost in the national race, LBJ could still remain an incumbent U.S. Senator. And, if he won on the ticket in the national race, he could then resign his position as a Senator. This devious plan allowed Johnson to win, even if he lost.

In addition to the "special Texas law for LBJ", he followed his typical pattern of securing victory for the Kennedy-Johnson ticket at all costs in the presidential election. According to most historians, Richard Nixon actually won the 1960 Presidential election until the Kennedy-Johnson ticket stole the election by vote fraud. This included deliberately jammed voting machines in Republican voting districts as well as discovery of floating ballot boxes containing Republican Presidential votes found in the Chicago river. While Chicago with its Democratic Mayor Richard Daley received the most national press for its election fraud, the state with the most voter fraud was none other than Texas. Eventually, the Kennedy-Johnson ticket claimed victory by less than 100,000 votes out of over 50 million cast, in the most corrupt presidential election in history. National magazines ran full page stories about the corruption, with such headlines as "How to Steal An Election."

Lyndon Baines Johnson began his political career by stealing a college election. He maintained political power for 30 years by the same practices. After it was all over, Johnson in reflecting upon his political career, acknowledged that most

Americans hated him. However, he hoped that future generations would view him differently and appreciate him as a "great leader". Fortunately, America's heirs will not be blinded by the Johnson propaganda that he left behind and will even more clearly see that Lyndon B. Johnson was a political thief.

13

Johnson—
The Bag Man

One of the easiest ways to become a millionaire is to become a politician. This cruel statement is more than a half-truth when one recalls the number of politicians who have amassed large fortunes while allegedly living on government salaries. It probably is even closer to the truth if one also considers that politicians spend millions to get elected to a job that pays less than the cost of just one campaign commercial. Why is this done? The answer is power. Power to control. And power to amass a fortune by selling influence, inside information, and collecting bribes. With enough political power a politician can maintain the public appearance of propriety while still stealing a fortune. This stealing can have the appearance of being perfectly legal by the use of exorbitant public speaking fees, lucrative contracts for spouses and relatives, and the ancient tactic of having the campaign adviser masquerade as the real crook (and thereby take the "fall" if something goes awry).

Lyndon Johnson was *not* an "honest" politician. For over three decades he was the political "bag man" for Texas political interests. When Johnson came to Congress in the 1930's he was a young politician from a poor family. He died leaving an estimated fortune of $14,000,000 to $20,000,000. Even if Lyndon Johnson had saved every single penny of all of his political earnings, he could never have amassed enough money to save one million dollars. Johnson obviously obtained his wealth by other means, and the other means involved political extortion, political kickbacks, and political bribery. To understand how he did this, two false claims must immediately be put to rest. One, Johnson did *not* marry into money. And two, Johnson's wife did *not* amass the Johnson family wealth through shrewd investment skills.

Johnson's wife Lady Bird was the daughter of a country storekeeper in a small village in East Texas. Her father did not die until 1960 and any inheritance that she received following his death was long after the Johnsons' had already amassed their fortune. One of Johnson's earliest maneuvers involved land located around his father-in-law's little village store. By obvious Johnson influence, a huge wartime ordinance plant was built, of all places in America, on Johnson's land next to his father-in-law's little store. To avoid being caught in a political scandal Lyndon and his wife conveyed the land to her father on July 27, 1942. Just days later her father sold the land to the United States government (August 5, 1942). But this was not the end to this federal windfall for the Johnsons. The ordinance plant created a huge profit center for Lady Bird's father. He owned the only store in the entire area where all of the military ordnance workers had to shop.[12]

It is true that a substantial portion of the Johnson family assets were in Lady Bird Johnson's name. But holding title did not make her the astute business woman she was portrayed. Rather, she held title in her name to allow Johnson to wheel and deal while still claiming that he did not have a conflict of interest because his "wife" was getting the huge profits from the ventures, not himself.

---

[12] The same Johnson "trick" was used when the space center was decided to be built in Texas. The space center was in fact built on worthless desert land "donated" by a Texas Oil Company. Fortunately for the oil company, the generosity was well returned since it owned all of the surrounding land which skyrocketed from valueless desert dirt into valuable commercial land adjacent to the center.

The group that helped make Johnson the wealthiest were two Texans who owned the Brown & Root Company, which became one of the largest recipients of Federal government contracts totalling billions in business. A direct time correlation exists between Brown & Root Company's rise to national business power and Johnson's rise from obscurity to the King of Capital Hill. The connection was so direct that a national investigation was started to investigate claims of illegal campaign contributions to Johnson. In typical Johnson fashion, the investigation ended when the evidence was destroyed.

However, one thing that was not destroyed were the documents that demonstrated how Johnson acquired his family's television and radio stations throughout the southwest. The Federal Communications Commission, made up of a few select people chosen to serve on its board, controls the right to broadcast radio and television signals. If a broadcaster has its license to broadcast revoked or not renewed the broadcast enterprise is worthless. A person with "connections" to control the licensing could extort majority control from any broadcast enterprise by arranging to detain or threaten to revoke the broadcast license.

Texas politician Sam Rayburn was not only one of LBJ's close friends, but also a Johnson political patron. During Johnson's television and radio acquisition period one of the few FCC members (who controlled all licenses) was a nephew of Uncle Sam (Rayburn). It is therefore not unusual that the Johnsons were able to buy their first radio station with no money down and at ten percent of its original price. Just before the Johnsons acquired the station, the FCC announced that it was going to revoke the station's permit, making it worthless. Within one month after the Johnsons' noncash purchase at only 10% of the station's value, the FCC reapproved the license based on the sale to the Johnson family. Similar practices and purchases followed and by the mid 1950's the Johnson family owned majority interests in a number of stations.

It is not unusual that one of the first post World War II

television licenses granted in the entire country was to the Johnson family for the Austin area. And, despite Austin's size and position as being the Texas state capitol, the FCC for decades refused to allow any other television stations in Austin (aside from LBJ's), thereby protecting the Johnsons' television monopoly for the region.

Johnson's fortune also came from actual cash kickbacks. As early as 1955, it was reported that Johnson was accepting bribes from organized crime elements. Even the "missing" teamster leader Jimmy Hoffa allegedly paid $100,000 for LBJ's help with his criminal problems. This was not surprising, since Gulf Oil Company was reported to have initiated one of its new executives with his first job assignment by having him deliver a $50,000 bribe to Johnson. Other bribe reports have also surfaced including a $100,000 spending spree by LBJ with bribe funds deposited in a Hong Kong bank for his benefit. Johnson spread bribery wealth to his brother who was hired as a "consultant" by Transport Company of Texas after it was awarded a multi-million dollar federal government "housekeeping" contract for some U.S. Military bases.

However, the biggest bribery scandal that erupted was the *seven billion dollar* military plane contract that Johnson pushed through Congress for a Dallas-Fort Worth company. While this topic will be discussed in a subsequent chapter, it is important to note that testimony by an independent witness under oath linked a satchel full of cash to then Vice President Johnson as a bribe for pushing the plane contract through Congress.

Johnson's rise to national power, however, came from his ability to dole out the money to other politicians. Early on wealthy Texans quickly realized that national influence for their Texas businesses could not be based on only their two U.S. Senators. They shrewdly determined that if they could get other U.S. Senators in the "hip pocket" of one of their senators it would result in strong political clout for him and them.

And of course, they selected Johnson to be the "bag man" probably based on their analysis of his character. Johnson became a master at doling out money in exchange for favors. LBJ's money bag was nonpartisan and he became so savvy that he only contributed to politicians who were certain to win, contributing heavily to those who were "shoe-ins" and giving little or nothing to those who might lose. This allowed Johnson and his Texas cronies to create a Congress that was stacked only with victors who owed Johnson favors. The money bag allowed LBJ to buy respect on Capital Hill and eventually seize the position of majority leader in the Senate, the second most powerful position in government.

14

The Capacity to Kill

It is difficult to conceptualize the character flaws that a man must possess to be able to plan and commit a premeditated murder. For this reason it is impossible to say with certainty whether Lyndon Johnson was a man capable of such an act. However, what is known about Johnson's character in this regard is troubling.

A person's respect for life can be seen by his treatment of all living things, big and small. In Johnson's case, in life, just like in politics, he believed there was no need to follow rules. Lyndon Baines Johnson was a hunter who did not believe in giving the prey any chance. In fact, it can be said that LBJ's only rule about hunting was that he would only hunt if a kill was guaranteed. For instance, Texas law required hunting to stop at sundown. Johnson hunted after sundown. Johnson and his friends owned a lavish glass enclosed hunting tower complete with an elevator. At nightfall, prey would be lured to the tower and huge search lights would then be turned on. Johnson would take careful aim with his telescopic rifle and murder the game which had no chance to escape. For Johnson, killing by his rules gave more pleasure than being a sportsman and taking his chances at a miss.

According to Billy Sol Estes, one of Johnson's close friends, LBJ was capable of executing a human being who

THE CHARACTER OF LBJ • 105

was performing his government job. In 1961, U.S. Agriculture Agent Marshall was found shot to death in his car in Texas.[13] Found next to Agent Marshall was a single action rifle. By autopsy it was determined that Marshall died from 5 gunshot wounds to the head, but Marshall's death was "determined" by a Texas county coroner to be "suicide." The coroner claimed that Agent Marshall killed himself with a single action rifle by placing a bullet into the rifle and then firing it into his head and repeating the entire process five separate times until he was dead. A scandal broke out when it was discovered that Agent Marshall was on the trail of a multi-million dollar swindle of the Federal Government's Agricultural Division. The scandal eventually became known as the Billy Sol Estes Affair since Estes was the culprit and LBJ's close friend.

Years later, Estes reportedly told a Texas grand jury that Vice President Johnson was directly involved in the murder.

In another case of mysterious death, Lyndon Johnson profited handsomely from the deaths of two pilots. The matter initially began in 1960 when Johnson was given use of an airplane valued at $500,000 by a wealthy Texas oilman for use by Johnson in his Democratic presidential campaign against John F. Kennedy. To avoid the public appearance of impropriety and negative press claims that the oilman was improperly backing LBJ, Johnson and the oilman signed a bogus plane lease. The bogus lease included a false option for Johnson to purchase the plane at $300,000 under its fair market value. Johnson used the plane until he lost his Democratic presidential bid to Kennedy and after the loss the oilman demanded return of the plane. However, Johnson refused to return it claiming that he had "exercised his option" to purchase the plane at its discounted price although he had paid nothing on the purchase.

---

[13] The Bill Sol Estes affair was the first major scandal to break during Johnson's term as Vice President under Kennedy. This scandal, along with others, will be discussed in greater detail in the *Motive* Section.

Though the oilman continued to privately protest the issue he quickly became silent after Friday, February 17, 1961 when Lyndon Baines Johnson ordered that the plane, now fully insured in his name, be flown to his ranch. When the pilot and copilot (whose lives were also heavily insured for Johnson's benefit) refused to make the trip because of terrible weather, Johnson let loose a tirade of profanities. When the Austin air tower informed the pilots not to make the flight due to the severe weather and because Johnson's ranch had no ground control instruments for safety, Johnson still demanded that the flight be made and he forced the pilots to take off. As may have been expected, the pilots were unable to find Johnson's ranch. They crashed and perished. However, it was not until three days later on Monday, February 20, 1961 that anyone at the Johnson Ranch noticed the plane "overdue" and reported it missing. To this day no one has ever explained the urgent need for the plane to be flown to the ranch in dangerous weather, since Johnson neither used nor apparently even missed the plane for the entire weekend. The end result was that Johnson pocketed a quick $700,000 in insurance money on the lives of two men and on a plane that he did not equitably own.

Lyndon Baines Johnson not only had the capacity to kill, but it seems he had character flaws that permitted him to do it in a calculated manner for his own benefit.

15 _____

A Distillation of Johnson's Character

Lyndon B. Johnson did anything and everything he wanted. He gratified his sexual impulses by repeated adulterous relationships. He quenched his thirst by out drinking all rivals. Johnson emptied his bladder wherever it was full.[14] He advanced politically by cut throat tactics that allowed him to steal everything from his first election (in student council) through his first U.S. Senate election (by judicial decree in his favor) to his victory as our country's Vice-President.

Johnson was a political schemer. His standard practice was to make bold illicit moves to his advantage and then rely upon his power to cover up the resulting problems. He did this time and time again. Lyndon Johnson had the character, temperament, and immoral nature to eliminate anything obstructing his path to power—including possessing the intellect, the capacity, and the creativity to successfully kill!

[14] Attempting to be sensitive towards some readers the chapter relating to Lyndon Johnson's obscene table manners and bathroom practices was deleted from this book. However, as a tidbit to others, it is sufficient to note that President Johnson used Secret Service Agents as a human shield so he could urinate outside while entertaining during White House garden functions.

SECTION 3

Johnson's
Motives

16

Motive in Criminal Investigations

A criminal suspect is a person who may be involved in a crime. Generally all persons who have a motive to commit the crime must initially be considered suspects. Police, criminal investigators, judges, and lawyers often refer to the word "motive" as it relates to two distinct elements. "Motive" means both the cause or power that induces the crime as well as the purpose to effectuate the result. However, in reality the word "motive" for a criminal investigation can simply be considered synonymous with the word—REASON. For what reason was the crime committed?

As all of us know from watching the TV crime shows, one of the fundamental principles in solving a serious premeditated crime is for the investigator to identify everyone who had a motive. These people are then grouped into the general category of criminal suspects. Investigators then rank the criminal suspects in decreasing order of suspicion starting with those with the strongest motive, who become part of the Prime Suspect list. If a criminal investigation skips this basic step, the chances increase that the crime may not be solved, because history and common sense have shown that rarely does a person commit a premeditated crime without a motive.

On November 29, 1963, Johnson as the new President appointed seven men to serve as members of the President's

Commission on the Assassination of President Kennedy (a.k.a. The Warren Commission). The seven Commission members had twelve staff members to aid them plus legal counsel and fourteen assistant counsel. These numbers increased six fold by the addition of clerical staff, court reporters, and consultants. In all the Commission reviewed over 2,300 F.B.I. interview reports and over 800 Secret Service reports, that constituted a combined interview total of over 26,000 people who had some possible information about the assassination. The Commission also conducted hearings and took testimony from 551 live witnesses. Unfortunately, the Commission with all of its staff people, with all of its exhibits, with all of the interviews and testimony, and with the concerted help from all police agencies—failed in its purpose by not offering a rational explanation as to why the President was murdered. They found no motive for Oswald's alleged act. Eventually the Commission just gave up and determined that Oswald, as President Kennedy's murderer, had a motive that was too obscure to discover.

Can you imagine that? The alleged murderer had no motive and the succeeding President had several strong ones? The Warren Commission claimed that it investigated all suspects and all theories relating to the assassination, but it completely ignored the most obvious suspect. And while they claimed to have interviewed or examined every single person who was an eyewitness to the assassination—they ignored one. And that one eyewitness, whom they did not question, a person ignored as a criminal suspect, was the only person in the world who directly benefitted from the assassination. Lyndon Baines Johnson should not only have been considered a suspect in the killing of President John F. Kennedy, but because of his strong motives, he should have been considered a prime suspect.

Since Johnson's character has already been considered and because it at least hints that he might have performed any act to advance his career, this section will examine his activities as a suspect to determine the extent and depth of his potential motives for killing the President. This job should have been done in 1963, but was not. However, as the evidence is reviewed, one should keep in mind the world situation in 1963 and try to forgive the members of Lyndon Johnson's Warren Commission for their failure to consider indicting their employer for murder.

17

Johnson's Obsession

Many children dream of growing up to become President of the United States. Lyndon Johnson's childhood dream was no different. Johnson made his first public proclamation about becoming President while still in grade school. However, in Lyndon's case his childhood dream never faded. Becoming President became his life's obsession. In fact, even before entering politics and when, as a young school teacher, he was mocked by his students, he would scold them saying they were looking at the "future President of the United States." Although few of the students believed Johnson, his statements left a lasting impression since they rarely heard a grown man still talking about childhood dreams.

The Johnson obsession to become President continued past his teaching days and when he finally made it to Congress his continuous patter on the subject shocked colleagues. According to one Congressman who knew Johnson, LBJ would sometimes just blurt out the fact that he was going to be President. To achieve this dream Johnson worked constantly towards it . . . rising from Congressman, to U.S. Senator, and finally to Senate Majority Leader. The only mistake that Johnson ever made in his march toward the Presidency was underestimating Jack Kennedy in 1960. According to Johnson's friend Bobby Baker, LBJ felt that when it came down to the actual 1960 Democratic nomination (or as Johnson put it "when it gets down to the nut-cutting") he would have enough power to steal the nomination from Kennedy by controlling the party captains from each state.

Because of his belief in his ability to steal the nomination, Johnson approached the 1960 Democratic Convention with the attitude "I am not running but I'm gonna win." However, his first ballot loss to JFK at the convention not only caused him deep humiliation, but created the bitter disbelief that he had been double crossed. The nomination loss left Johnson with only two avenues towards still achieving his obsession to attain the Presidency. LBJ could either wait for a future election or he could take the chance of obtaining the subordinate position as the Vice-Presidential candidate with Kennedy in hopes of fate intervening. Johnson chose the latter option and became Kennedy's subordinate running mate. While most political analysts were shocked by Johnson's choice, Johnson took the lesser position since it was his only chance to become President in the near future. Insiders to the Johnson camp have stated that while political observers viewed the Vice Presidency as a dead end position that was not worth a "warm bucket of spit", Johnson saw it as his opportunity to obtain the impossible.

His obsession was fulfilled by the suspicious murder of the President, but his bizarre actions both before and after attaining the office confirm that his drive was truly an obsession.

While Johnson erred by underestimating Kennedy's power in 1960, perhaps President John Kennedy's greatest failure was his inability to perceive his successor's ego as a danger, rather than a mere character defect. When Kennedy took office he was immediately met with Johnson's first unreasonable request. Vice President Johnson proposed to President Kennedy that he should be allowed to move into the White House and to share the presidential power with President Kennedy under a two person presidential system. At first Kennedy thought Johnson was joking, but when the Vice

President persisted, President Kennedy flatly refused to create a new governing duet for America.

But Kennedy's refusal did not deter Lyndon Johnson. Johnson routinely demanded that he be allowed to travel together with Kennedy even though national security dictated separate travel. And, when Vice President Johnson finally discovered that he was not the President, he refused to admit it. Rather, each day Vice President Johnson would have his driver take him to the White House (where he did not have offices and where he did not work). Johnson would then exit the vehicle and proceed through the White House grounds. He would enter the White House and walk down the halls deliberately passing in front of the Oval office. LBJ would then exit the White House out the back door, walk off the grounds, and walk the block to the building where he actually worked. This curious daily practice has never been followed by any other Vice President in history! However, perhaps Johnson was practicing for his big day.

Johnson's big day came on November 22, 1963 when the President was executed on the streets of Dallas. Within 12 hours of Johnson's return to Washington, as the new President, he had already hung a gold framed portrait of himself in Kennedy's Presidential office. And, to add to this Napoleonic complex, Johnson:

1. Immediately fired the President's secretary and then ordered Kennedy's widow to vacate the premises by Monday, the day of her husband's funeral;

2. Ordered the removal of President Kennedy's belongings from the Oval office less than 24 hours after his death;

3. Vividly recalled the exact instant in the assassination crisis when someone first called him ''Mr. President'';

4. Claimed that on the assassination day Americans were not only upset with Kennedy's death, but were con-

cerned about a rumor that he had suffered a heart attack; and

5. Claimed that it was his skill as a world leader after the assassination that prevented the New York Stock Exchange from dropping.

When Johnson succeeded to the Presidency, for the first time in U.S. history a professional photographer became a permanent fixture in the White House as a government employee. The new government photographer did his job well since within just the first few weeks of Johnson taking office over *11,000* photographs of Johnson were snapped.

Johnson's official rise to the Presidency completely unleashed his monstrous ego which was the only thing larger than the State of Texas. Everything Johnson touched he had to put his own initials on to make sure that everyone knew it was his. This included: his wife (Lady Bird Johnson); his daughters Luci and Lynda (LBJ's); his best friend John Connally (who was called Little Boy Johnson); his ranch (the LBJ); his dogs (beagles initialed LBJ); his household flag (an LBJ logo); and, even his office furniture (that was emblazoned with his LBJ brand). Johnson was so egocentric that not only did he claim that Johnson City his hometown was named after his family (which was untrue), but he also managed to have the Federal Space Center in Texas named after himself (The Johnson Space Center).

Not to be outdone by predecessors, Johnson hired five secretaries to President Kennedy's two. He created the largest and most expensive White House staff in history with over 1,500 workers. He ordered the construction of a Roman emperor style bathroom complete with handpainted murals depicting a banquet for an emperor along with installation of golden chandeliers in the bathroom. And, in furtherance of Roman tradition Johnson ordered the use of a United States serviceman to act as his valet which included the requirement that the soldier groom Johnson's feet. Even in public the soldier would silently approach Johnson and kneel before him. The soldier would then remove Johnson's socks and shoes, cleanse his feet, pat them dry, and conclude by placing fresh socks and shoes on Johnson.

President Johnson had a throne or "special chair" and he demanded that it travel with him to all functions in order to retain a regal appearance. Johnson ordered that one military soldier be assigned to the sole duty of caring for the throne. Aboard Air Force One another "special chair" was constructed for Johnson. That chair had automatic buttons that allowed Johnson to raise the chair above his passengers. And, in conjunction with the airplane throne Johnson demanded that all the other seats on the plane be reversed to face the rear of the plane where he had his desk and that a clear glass divider be installed between him and the passengers. Thus, all passengers riding with Johnson were forced to remain looking at him at all times, even when he had private conferences behind the glass divider. The total costs of these extravagances to the taxpayers is unknown. However, it is known that Johnson spent over one million dollars in materials alone, customizing another government plane that was used solely as a backup.

During one plane flight, President Johnson shocked the crowd of passengers flying with him when he shouted from his special chair that all of the good leaders in the world were dead, except for him, and in King of the Jungle style fashion he began to thump his chest and cry out "I am the King". These acts were consistent with predictions of some national broadcasters dating back to 1960 recognizing that LBJ was unfit to govern. For instance, NBC in its program Emphasis USA concluded that Lyndon Johnson was a man incapable of governing America because of his ego, temper, and sarcasm. Johnson's staff knew of his irrational character and they classified it among themselves as a "mad on". When Johnson had a "mad on" everyone stayed away since LBJ would explode at the nearest target. These "mad ons" included: throwing a telephone into a swimming pool because it transmitted bad news; violently swearing at a photographer who snapped a picture of his "bad side"; grabbing Secret Service agents by their coat lapels; and belittling citizens who asked him questions, with responses such as, "why would you ask me, the leader of the western world, a chicken shit question like that?" Members of his staff privately consulted with a psychiatrist about his mental health.

Lyndon B. Johnson had a character disorder so severe that he committed acts that absolute monarchs would dare not do. Once, Johnson demanded that the Presidential yacht travel backwards down the Potomac River, because the wind was apparently disturbing him while on deck. Johnson insisted that his aides keep exact count of each time that he received applause during a speech and he would severely reprimand them if their tally totalled less than his (LBJ's tally was always higher).

Perhaps because Johnson believed that he was the "ruler of the western world", he thought that he was also entitled to its assets. One glaring example of Johnson's use of federal funds for his own use was his misappropriation of money set aside for construction and maintenance of Presidential bombshelters. Johnson took the money, millions, for his own use. He used the bombshelter funds to install an irrigation system throughout his Texas ranch, resurface his ranch roads, install showers, and even build a personal air conditioned movie theater on his ranch. The *Washington Star* proclaimed that LBJ was the most blatant personal abuser of government funds and services in U.S. history.

This included Johnson's use of the Internal Revenue Service as a vehicle to carry out his grievances against others. IRS agents were turned loose against U.S. Senators and news commentators with whom Johnson disagreed. The F.B.I. was made into a personal LBJ detective agency. This included directed F.B.I. investigations into:

1. Obtaining defamatory material against any U.S. Congressman as well as all individual citizens who publicly opposed the Vietnam war;

2. Looking for "fags" and "perverts" in the Republican party;

3. Use of special squads of F.B.I. agents for Johnson's personal use during both the 1964 and 1968 Democratic conventions; and

4. The background and sexual habits of the boys who dated Johnson's single daughter.

Once Johnson announced that he would not seek re-election in 1968 his misuse of government funds increased. Johnson began using C-141 military transport planes to haul tons of cargo back to his ranches. The cargo even included such things as crates of stolen government toilet paper. And, while by rule an ex-President can have the use of a telephone switchboard for up to six months after leaving office, Johnson managed to keep his government switchboard open for another 4½ years while using the services of 12 men from the White House Communications staff to operate it. LBJ also somehow secured the full time use of a government helicopter complete with a crew for his personal purposes.

Even after Johnson's death, the abuse continued for years. It included personal use at the Johnson ranch of a full time Navy cook to prepare family meals and to give family massages at taxpayer expense, as well as the assignment of two military boats on LBJ's personal lake with a full time Naval officer on the boats for the sole purpose of operating them for the family.

Lyndon B. Johnson made sure that his ego would survive his life. In Texas, there is Lake Lyndon Johnson as well as the Johnson Space Center. In Austin, Texas, the LBJ Memorial Library stands complete with five floors of boxes containing over 30 million documents about LBJ. Also located in the library is the LBJ Museum where visitors can learn about the "great accomplishments" that Johnson achieved. Contained in the museum is a display dedicated to his high school career as well as another consisting of a replica of his White House office. Down the road from Johnson's hometown is the LBJ National Historic Site. Federal park rangers give tours of the Johnson homestead. The only problem with these self-created remnants of Johnson's legacy is they do not supply an inkling of truth about the real Lyndon Baines Johnson.

It is abundantly clear that from childhood on Lyndon Baines Johnson lived and worked towards only one goal—his dream of becoming President. He accepted the subordinate position of Vice-President to keep his dream alive. And, on November 22, 1963 when he finally achieved the dream, LBJ grabbed all the rewards that anyone could ever fantasize about, and when that was not enough to satisfy his obsession . . . he seized even more.

18

Johnson's Family Health History

On November 22, 1963, President John F. Kennedy was 46 years old. Lyndon Johnson was 55 years old. Eight years before this date, in July of 1955, Johnson at the young age of 47 had suffered a massive heart attack. At that time he was rushed to the hospital in shock and remained in critical condition for days. Johnson's serious heart attack required a full six week hospital stay. After hospitalization his poor heart condition demanded complete rest for another three months. Therefore, Johnson knew as early as 1955 that he was a man with a weak heart. At that time he was also aware that he was following the health pattern for all Johnson men.

Johnson's uncle only lived to the age of 57 when he died from a massive heart attack. His father followed suit by dying at age 60 from heart disease. And, Johnson in 1955 at the age of only 47 had already suffered a massive heart attack that almost killed him. It was for this reason that in 1960 Johnson at the age of 52 made a bid for the Presidency. With the Johnson family heart history and with his own major heart problems he knew that the odds were very slim that he would live a long life. His 1960 Presidential bid was surely based on his knowledge that statistically he had only 5 to 10 more years to live!

When young Jack Kennedy defeated Johnson to achieve

the 1960 Democratic nomination, Johnson did the only thing he could do to still attain his dream. He forced his way onto the Kennedy ticket. After his 1955 heart attack, Johnson's long forgotten childhood fear of being paralyzed from a heart attack not only returned but developed into adult nightmares. Johnson reported, "They got worse after my heart attack . . . for I knew then how awful it was to lose command of myself."

By November of 1963 the presidential dream of Vice President Lyndon Baines Johnson faced two major problems. While Johnson was close to being the President, he still was not President, because fate had not intervened. And, time was running out. Johnson knew that three years had already passed since he first took the position of Vice President. And that while the younger Kennedy had some health problems, his health had not faltered enough to allow "fate" to intervene.

Johnson also knew that with President Kennedy as an incumbent president, the most he could hope for was to again be JFK's right hand man on the 1964 ticket. It would have been virtually impossible for Johnson to wrestle the 1964 Democratic nomination away from President Kennedy. Therefore, at best, assuming that Johnson was able to hang on to his health and his fading political career, 1968 would be the next time that he could again try to run for the Presidency. And, of course in 1968 Johnson would be 60 years old. At 60 he would have lived three years longer than his uncle, and would have survived a full 13 years after his own massive heart attack. To run for President in 1968 would have required Johnson to run a strenuous campaign at the exact same age that his father was when he died.

From a practical standpoint, Johnson had to have known that his best and perhaps only chance to obtain the Presidency was to step up to the position. It avoided both the time risk of waiting as well as losing another nomination while attempting to obtain the coveted position.

Time waits for no man and Lyndon Johnson knew that his time was running out.

19

LBJ's Hatred
of the Kennedys

Lyndon Johnson desperately wanted to be a President. And, although Johnson waited until the eve of the 1960 Democratic Presidential Convention to "announce" his candidacy, the announcement was not at all impromptu. The truth is that LBJ ran a national presidential campaign for almost one year before the actual announcement of his candidacy. Johnson's political plan involved maintaining a low profile during all of the presidential primaries. He expected the other democratic presidential candidates to bitterly fight among themselves in the primaries. If this occurred, no front runner would have emerged by the convention, at which time Johnson planned to steal the nomination for himself by use of his political power. The strategy almost worked. Unfortunately, for Johnson, on this occasion he underestimated John Kennedy's power and overestimated his own.

In preparation for Johnson's "unannounced" presidential campaign (that he ran for almost a year before the Democratic Convention), he initially raised over one million dollars. The funds were principally contributed by a small group of conservative Texas oil men. As early as 1959 a small group of Johnson's friends were called together and told about his plans to run an unannounced presidential campaign throughout the primaries and attempt to steal the nomination right on the convention floor. This band of Texas men loved the LBJ strategy and formed a private political group for Johnson called the "Texas Rangers." The lead "Ranger", who proved to be the most effective, was Johnson's friend John Connally. Part of the ground work performed by the Texas Rangers was the continued public dissemination of laudatory press releases about Johnson to keep his name before the public. One press release boasted that Johnson was the greatest Senate Majority Leader in the history of the United States and would therefore make a great leader. The intent was to convince the public of Johnson's presidential leadership qualities. The base city for LBJ's Texas Rangers was none other than Dallas. Starting in October of 1959, Dallas was also the headquarters for the official Johnson for President Committee. This official campaign committee was also composed of Johnson's old Texas friends.

While Johnson and his Texas Rangers were laying the ground work for his power move at the Democratic Convention, John F. Kennedy was busy tallying up supporters nationwide. In Pittsburgh's preferential Democratic presidential primary, Kennedy slaughtered Johnson by a hundred to one margin (JFK received over 76,000 write-in votes to LBJ's mere 745 votes). In another primary on April 12, 1960, Kennedy again destroyed Johnson by receiving 34,000 votes to Johnson's 442. When it became clear that Kennedy was breaking away from the other Democratic candidates and developing a strong following, attempts were initiated by Johnson to destroy him as a candidate. This first began with Johnson's aides obtaining and mailing out to both voters and delegates damaging material about Kennedy (the material was originally prepared by the Republicans). Following this were verbal attacks by Johnson calling Kennedy the "Absentee Senator." When none of these tactics were successful in slowing Kennedy's ground swell of support, Johnson's attacks became more vicious. He not only attacked Jack Kennedy as a candidate, but attacked the Kennedy family with slurs such as the "Catholic Conspiracy." His hope was that this would draw Protestant support to him. And, in an attempt to win an even broader range of prejudiced supporters, Johnson appealed to American patriotism by relentlessly attacking Kennedy's father claiming that Joe Kennedy was sympathetic to the Nazis during World War II. This, in spite of the fact that not only was Jack Kennedy injured in combat but he also lost his older brother in the war.

When Johnson's mudslinging failed things got worse. While most Americans recall the Watergate break-in scandal during the Nixon era, few people today remember the 1960 Manhattan break-in that was even more scandalous. Just before the Democratic National Convention "someone" committed two separate break-ins into the medical offices of Jack Kennedy's doctors. While no one was caught, the burglars were obviously after Kennedy's medical files and the culprits were obvious. The break-ins were consistent with what Johnson later did at the Democratic Convention. Johnson began the Convention by spreading rumors that he knew that JFK was seriously stricken with Addison's disease. And, on other occasions he would go to great lengths to tell the press and delegates that Kennedy was suffering from a terminal illness and that voters should not support a man who was likely to die.

John Connally, as the key Texas Ranger, also did his part to support his friend. At the Convention, Connally called his own press conference where he confirmed to the press that the health rumors that they had heard about Kennedy from LBJ were true. Connally claimed that JFK was a "very sick man" and implied that JFK would soon die. When the press did not fall for the ploy, Connally pleaded with them to print the stories about the Kennedy's health problems anyway, with the promise to supply proof later to support the news stories.

When this plan failed, Johnson got meaner. He conducted obscene verbal attacks against Kennedy that were so severe that they could not be printed. He also publicly referred to JFK as the "scrawny little fellow with rickets" demonstrating Kennedy's body size with his fingers. When the Kennedy camp heard of Johnson's statements, Bobby Kennedy finally exclaimed, "I knew he (LBJ) hated Jack, but I didn't know he hated him that much." Johnson even got one of his Texas multimillionaire supporters into the act. Texas millionaire H. L. Hunt violated federal election laws to help Johnson. H. L. Hunt anonymously printed and mailed over 200,000 copies of a speech lambasting Kennedy as a Catholic, which claimed that if he became President, he would destroy America's religious freedom. As a result of this illegal election action, the United States Senate began a federal investigation into Hunt's conduct with Hunt eventually apologizing for his federal election law violations by simply claiming that he was just trying to "help Lyndon."

During the entire 1960 Democratic Convention Johnson only obtained one short lived success against Kennedy. This occurred when he baited John Kennedy into a debate at the Biltmore Ballroom with the entire room stacked with Johnson's friends. When Kennedy appeared to debate Johnson, LBJ did not debate but rather conducted a bitter attack on Kennedy to the cheers of his friends. However, the Democratic Convention hall was not packed with Johnson supporters and John Kennedy rolled to a first ballot victory. Johnson's political strategy had failed. In defeat, LBJ, rather than go to his convention headquarters to thank his few loyal supporters, chose instead to brood in his hotel room with—H. L. Hunt. But Johnson as the loser did not fall by the wayside. Though John Fitzgerald Kennedy had endured months of Johnson's name calling, dirty tricks, and personal hatred, he finally ended up with Johnson as his running mate. How this actually occurred has always been the subject of great debate among historians, but regardless of the correct version—Johnson had his hand in obtaining his Vice Presidential position since it is without doubt that Johnson was not one of Kennedy's top Vice Presidential choices.

One version as to Johnson's grab of the Vice Presidency involved a pay off by Johnson to Kennedy for the position. Thus, if this version is believed, Johnson paid for the privilege of obtaining the second position which thereby allowed him the chance to still attain his dream. A second version involved Johnson's use of political power rather than payola to obtain the spot. It has been claimed that while Johnson failed to have enough political clout to steal the nomination from Kennedy, he had enough political muscle to fight for the Democratic Vice Presidential position on the convention floor. And, because Kennedy did not want to split the party he reluctantly accepted Johnson as his running mate.

A third version appears to have strong validity because it has been supported by several witnesses who were present at the convention. Unfortunately, each witness' account differs slightly making it a version with several versions. But the basics are all the same with John F. Kennedy knowing that he needed unity in the party to achieve success in 1960. To accomplish this task, Kennedy strategists thought that unity could be accomplished if Kennedy offered the second position on his ticket to Johnson which would appease fractionating Democratic groups and also placate LBJ. It was expected that Johnson would turn down the offer and would then return to the Senate as its powerful majority leader. The offer was only to be a token gesture and everyone knew it. In fact, until only hours before Kennedy's actual offer Johnson had publicly told reporters that he would never accept a position on the Kennedy ticket. Whether LBJ was so cunning that he actually baited Kennedy into making a public offer to him which he then would publicly accept, or just changed his mind, will never be known. What is known is that no matter what version is accepted as true, once Kennedy offered the job to Johnson, rather than decline it, to the surprise of everyone, he accepted it. This created shock waves at the convention.

Thus, the Kennedy-Johnson ticket was formed. It consisted of a charismatic man who had won his party's nomination with overwhelming support, and a bitter Texan who publicly belittled and hated the winner. What discussions ensued in Johnson's hotel suite after he lost the nomination to Kennedy is not exactly known. But one Johnson subordinate who was present said that LBJ demanded the right hand man position saying, "tell um . . . that I deserve the Vice Presidency and intend to get it." Perhaps the strangest and most mysterious premonition came from Johnson after publicly accepting the position of Vice President. Just hours before, Johnson emphatically told one reporter that he would never accept the subordinate position. And, when questioned by the same reporter moments after he accepted the position, Johnson hinted at what later became a tragic reality by saying:

". . . I have now learned that one out of every four Presidents dies in office . . . and I am a gambling man!"

Bygones were not bygones for Lyndon B. Johnson after his nomination loss to Jack Kennedy. This was true when the two were running mates, and even after they were elected to office together. On the surface it was necessary that the two showed a smooth and stable relationship. But underneath there was intense hostility existing. Just days after Kennedy's defeat of Nixon, as the new President-elect, he visited Johnson in an attempt to develop a cordial relationship. Unfortunately, Kennedy's trip was wasted since Johnson started things out by stubbornly failing to remove his hat to the newly elected leader. From that moment on things worsened with Kennedy not only having to handle the nation's problems, but also having to tolerate Lyndon Johnson's embarrassing public actions.

The two men were opposites. President Kennedy was well educated, well bred, and well mannered. As a gentleman he tolerated Johnson who at best was considered a crude cowboy. And, when Johnson created a political embarrassment all JFK could do was shrug and say "that's Lyndon." But while President Kennedy was capable of tolerating LBJ as his subordinate, Johnson was incapable of accepting Kennedy as his superior. Johnson was jealous, not only of the President's position, but of his charm, appearance, and public admiration.

Privately Johnson referred to the President and his friends as "red hots" and "lib-lab boys." He also constantly called the President's brother "the little shit." To Johnson the Kennedys were his enemy and he perceived every action by them as an attempt to humiliate him and to reduce his future chance for the Presidency. By 1963, Johnson in tears declared to Senator Dodd from Connecticut that the Kennedys were "sadists." Reports eventually filtered into the White House that Johnson would often fly into temper tantrums and kick doors while screaming about the Kennedys. This included such conduct as shouting into occupied reception rooms with paranoic phrases like, "why does the White House always have it in for me?"

Johnson hated the Kennedys because they destroyed his plan to steal the 1960 Democratic Presidential nomination. He viewed Jack Kennedy's elected position as President as one rightfully belonging to him. His hatred for the Kennedys was so intense that even after he obtained Presidential power by succession he treated the surviving Kennedy clan with immense disdain. LBJ's treatment of Jackie Kennedy immediately after her husband's death has always been considered socially and politically distasteful.

20

LBJ's Loss of Power

Perhaps the major reason for Johnson's intense hatred of the Kennedys was that he believed that they were the cause of his loss of political power. Prior to demanding and then obtaining the politically unimportant position of Vice President, Johnson held the second most powerful position in the United States as the Senate Majority Leader. From this mighty position, Lyndon Johnson took a big step down to become the Vice President. In this lowest of the low political position, Johnson's basic job was to be ready as the President's successor while making public appearances essentially on the President's behalf.

Until the recent Presidential elections of former Vice Presidents Richard Nixon and George Bush, the Vice Presidential role in American politics was considered to be the road to political ruin. This was one of Lyndon Johnson's major problems when he first took office, because he refused to accept the fact that he held an office with no political power and one that normally led nowhere. He mistakenly predicted that even without legitimate political power, as the Vice President, he would still be a major power force in Washington because his ego convinced himself that he, as a person, and not as an office holder, was the source of power and "power is where power goes.'' However, Johnson's opinion of himself was similar to a military general re-enlisting as a private under the mistaken belief that his power would remain with him. To Johnson's disbelief, the power did not follow. When LBJ soon realized that nothing followed and that he was wrong, he became even more bitter.

Lyndon Johnson's power rapidly diminished to such an extent and he became so unimportant in Washington circles, that though he was the Vice President, his home telephone number was published in the Washington telephone directory. Rather than having a job where he could order others, Johnson for the first time was stuck in a position that required him to accept orders. And he was repeatedly ordered out of the country on such non important ventures as goodwill fact finding and fence mending tours. By 1962, Johnson was so disgusted with his new job that he began talking openly about returning to Texas to either retire or to run for his U.S. Senate seat again. However, a plan to run in another U.S. Senate race posed great problems since many believed that Johnson was already losing his political power in Texas.

By the third year of John Kennedy's term the total time Johnson spent with the President in private conferences amounted to only one hour and fifty-three minutes. Thus, in 1963, the President and his ''forced'' Vice President spent less than two full hours together. From this alone it should have been clear to Johnson that his political expertise was not valued by the Kennedy administration. During the Bay of Pigs invasion, Johnson was not asked to offer advice in managing the crisis. During the invasion Johnson went to a flower festival in Virginia and then flew home to a barbecue in Texas. By 1963 Texas Democrats were conceding that Johnson had outlived his usefulness and that he would not be able to hold his home state for the party in the next presidential election. Clearly by late 1962 Vice President Lyndon Baines Johnson had lost most of his Washington political power. He became the butt of television jokes because of his political impotence. To make LBJ's political free fall worse was that by this time he knew that he was caught in a powerless position with a job terminable at the will of another.

21

Dump LBJ Campaign

After Johnson became president he claimed that if President Kennedy had not been killed, Kennedy would have kept him on the 1964 ticket. As proof, Johnson offered his "word" that Kennedy had promised him this. But Johnson's claim was directly contrary to the facts.

When the Kennedy-Johnson ticket barely won the 1960 election, it was already evident that Lyndon Johnson was not an asset in a national election. The 1960 ticket barely captured Texas. This surprised Kennedy and his staff who expected Johnson to at least provide strength in his own state.

By 1962, news articles were already reporting that Johnson would be dumped from the 1964 ticket. In a press conference in May of 1962 the President was asked whether he was going to dump Johnson. By July of 1962 the *New York Daily News* ran a story that Johnson would loose his position on the 1964 ticket based on statements by one of the President's sisters.

Compounding these reports in 1962 were the serious scandals encircling Johnson, each one more serious than the last. Republican Richard Nixon predicted that LBJ would not be on the 1964 Democratic ticket.

As the 1964 election approached, political analysts were already predicting that Texas would swing to the Republicans if Johnson was on the Democratic ticket. It was clear to everyone that Johnson had to "go". In final confirmation of this are the last dictated words that Kennedy's personal secretary ever took from him, '*Johnson would not be his running mate*' in the 1964 election!

With all of this public information to the contrary, why did Johnson, after the assassination, claim that Kennedy would have kept him around? The obvious answer is that he created this lie in an effort to eliminate himself as one of the murder suspects.[15]

---

[15] Some readers may wonder why, if Johnson was a liability as the Vice President, did he win by such a wide margin in 1964 as President? The answer is timing. In 1964, Americans did not vote for LBJ, rather they voted for the stability of a temporary incumbent in a time of turmoil. Johnson's campaign strategy brilliantly played on that fear.

22

The Vice President of Scandals

In 1973 Vice President Spiro T. Agnew was forced to resign in disgrace from the Nixon Administration as a result of one scandal.[16] The only difference between Vice President Agnew's resignation in disgrace when compared to Vice President Johnson's tenure 10 years earlier, was that Johnson, in the midst of several scandals, rather than resigning in disgrace, stepped up to the Presidency. Johnson's tenure as Vice President was so clouded by turmoil that he was branded as the Vice President of Scandals. And these were not merely Washington "sweep under the rug" scandals. Rather, they were matters of national significance that were publicized across the country. Three major scandals rocked Johnson while Vice President and all three surfaced less than 18 months before Kennedy's death. The scandals were the Billy Sol Estes affair; the TFX Missile Scandal (a.k.a. "the LBJ"); and the Bobby Baker scandal. Each scandal, as it surfaced, came closer to directly centering on Lyndon Johnson until John Kennedy was murdered.

Billy Sol Estes was a "good old Texas boy." He and Lyndon Baines Johnson were long time friends. The center-

---

[16]Vice President Spiro T. Agnew resigned on October 10, 1973 after pleading no contest to the charge of income tax evasion. He had been accused of accepting bribes while Governor.

piece in Estes' home was an autographed portrait of LBJ which perhaps signified their mutually profitable relationship. Estes helped finance Johnson's campaigns and allowed Johnson to use his private plane for campaigning. On a reciprocal basis Billy Sol Estes was then "federally privileged" to make millions of dollars on fees for storing federal government grain and on federal cotton allotments. The economic relationship between Johnson and Estes was so open that at Kennedy's first Presidential anniversary celebration, Estes was not only invited to the premier event but was seated at the table immediately next to Johnson.

Estes began his first federal fraud scandal in 1959 by building grain warehouses and buying up federal cotton allotments to grow cotton on submerged lands. He then, somehow, was "blessed" with contracts from the United States government to store surplus grain in his warehouses. He also was permitted to trade his rights to grow cotton on his submerged lands (which were useless), for the right to grow cotton on fertile fields, an extremely profitable exchange for Estes because it immediately raised the value of his otherwise worthless cotton land into a productive exchange commodity.

By 1961 government officials suspected that Estes was doing something illegal, but Vice President Johnson intervened and on January 31, 1961 he wrote a letter to the Secretary of Agriculture supporting Estes' practices with respect to his cotton land. The letter eventually became the impetus for an Agriculture Department investigation involving both Billy Sol Estes and Vice President Johnson. Typical when Johnson was involved, the major investigatory problem with the Estes' case was that the records of land holdings and transfers were so jumbled that it was difficult for the government to assess it. As a result, Agricultural Agent Henry Marshall was assigned to investigate and issue a full report of his findings. Marshall conducted a thorough investigation, completed his assignment in the Spring of 1961, and issued a written report to Washington.

The Washington commendation that agent Henry Marshall

received for his excellent work was five bullet holes to the head. On June 3, 1961 Marshall was found dead in a ditch in Franklin, Texas. A bolt action rifle was beside him. This five bullet killing and its cover up was more than a warning to other investigators. It also served as an example of Texas power and political corruption. On June 8, 1961, the local Justice of the Peace investigated the killing and miraculously declared that Marshall committed suicide. The absurdity of this determination was obvious, because it was impossible for Marshall to commit suicide by shooting himself in the head five separate times with a bolt action rifle. In essence, what the Texas Justice of the Peace found was that Henry Marshall loaded a rifle with a bullet, shot himself in the head, discharged the shell from the rifle, and repeated the process over and over again five separate times until he was dead.

Marshall's widow violently protested, the public complained, but the "suicide" of Henry Marshall completely stalled the government investigation. For a time it looked as if the whole matter was going to be dropped until a House Subcommittee decided to begin its own investigation. However, the Subcommittee's investigation was deliberately "dead ended" from the powers above and again it looked as if the matter was going to be dropped until several members of the Subcommittee, upset with the cover-up, leaked a report on the Estes affair to the press. The press then took over and went after Estes faster than boll weevils in a cotton patch. It was America's free press that finally broke the cover-up and pointed public attention in the right direction.

As a result, the past investigations of the cotton land transfers were renewed, and new investigations were instituted looking into Estes' grain storage profits from his federal contracts. This lead to further sensational discoveries about Billy Sol Estes including concern that he may have sold the government grain that he was being paid to store.

By March of 1962 Estes was arrested and charged with a host of crimes, and by May of 1962, the Estes affair had reached such a boiling point that Vice President Johnson flew to Dallas aboard a military jet to privately meet with Estes and his lawyers on a plane parked away from the terminal. What was discussed has been kept secret but it has long been suspected that during this meeting LBJ told Estes to keep his mouth shut and leave Johnson out of the scandal.[17] After Billy Sol's arrest the FBI had begun to acquire evidence linking Johnson to the matter. However, the FBI investigation reached an impasse when:

- **LBJ's personal legal counsel showed up as Estes' principal attorney;**

- **Billy Sol Estes refused to talk; and**

- **Billy Sol Estes' accountant (who was the only other man besides the dead Henry Marshall who could unravel the fraud) was found dead in his car.**

Throughout the remainder of 1962 and into 1963 the Estes' investigation was inactive. Governmental investigators could go no further because Estes refused to talk and all other avenues of uncovering the fraud were either dead or blocked. After Johnson became President, he issued an order stopping all federal investigations into the Estes matter. This prevented all links to Johnson from being discovered and stopped Estes from being charged with a federal crime. From a criminal standpoint, the only charge left pending against Estes was a state criminal charge of defrauding farmers. Estes was ultimately tried for the state crime, and convicted by a Texas jury. Estes then appealed to the Texas Court of Criminal Appeals and lost the appeal. In 1965, during Johnson's Presidency, Estes took another chance by appealing his conviction

---

[17]This incident would probably have remained secret except that LBJ's plane suffered a mishap in landing at Dallas. When investigative reporters attempted to obtain the tower records for the flight mishap, the records were "sealed by government order."

to the United States Supreme Court. The Supreme Court was not required to accept Estes' appeal, nor did it accept such cases except in rare situations. Yet, to the surprise of many (but not all) it agreed to review Estes' case as a "discretionary" matter (called certiorari). The Court's decision to accept the case may have been influenced by President Johnson's request that it at least look at his friend's case.

The Estes case was argued to the U.S. Supreme Court on April 1, 1965 and two months later the Court concluded that Estes' "rights had been violated" and he was entitled to a complete new trial. Typical Johnson, the Supreme Court Justice who wrote the opinion finding that Estes' "rights had been violated" was Justice Clark, a Dallas native. And, not surprisingly, the Justice who concurred with Clark that Estes deserved a new trial, was none other than the head of LBJ's Warren Commission—Chief Justice Earl Warren. It has long been said that politics is played in many forms. This judicial decision may have just been one of the many political mutations.

However, the U.S. Supreme Court's reversal of Estes' conviction did not help him. He was retried, again convicted, and eventually sentenced to a 15 year prison term for fraud. He was paroled in 1971 but his parole was revoked in 1979 and he was sent back to prison. He was finally released in 1983. Recently, Billy Sol Estes has again been indicted on other criminal charges.

While Billy Sol Estes did not ultimately escape jail, he was never charged with the murder of Agent Marshall, which was later re-determined not to be a suicide. Marshall's body was exhumed and his remains tested. The results proved that in addition to the five bullets to his head, before his death Marshall also received a severe blow to his head, and was asphyxiated with carbon monoxide. While this did not solve the crime of who killed Marshall, twenty three years after Marshall's death it was at least determined that the suicide story was a cover up for murder.

In March of 1984, one year after release from prison Estes

was subpoenaed to testify before a grand jury concerning the death of Agent Marshall in 1961. Because grand jury testimony is secret, only reports of his testimony, and not actual transcripts are available. However, the reports of Estes' sworn grand jury testimony are that decades after the murder Estes *linked Vice President Johnson* and two other men *to the execution of Henry Marshall*. While it is entirely possible Estes in his old age decided to lie about the event, another possibility is that after years of silence and with Johnson dead and nothing to fear, Estes finally decided to talk and tell the truth. And his talking revealed that in 1961 Lyndon Baines Johnson, as our Vice President, had both the need and the Texas power to kill agent Marshall and then cover it up.

The second major scandal during Johnson's Vice Presidency also involved Texans making huge amounts of money from federal contracts. As most of us know, to avoid favoritism, undue influence, and to achieve fairness in the purchase of goods and services, the federal government regularly uses either an open public bidding process or a selection system which is supposed to be neutral. Unfortunately, in many instances the government selection system is corrupt, the private businesses involved are corrupt, and so are the politicians who are supposed to guard against the corruption. This was the case in the early 1960's when two private companies were vying for a huge federal contract to build the military fighter plane known as the TFX (the TFX plane on Capital Hill was dubbed the "LBJ" for Johnson's "activities" in securing the contract for a Texas company).

Background to this national scandal starts almost immediately after Johnson took his oath as Vice President in 1961. As Vice President, he was allowed only a few political appointments in the Kennedy administration and one involved selection of the Secretary of the Navy. The position is politically insignificant but it has always carried economic clout in the billions of dollars for those businesses who compete in providing military hardware to the Navy. From experience, Lyndon Johnson knew this and asked for the right to appoint one of his friends to the post. Lyndon Johnson initially had John Connally appointed to the position. Connally was not only Johnson's long time friend, past campaign manager, and political ally, but he was also from Fort Worth, Texas—the home of General Dynamics, a company deeply involved in supplying America's military with equipment, and of course, one of the two companies attempting to secure the huge TFX plane contract.

The other company battling to secure the TFX contract was Boeing located in Washington state. As could have been expected with Johnson's involvement, when groups took sides to support the two competing companies, almost everyone (including the military engineers) supported Boeing. Opposed were only three Texans supporting General Dynamics, but what a trio. The three Texans were: Vice President Johnson; his appointee, Secretary of the Navy John Connally; and Fort Worth Congressman Jim Wright.[18]

Before the government selection between the two competing firms could be made, John Connally decided to resign as Secretary of the Navy and run for Governor of Texas, but the resignation did not stop Johnson. He merely selected another Texan for the same post. The second time Johnson selected his old friend Fred Korth. Korth, the new Secretary of the Navy, picked up where Connally left off by again strongly advancing General Dynamics' interests. It was during Korth's tenure as Secretary of the Navy that General Dynamics was finally selected to build the TFX plane and was awarded the contract. As a result, a "minor" scandal arose in Washington, D.C. where it was rumored that not only had Johnson put the "fix" in to get the plane contract for General Dynamics, but that he was personally rewarded for his efforts with satchels full of cash.

The full TFX scandal developed later when it was discovered that General Dynamics' test data was "suspect," or in

---

[18]If one recalls more recent events in history, House Speaker Jim Wright was caught in a political scandal in 1989 that completely destroyed his career.

President John F. Kennedy in foreground. At his side his right hand man, Vice President Lyndon B. Johnson. *UPI/Bettman*

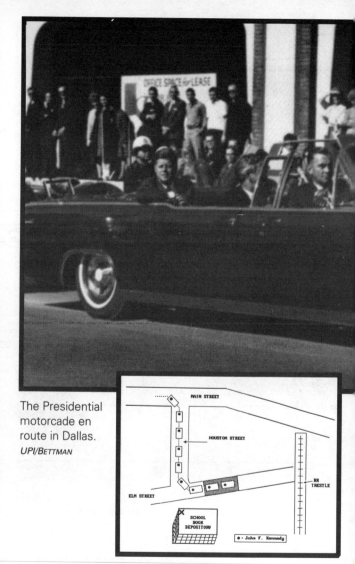

The Presidential
motorcade en
route in Dallas.
UPI/Bettman

Diagram 2:1
The end to the Dallas motorcade.
Sherris Service

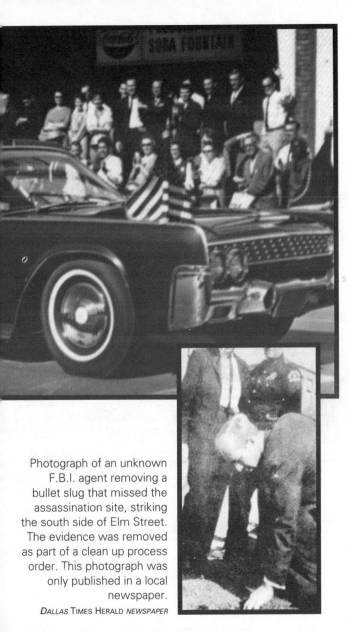

Photograph of an unknown F.B.I. agent removing a bullet slug that missed the assassination site, striking the south side of Elm Street. The evidence was removed as part of a clean up process order. This photograph was only published in a local newspaper.

DALLAS TIMES HERALD *NEWSPAPER*

The alleged
assassination rifle.
NATIONAL ARCHIVES

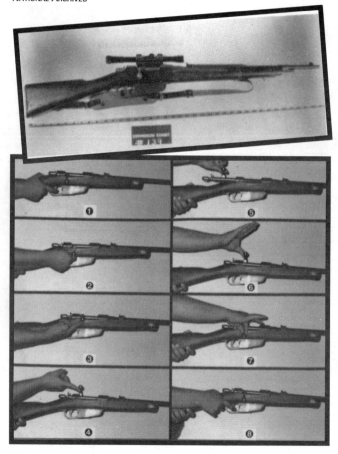

Firing sequence for one round from a Mannlicher-Carcano
rifle. *NATIONAL ARCHIVES*

COMMISSION EXHIBIT NO. 887
The reenactment rifle camera. NATIONAL ARCHIVES

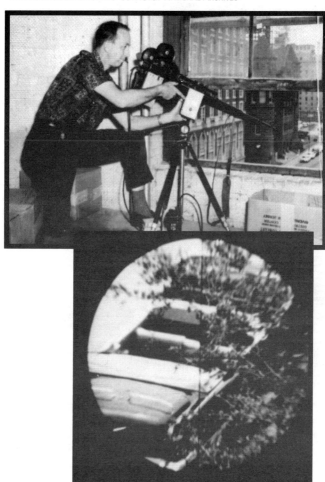

COMMISSION EXHIBIT NO. 889: A PORTION
A reenactment photograph as seen through
rifle scope. Note the tree branches blocking
view. NATIONAL ARCHIVES

The Presidential limousine moments before the assassination. Note the close distance of the trailing security car containing agents. This vehicle with its occupants also partially impeded views. *AP Photographer*

COMMISSION EXHIBIT NO. 900
A Warren Commission reenactment photograph. Note no closely trailing car was used which would have blocked portions of the Commission's rifle scope photographs. *National Archives*

Warren Commission exhibit depicting the alleged sniper's outpost in the Texas School Book Depository as identified by "A." The President turned to the left directly in front of this building. The obvious "killing zone" was in this photograph area. *NATIONAL ARCHIVES*

Diagram 6:1
The actual "kill zone" versus the optimum target area. *SHERRIS SERVICE*

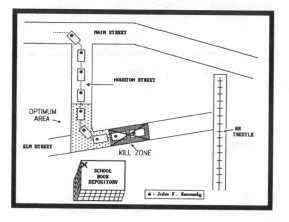

COMMISSION EXHIBIT NO. 237
Photograph taken at the Russian Embassy in Mexico City. Unknown to the Commission the photograph apparently depicted a professional assassin called "Saul."
NATIONAL ARCHIVES

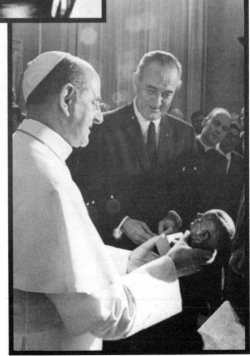

President Johnson presents his own bust to a shocked Catholic Pope.
LBJ LIBRARY

U.S. President John F. Kennedy with his successor Lyndon B. Johnson. Under standard police practices, Johnson could have been considered a prime suspect in President John F. Kennedy's murder. As a prime suspect, Johnson should have been investigated by his own commission.

Art Rickerby/Life Magazine

Life magazine's cover and cover story of November 8, 1963.
ROBERT STRAIR/CITY NEWS BUREAU

Bobby Baker and Lyndon Johnson together. The photograph was the lead to *Life* magazine's detailed investigation against Baker which was beginning to center on Johnson.
ROBERT STRAIR/CITY NEWS BUREAU

The President and Mrs. Kennedy smiling in Dallas with Governor John Connally standing between the couple moments before the start of the Dallas motorcade. Moments later the President was dead and Connally was wounded.
UPI/Bettman

The Presidential open limousine in downtown Dallas. Note the Dallas motorcycle policeman, on order, trailing off the back bumper. In conjunction with this the Dallas police ended their security just short of the assassination site and officers "protected" the President by turning their backs to the crowd.
UPI/Bettman

Dallas patrolman J.D. Tippit. At the time of the assassination Tippit, Jack Ruby's friend, was ordered away from the assassination scene and into Oswald's neighborhood and told to remain at large. *UPI/BETTMAN*

The miracle bullet. No distortion. It allegedly linked Oswald's rifle to the assassination. It was mysteriously found in Parkland Memorial Hospital. *NATIONAL ARCHIVES*

COMMISSION EXHIBIT NO. 723
The hidden sniper's den in the Texas School Book Depository. Note the shield of book cartons weighing 50 pounds each. It has been alleged that the Dallas police actually moved the boxes to take better photographs after the slaying. *NATIONAL ARCHIVES*

COMMISSION EXHIBIT NO. 2424
Photograph taken from movie footage at the Friday, November 22, 1963, press conference of Oswald in the Dallas police station. Jack Ruby is situated among the press corps with a revolver in his pocket. *NATIONAL ARCHIVES*

At 11:19 A.M. Oswald entered the prison basement, steps away from his execution.
UPI/BETTMAN

Oswald was then openly exposed towards the transfer vehicle. *UPI/BETTMAN*

The execution on live television, Jack Ruby shoots Lee Harvey Oswald once in the abdomen. Oswald is pronounced dead at 1:13 P.M. *UPI/BETTMAN*

Jack Ruby is wrestled to the ground as he shouts, "I had to do it." An officer pulls the gun away. *UPI/BETTMAN*

A poor copy of Oswald's handwritten letter to John Connally. *UPI/BETTMAN*

Police Chief Curry with LBJ aboard Air Force One instead of helping his men solve the crime. *LBJ LIBRARY*

Within hours of the murder, Johnson ordered the removal of President John F. Kennedy's symbolic rocking chair from the White House. It was slipped out through a side door unbeknownst to mourners who stood watch. *UPI/Bettman*

lay terms "falsified." From this initial discovery, investigations centered on everything from General Dynamics' cost overruns to the original selection process. As more evidence surfaced, the new Secretary of the Navy (Fred Korth) was accused of improper conduct. Mr. Korth was charged with conflict of interest by advancing the TFX, awarded to General Dynamics, at the same time when he was involved with General Dynamics' interests in Texas. With this discovery the scandal grew worse and closer to Johnson. However, Korth just like Billy Sol Estes kept his mouth shut. He resigned in disgrace and went back to Texas.

Even though the Billy Sol Estes and the TFX scandals did not politically destroy Johnson, it may have been only because Estes and Korth refused to cooperate and this kept the investigators from tying Johnson in. And, while the bulk of the publicity from each of the scandals ended before Kennedy's death, the political repercussions continued and President Kennedy knew, and the public suspected, that his administration had a "bad apple" occupying the right hand man position in the White House. It had become clear to everyone that Johnson and his friends were tainting the Kennedy presidency.

In fact, on the day of the President's death the reason Kennedy flew the few miles from Fort Worth to Dallas rather than drive, was because his advisors realized that any drive between the two cities would require the President to travel right past the front door of the General Dynamic's plant. Kennedy flew because he did not want to be reminded nor did he want the public to remember anything about the fiasco*.

---

*To read a full account about Billy Sol Estes, his encounter in the middle of a political squabble, and resulting problems from refusing to publicly talk, please read "Billy Sol: King of Texas Wheeler-Dealers" by Pam Estes, and published by Noble Craft Books of Abilene, Texas.

23
Into Seclusion

With the Billy Sol Estes scandal temporarily buried in the coffin with the body of agricultural agent William Marshall and with the TFX scandal subsiding, the remainder of 1963 looked like it might be improving for Vice President Lyndon Johnson and his friends. Besides, what more could go wrong? Plenty! It occurred with the bombshell scandal that blew onto the scene just months before Kennedy's death. This new scandal centered on a man by the name of Robert G. Baker (Bobby Baker). Bobby Baker was not only Johnson's close friend, neighbor in a nearby Washington mansion, and Secretary to the Democratic Senate Majority leader, but he had previously worked for Johnson. As a man who was only earning $20,000 a year in his salaried job, Bobby Baker was caught in the midst of an influence peddling and high living scandal.

The problem for Vice President Lyndon Johnson was not only Baker's: ownership of a mansion near LBJ's; purchase of a four bedroom townhouse for his mistress; interest in a North Carolina motel; ownership of a seaside resort (the Carousel) all on a government salary . . . but it was Johnson's close relationship with Baker. This included LBJ's sponsorship of Baker as Secretary to the Senate Majority leader. It was Johnson who publicly proclaimed in front of the entire

U.S. Senate that Baker was his most trusted, most loyal, and most competent friend. In fact, Johnson told the whole world that if he had a son, Bobby Baker would be him. And it was Johnson who had proudly told the American people about "Lyndon's boy" (Bobby Baker) and proclaimed:

> *"Bobby is my strong right arm. He is the last person I see at night and the first person I see in the morning."*

It was for these reasons that when the Senate and later the media began investigating Bobby Baker, the connection to Lyndon Johnson was too close for comfort.[19] And, until President Kennedy was killed, the scandal was so closely tied to Johnson that it appeared impossible for him to escape. Unfortunately for America, with John F. Kennedy's murder, Johnson achieved the impossible by effectively quashing the scandal.

The Bobby Baker scandal came to public attention less than two months before John Kennedy's death. In September of 1963, it was discovered that Bobby Baker had been sued for $300,000 by Ralph Hill. Hill was the owner of a vending machine company and claimed that he paid Baker bribe money for Baker's "influence" to keep Hill's vending machines in government buildings. Hill also claimed that Baker not only failed to do the "influence" job, but when Baker realized the amount of profits that could be made from the vending machines, he "influenced" the government into replacing Hill's machines with those Baker then began owning. Thus, it was not only a case of Baker allegedly taking bribes to improperly influence others, but where Baker kept the bribes and used his influence for his own gain.

Once word of the Hill lawsuit got out, investigative report-

---

[19]The association between the two was so close that not only did Baker and Lyndon share personal secrets and gifts, but Baker even named two of his children after LBJ and his family.

ers discovered that Bobby Baker was involved with a new vending machine company that had obtained over $3,500,000 in business from federal contractors in California alone. And, while Bobby Baker did *not* personally own any stock in the company, his wife, brother, and his law partner did. What made Hill's allegations even more damaging was that it was learned that the Baker vending machine company had obtained almost all of its business from private companies with federal contracts. It was discovered that each company had replaced existing vending companies with the new Baker vending machines. The companies involved read like a list of "Who's Who Among Defense Contractors" and included the likes of Northrop Corporation, North American Aviation, Space Technical Laboratories, and Melpar.

But getting caught in the middle of an influence peddling scandal was only the beginning of the problems for Baker and Johnson. As September 1963 wore on, Congressional Committees, the Justice Department, a Federal Grand Jury, and investigative journalists all began looking into the affairs of Bobby Baker and his friends. This made matters too hot even for Vice President Johnson.

When reporters began publicizing: Johnson's direct links to Baker; the fact that only the year before LBJ was the guest of honor at the grand opening of Baker's seaside resort; and, that Baker and Johnson together controlled the Democratic Party Senatorial Campaign checkbook, Johnson began to panic. When a U.S. Senate investigation was initiated into the affair, Johnson immediately ended a foreign junket and returned home to try to stop the investigation and save his political skin. However, it was too late for Johnson to stop the investigation and when it was clear that Bobby Baker would be destroyed, Johnson adopted a typical strategy—he practically denied even knowing Bobby Baker and pretended that the two had hardly met. But this tactic did not stop the investigation from examining the relationship between the two. Once the Baker scandal publicly surfaced President Kennedy became so disgusted that he "gave the green light" to allow all investigations to continue to their final conclusion. On October 7, 1963, Bobby Baker finally resigned in disgrace as the Secretary to the Majority Leader of the Senate. In response, the Senate Rules Committee announced that the resignation ended nothing and that it would continue to investigate Baker's financial accumulations, his political career, and his relationships. The Chairman of the Committee stated:

> *"We are starting with the Bobby Baker case . . . where it spreads from there we don't know."* [Emphasis Added]

During this period Johnson fled from Washington and headed for his Texas ranch. With the exception of a few short trips for speeches, Johnson stayed secluded away from Washington at his ranch until after Kennedy's assassination. When *Life* magazine's November 8, 1963 cover story ran as "The Bobby Baker Bombshell," Johnson refused to comment on the matter in spite of a full page photograph of Johnson and Baker together.

As the remaining days of Kennedy's life went by, John Kennedy flatly told the press that when the Baker investigation concluded others would also be fully investigated. By this Jack Kennedy gave clear warning that he had no intent to stop any investigation prematurely to protect LBJ. On the day of JFK's murder, *Life* magazine issued another cover story about the Baker scandal entitled, "Scandal Grows and Grows in Washington." Unfortunately, JFK's murder overshadowed the work of a nine member *Life* magazine task force who had spent close to a month loosening the Bobby Baker trail even further. The team reported:

> *"Nevertheless, the Baker scandal, gathering both bulk and momentum, has been enough to embarrass severely . . . It has scared numerous other individuals into funk holes from which they may never emerge—at least not without scars."*

* * * *

"From 1955 to 1961 he (Baker) was secretary to the Democratic Senatorial Campaign Committee. It was a committee in name only, for Johnson controlled it absolutely—and Baker handled the committee's funds."

* * * *

"It is frequently customary when . . . contributions are made for the donor to earmark . . . his gift. But under the operation of the Johnson-Baker axis the earmarking did not always stay put." [Emphasis Added]

Clearly, *Life*'s reference to the scandal scaring individuals "into funk holes" was a direct reference to Lyndon Johnson's seclusion on his ranch. And, by the day of the assassination the *Life* reporting team was beginning to center its attack on Lyndon Johnson. On the day of Kennedy's death not only was Johnson's involvement with Baker making national headlines, but the *Dallas Herald Tribune* had three separate news articles about the Baker matter. But upon Kennedy's demise, the attack as well as the entire scandal was ended by Johnson's rise to power. While Lyndon Johnson had been run out of Washington and was within weeks of complete political destruction, fate from a few ounces of lead returned him to Washington with the power of the presidency.

When Johnson seized power the Senate investigation into Baker was temporarily stopped. It was then "deferred" until after the 1964 presidential election because of the assassination. Even the criminal pretrial hearings against Bobby Baker were deferred for no other reason than that was what Johnson wanted. And in a direct threat to the Republicans, Johnson told them to leave the Baker scandal alone during the 1964 campaign because he had the goods on them. How Johnson stopped the press from continuing their investigation is unknown, except the facts demonstrate that this did occur. What is known in retrospect is that Johnson's order was obeyed by all.

If Jack Kennedy had not been murdered the Baker investigation would not have ended. If Jack Kennedy had not been murdered the Baker scandal would have either destroyed or tarnished Johnson's image so completely that he would not have been on the 1964 ticket. If the President had not been slain, the truth about LBJ may have put him in prison, as his grandma predicted, rather than into the White House.

24

Conclusion
as to Motive

While the Warren Commission was unable to find a motive for Oswald's alleged assassination of the President, the Commission, if it had tried, would have had no trouble finding a motive for Johnson, the man who had the most to gain from Kennedy's death.

Johnson had *personal motives*. He had an insatiable life long desire to become a U.S. President and an egocentric belief that destiny demanded it. Johnson felt that Kennedy had interfered with destiny by winning the 1960 Democratic nomination. He was acutely aware of his family's poor health history along with his own, and knew that statistically, unless he gained the Presidency by succession, he would either not be alive or healthy enough to win a 1968 election. From a personal standpoint, Johnson did not like Jack or Bobby Kennedy, and his dislike for both men increased over the years. The Kennedys: deliberately kept him outside the intimacies of the Administration; privately belittled him; and, from Johnson's perspective, were responsible for the scandals encircling him.

Johnson had *political motives*. As the Vice President he lost his political power. He left the second strongest political position in the United States (Senate Majority Leader) to accept a position of political impotence. He went from being the powerhouse on Capitol Hill to the laughing stock of Washington. And, without political power, there was nothing he could do to change things. For his three years as the Vice President, Johnson once again began to relive his childhood nightmare of being paralyzed and helpless . . . only this time in real life he was politically helpless. This hell hole was only made worse by his belief that he was "ten times the leader compared to President Kennedy."

Johnson (and his cohorts) also had *economic motives*. Johnson had always bartered his political power to increase his net worth. While this system had worked in the past, as Vice President, he soon found he had little to offer. While he used what few appointments he had to their utmost (i.e. Secretary of the Navy . . . TFX contract to General Dynamics), it was not even close to what LBJ and his cohorts were used to. As the Vice President he could do very little, yet he was only a heart beat away from the "King of the Hill" position for himself and his friends. He was frustrated by the knowledge that if he was dumped from the 1964 ticket his years of political maneuvering and vast contacts in Washington would be wiped out. A Johnson Presidency represented the potential of additional millions for himself and billions in contracts for his Texas friends. Many have killed for much less.

If a man sees his life long dream crumble before his eyes, if he perceives his rival as unqualified but cast by sheer luck into "his" position, and if he believes that this rival is now belittling, taunting, and destroying his career, that man might be tempted to strike back. And depending upon the person's moral character along with the risks and rewards, the retaliation may be violent. History has taught, "desperate men do desperate things."

The Warren Commission's members surely knew this as did many Americans who felt then, as now, that something was not right about what we were being told. But Americans believed the Warren Commission because we also knew that, if you accuse the new king, you also accuse his country and its political system. And, if you convict the new king, you

September 24, 1964

The President
The White House
Washington, D. C.

Dear Mr. President:

Your Commission to investigate the assassination of President Kennedy on November 22, 1963, having completed its assignment in accordance with Executive Order No. 11130 of November 29, 1963, herewith submits its final report.

Respectfully,

Earl Warren, Chairman

The President's Commission on the assassination of President Kennedy supposedly accomplished its purpose on September 24, 1964. It submitted its final report directly to President Johnson.

risk turmoil and political change of unknown dimensions. To the politically astute, 1963 was a delicate period in American history. Therefore, while Johnson was a logical suspect because of his known strong motives, everyone remained mute to save the country, letting the one who benefitted the most from the killing avoid scrutiny.

Opportunity

25

Basics of Opportunity

After all of the criminal suspects have been evaluated for motive and the Prime Suspects have been determined, the next phase of a criminal investigation involves evaluating the opportunity that each Prime Suspect had to commit the crime. This is called determining criminal opportunity.

Criminal opportunity is a state of facts which demonstrate the likelihood that a criminal suspect may have committed the crime. It is an attempt to determine which, if any, Prime Suspect had the ability to perform the act. For example, if a Prime Suspect with a strong motive was in jail when the crime was committed, it could be said the suspect lacked opportunity to do the act, at least by himself. On the other hand, evidence that shows that a Prime Suspect could not have physically committed the crime does not itself completely absolve the suspect from possessing criminal opportunity. In such instances, a criminal investigation might have to delve deeper to determine whether the Prime Suspect could have been involved in the crime by planning, by association, or through a conspiracy. A person *does not* have to commit the final physical act to be guilty of the crime.

Before a Prime Suspect should be excluded from an investigation based on lack of physical opportunity, an analysis must be made to determine if the Prime Suspect (the one who had the most to gain by the crime): was involved in any of the planning leading up to the crime; had more knowledge of the intimate facts that others; or had an indirect ability to carry out the crime. If a criminal investigation deliberately ignores a Prime Suspect who had the opportunity to commit the crime, the chances are even stronger that the crime may never be solved.

The Warren Commission allegedly "solved" the assassination by attempting to perform a standard criminal investigation. But as demonstrated in the preceding chapters, Johnson should have been classified as a Prime Suspect because he certainly had a multitude of motives for wanting Kennedy dead. Yet, the Commission failed to consider Johnson as a suspect, let alone a Prime suspect. Because of this omission by the Commission, it did not take the customary next step in its investigation. It never determined whether Johnson, as a Prime Suspect, had the opportunity to commit the crime. The Chapters in this Section will undertake the failed task of the Warren Commission to investigate Johnson's opportunity to commit the crime.

This can begin by noting that in 1963 there were well over 180 million people living in the United States. But of all of these people, Texans were involved with each aspect of the Kennedy assassination and, for the most part, were responsible for each error, mistake, and misjudgment leading up to, during the course of, and after the assassination. Each participant in this "Texas Connection" can be linked to Johnson and it would be difficult for any reasonable person to conclude that such connections were merely coincidental. It is also difficult to believe that by sheer coincidence:

- **Johnson was the one directly involved in planning the President's death trip;**

- **Johnson was one of the main figures involved in urging the President to make the trip;**

- **On the day before the assassination, Johnson and the President got into a fight over switching seating positions in the vehicles for the upcoming motorcade. Johnson wanted Connally out of JFK's car and his enemy Senator Yarborough to sit in Connally's seat.**[20]

- **Johnson's strongest supporters for his Presidency lived in Dallas;**

- **Some of Johnson's strongest supporters in Dallas made threatening remarks against the life of President Kennedy;**

- **Johnson's appointees as Secretary of the Navy each had preassassination contact with the Oswald family, and one appointee even had contact with Oswald less than 2 months before the assassination;**

- **One of Johnson's strongest supporters in Dallas was visited by Oswald's murderer (Jack Ruby), the day before the assassination;**

- **Oswald's murderer (Ruby) was found to possess evidence directly linking him with one of Johnson's strongest supporters in Dallas;**

- **Johnson's friends had contact with Ruby's trial court judge (who committed reversible error) and**

---

[20] It is uncontested that the argument occurred. Some historians of Johnson's presidency placed the blame on Senator Ralph Yarborough. Others, with witness support, placed the "trading places" fight on Johnson. This historic conflict has unfortunately resulted from mistaken use and reference to the "authorized" assassination account. This conflict is more clearly resolved in Chapter 38 which explains why the inaccurate but "authorized" assassination account deliberately replaced the truth on this subject for political purposes.

gave him a California resort trip and a book contract; and

- Johnson created the Warren Commission which seized the evidence, investigated the murder, and only reported to him.

26

Timing

The importance of timing of controlled events such as assassinations cannot be overlooked in seeking to explain the Kennedy murder. It often provides strong indication as to why the event occurred when it did, which can then supply a clue to determining the person who may have caused it to occur when it did.

In the Kennedy assassination analysis, a number of the assassination conspiracy theories as discussed before can be dismissed as not being credible merely because the timing of the killing did not specifically benefit those allegedly involved.

Conversely, the assassination of November 22, 1963, was almost precisely one year prior to the 1964 Presidential election. From a political standpoint, Kennedy's death, at that exact period in time directly benefitted one person more than anyone else—Johnson. The Kennedy killing overshadowed several mushrooming scandals and saved LBJ's political skin. The killing at that time also stopped Kennedy from publicly announcing his intent to dump Johnson from the 1964 ticket, or in fact doing so. Further the November 22, 1963 murder was perfectly timed since it was sufficiently removed from the November 1964 Presidential election to allow Johnson the opportunity to establish himself as a leader in his own right, but yet not so far removed from the coming election as to alleviate the public's concern about transferring Presidential leadership to anyone other than Johnson.

Without question, timing of this killing best benefitted Lyndon Baines Johnson above all others. It not only allowed him to shut down the furor of the scandals surrounding him and survive politically, but to prosper from it.

27

Planning the Death Trip

Following the assassination, Lyndon Johnson always denied participation in planning President Kennedy's death trip. Johnson also denied arguing with Kennedy about which car Connally was going to ride in. These denials and minimizations were grossly untrue since Johnson was a major participant in urging and planning the trip.

The post-assassination denials by Johnson are important to show that Johnson knew his involvement with planning the trip was important from a criminal investigation standpoint. It demonstrated an opportunity to commit the crime.

It is uncontroverted that Johnson had substantial control over Kennedy's Texas trip and his itinerary. Kennedy placed the trip in Johnson and his friends hands since Texas was their home state. The trip had been under consideration for almost a year when, on April 23, 1963, Johnson announced that the President would visit Texas in the near future. Less than 45 days after this announcement the basic outline for a November trip to Texas was agreed upon in a private meeting between Kennedy, Johnson and Connally at the Cortez Hotel in Texas. The Secret Service, the bulk of the White House Staff, and the public, however, were not informed about the details of the trip until just weeks before it occurred. From the outset, only the three knew the details.

The three also agreed that since Texas was the home state of Johnson and Connally, they would be in charge of the planning. Subsequently, the length of the trip was extended from only one day to a tour of Dallas, Fort Worth, San Antonio, Austin and Houston.

By September of 1963 in conjunction with the lengthened trip, Governor Connally proposed a motorcade through Dallas followed by a luncheon, and then a flight to Austin.

The motorcade was to follow the traditional Dallas parade route that had been used since at least 1936. However, because few spectators were expected at the end of the traditional route, it was originally proposed that the motorcade would avoid the Texas Book Depository area and would proceed straight ahead on Main Street, allowing the motorcade to build up speed on a straightaway before getting on to the expressway (Stemmons). But the route that was eventually selected for the end of the motorcade required a turn off the parade street (Main Street), travel on a side street for one block (Houston Street), a sharp turn onto another street (Elm Street past the Texas School Book Depository), and then a procession straight for one block on to the freeway.

The turn onto Elm Street past the book depository violated the safety policy of the Secret Service which discouraged 90° or greater turns because it created a slow down for the Presidential vehicle and made the President an easier target.

If the straightaway route had been followed, the motorcade would not have slowed to a crawl for the 90° turn onto Elm, but would have proceeded straight to the freeway. It would have avoided the assassination site by over a block. The straightaway route was the only logical route if the White House staff's proposed noon luncheon site for the President would have been accepted. But the Texas planners would not agree to change either the end of the motorcade route, or the proposed luncheon site. Their strange insistence in demanding that these details not be adjusted has to this day bothered members of Kennedy's White House staff.

Kennedy had a personal advanceman, Jerry Bruno, whose

job was to travel to the site in advance of the President's trip to insure that all aspects of the trip would run smoothly and safely. Over a month before the trip, Bruno demanded that the Texas planners' motorcade route not be taken. Bruno felt that the Texas planners' route created unnecessary risks for the President by making him a slow moving target in an open area. In late October, Bruno flew to Dallas to specifically meet with Connally to discuss more details of the President's trip. Before Bruno met with Connally, he talked with U.S. Senator Ralph Yarborough of Texas. Their discussion ended with Yarborough warning Bruno that Johnson and Connally would be ". . . after John Kennedy in a minute if they thought they could get away with it politically." Bruno then left Yarborough and went to see Connally as planned.

In his book, *The Advanceman*, Bruno described the unusual and bitter fight that he had with Connally over the Texas planned motorcade route. To this day, Bruno has not been able to understand why Governor Connally was so adamant that the death route be taken. According to Bruno, Connally became so insistent that the Texas planned parade route and luncheon site be followed that a strong argument broke out.[21] When the Connally-Bruno dispute reached heated stages, according to Bruno, Connally got on the telephone to the White House and in Bruno's presence (with him hearing only one side of the conversation), it appeared that the White House agreed with his plans since he was in charge of the trip. Bruno then relented and let the proposed motorcade and luncheon site proceed as planned by the Texans. After the assassination Bruno learned that the White House Staff had *not* agreed with Connally at all. Bruno then realized that somehow he had been talked into accepting plans that were against his better judgment.

In his three years of serving the President, Bruno claimed

---

[21] If the luncheon site proposed by the White House staff had been chosen, the parade route dispute would have become a moot issue, because the motorcade would have had to have gone straight to get to the luncheon site.

he never encountered any other group who refused to alter plans to accommodate concerns for the President's safety. Aside from the Texas planners, neither a particular parade route nor a specific luncheon site was ever of any importance to the hosting locals. But the Texas planners got their way. They got their luncheon site and their parade route.

On October 4, 1963, Connally flew to Washington to finalize plans and meet with the President. According to members of the White House staff, Kennedy had been advised *not* to make the trip and those involved in his administration still insist that it was Johnson and Connally who urged that the trip go on as planned. On that same October 4th evening, after Connally left the White House, he met Johnson for dinner. What was discussed between them has never been publicly disclosed nor whether LBJ inquired about the Texas trip. However, after this meeting, and as the Bobby Baker scandal surfaced in Washington amidst rumors tying Johnson to the scandal, Johnson left for his Texas ranch to get ready to give President Kennedy a "Texas Welcome." Aside from one or two short trips out of Texas, Johnson did not return to Washington and had nothing to do but prepare for Kennedy's trip the next month.

The Warren Commission deliberately ignored most of these important facts. Its 1964 report all but ignored the parade route controversy and the exceptional efforts undertaken by the Texas planners to make sure the route that was chosen by them was used. The Commission's statement that the "appropriate route was chosen" was the pinnacle of sophistry. It was only appropriate (ignoring the 90° turn issue) if the luncheon site chosen by the Texas planners was appropriate. And the luncheon site dictating the route selected was a safety risk according to Kennedy's advanceman Bruno.

The Warren Commission justified the three block detour at the end of the route as "necessary" because it prevented the motorcade from making an illegal turn. This was preposterous. Even school children know that when parades and important motorcades occur—especially when the President is involved—roads are blockaded, speeds are exceeded, and traffic rules are ignored. If it was safer for the President's car to make illegal turns this would have been done.[22] The route selected was improper and the Warren Commission's attempts at justifying it are beyond comprehension.

The Warren Commission's handling of Oswald's employment in the Texas School Book Depository, at the end of the parade route, is just as incomprehensible. Oswald started his job on October 16, 1963, *days after* Connally's visit in Washington with Kennedy where parade plans were confirmed (and his dinner with Johnson). He got his job in the specific building on the motorcade route when a job opening did not exist. In spite of this, the Warren Commission found that Oswald's employment in the Texas School Book Depository occurred without Oswald having advance knowledge of the President's parade route. This finding was based solely on the premise that Oswald could not have known about the motorcade route because at that time, neither the general public, nor even the Secret Service were told the route. But this premise ignored the fact that the Texas' planners knew, and insisted, that the motorcade travel the specific route that would take it past Oswald's new place of employment.

One of the most perplexing actions before the assassination that the White House Staff was unable to comprehend was why Johnson and his friends, who had arranged for and planned the trip, did little during the weeks preceding it to drum up luncheon support. The Dallas luncheon tickets were

---

[22]To those who have read the actual Warren Commission report, another factor was raised by the Commission in finding the selected route appropriate. That factor was a concrete riser which the Commission claimed would have impeded the motorcade if the alternate route would have been accepted. However, the Commission's claim was false. The riser was not an impediment to traffic flow. Rather, the mounded concrete riser similar to a speed bump, was illegally traversed everyday by Dallas motorists to get onto the expressway from Main Street. As proof of this fact are photographs which depict the speed bump as well as traffic signs directing motorists not to make the illegal turn. This routine crossover practice would therefore have been extremely safe for the motorcade especially without other traffic in the area.

selling slowly even though the proceeds would help the party. The administration began speculating that Johnson and some Texans were intending to embarrass Kennedy by not having visible Texas support for the President. Of course, in hindsight, ticket sales for the Dallas luncheon were unimportant since Kennedy never made it there.

The Johnson trip planning was only part of the broader picture. If Johnson had gotten his way, the assassination tragedy would have been even worse! On Thursday evening, November 21, 1963, Johnson entered Kennedy's suite. Only hours before JFK's death, an argument erupted in the suite so violent that the First Lady heard the shouting in the next room. Even the hotel staff heard the two men having an exceptionally forceful argument. The noise suddenly abated and Johnson left the presidential suite "like a pistol" with his arms and legs pumping up and down, and looking furious.

What did the two argue about? They fought about Johnson's demand to change the seating position in the cars on the morning of the motorcade. Kennedy had Johnson riding with Johnson's enemy, U.S. Senator Ralph Yarborough. Johnson however demanded that Senator Yarborough ride with Kennedy . . . leaving Johnson and Connally traveling together in a trailing car. Kennedy refused to accept the seating changes demanded by Johnson, and inexplicably Johnson refused to abide by Kennedy's plan. Ultimately, Kennedy prevailed, and Kennedy and Connally were shot.

If Johnson had prevailed, the assassination results may have been even more tragic. Kennedy still would have been killed, but Connally would have been safe, and the older Senator Ralph Yarborough, as LBJ's enemy, would have been the other one shot. Yarborough, because of his age, may not have survived the wounds Connally received, or at least may have been so seriously incapacitated that he would have been unable to run for re-election.

At the time of the shots, Connally was sitting in the seat directly in front of the President. Connally has repeatedly sworn that when the shots were fired and he was struck by a bullet, he was unaware that the President had been hit. Yet, upon being hit, Connally immediately exclaimed:

"Oh no, oh my God, they are going to kill us all."

The exclamation by Connally is known in the law as an "excited utterance." Excited utterances are regularly accepted as valid evidence in courts (as an exception to evidentiary hearsay rules) because of the spontaneity of such statements following an event. Experience has shown that what a person blurts out in immediate response to a crisis is normally reliable and truthful since there is not time to think or make up a story. On examination, Connally's exited utterance is very unusual. Look at the words. Why, after immediately being hit by a bullet, and without knowing that anyone else was shot at or injured, did he say *"they"* and *"kill us all."*

Most accident victims, if they are unaware of other people's injuries, immediately revert towards self-preservation by thoughts, words, and deeds (i.e. a gun is fired, everyone ducks). Psychologists confirm this self-preservation action as part of human nature. Therefore, the more appropriate spontaneous utterance from Connally (especially not knowing that Kennedy was hit) should have been "I am shot", or "I've been hit", or "I am hurt", or even "they are going to kill me." Because Connally was originally unaware that the President, who was behind him, was also shot, why were his first words "they" are going "to kill us all." Is it possible that at the immediate instant when the bullet struck, Connally finally put together the pieces realizing that he had been duped by Johnson into innocently supplying him with information that LBJ had now used for political destruction? Or, maybe other rational explanations exist?

If Johnson had gotten his way with the motorcade seating, he would not only have succeeded Kennedy as President, but his enemy Ralph Yarborough may have also been destroyed. As usual, after the murder, Johnson denied that a confrontation had occurred between Kennedy and himself about car seating positions. In fact, Johnson began telling the press that on the morning of Kennedy's death, the two had allegedly talked about running together again in the coming election (Kennedy's last dictated words to his secretary were that Johnson would *not* be on his ticket).

In any event, it is without dispute that Johnson had a direct hand in the death trip. He knew the exact itinerary and route; and, if one believes other witnesses excluding Johnson, he had an intense interest *before* the slaying in having certain politicians ride in specific motor vehicles in the motorcade.

28

The Dallas
Police Force

In 1963 the Dallas Police Department was headed by Police Chief Jesse Curry. Chief Curry began his working career as a teamster trucker but quickly switched occupations to become a Dallas police officer. He rose within the ranks to eventually head the department. He held an appointed position reporting to Mayor Cabell.[23] Beneath Mayor Cabell and Chief Curry was Captain William Fritz who controlled the everyday police operations.

Curry and Fritz under Mayor Cabell were responsible for the local security protection of the President during his trip. It was also Curry and Fritz who headed the Dallas Police Department's investigation into Kennedy's death. And, it was these two men who were in charge of the illegal incarceration and jail transfer of Oswald resulting in his death.

Many believe the actions of the Dallas Police from the start of the President's visit in Dallas until Oswald's murder two days later went beyond the bounds of even gross negligence to unexplainable deliberate actions. Leading Dallas citizens publicly stated that Dallas' top ranking police officers ''delib-

---

[23] As a side note, the mayor's brother was none other than General Cabell, who was intimately involved with the embarrassing Bay of Pigs Invasion. General Cabell was one of the men who Kennedy forced to resign as a result of alleged military mismanagement following the Bay of Pigs fiasco.

erately let Lee Harvey Oswald be killed while in their custody by orders from those higher up.'' Even Chief Curry, who started out claiming that Oswald was a lone assassin, years later admitted that ''sooner or later some evidence will probably come forth indicating that there was more than one gunman.'' Either Chief Curry was an excellent predictor or he knew more than he originally claimed at the time of Kennedy's death.

To properly evaluate the Dallas Police Department's actions it is necessary to look at all of the facts including what went on even before the trip began. Since it was Chief Curry's police who were to supply the local protection for the President, it was necessary for Chief Curry to work closely with the trip's key organizers, which of course included fellow Texan Lyndon Johnson. On the fateful November 22 day, it was readily apparent that the Chief had worked extremely close with the trip's organizers since it was Curry who: elected to drive the lead car in the motorcade; decided how local security would be handled in Dallas; and had previously demonstrated to Secret Service agents in early November the exact motorcade route that would be taken. It can be stated without a doubt that Chief Curry had direct close contacts with the trip's planners prior to the assassination and in addition was connected to an assortment of leading Dallas citizens, including Mayor Cabell and the oil rich Hunt family (who after the assassination were advised by the police to get out of town for their own safety).

While never discussed in much detail, the security protection by the Dallas Police Department implemented to protect the President while traveling in the motorcade was bizarre. For some unexplainable reason, the Dallas police were instructed to stand *with their backs to the crowd* and face the motorcade. This curious order and resulting police positioning was not used in any other major city and violated standard Presidential security measures since it did not allow the police to watch the crowds or buildings behind them for any unusual activity. While the patrolmen could watch the motorcade and the crowd and the buildings across the street, if a crisis arose, all an officer could do was watch from afar. If an officer had spotted an assassin in the crowd or in a building, the officer would have had difficulty in preventing action from the opposite side of the street.

Also bizarre was the reduction in number of motorcycle policemen encircling the Presidential limousine. Motorcycle officers, known as outriders, around a President in a motorcade serve both as a protective screen as well as a break off unit in case of trouble. While the original plans called for eight motorcycle officers encircling the limousine, the number was reduced to four with the police cyclists being strictly ordered to stay to the rear of the President's limousine. This token Dallas police protection has never made any sense if the purpose was to protect Kennedy. In an after the fact public explanation for this conduct, Chief Curry blamed Kennedy's Secret Service Agents, who he claimed demanded the security changes. Since the Secret Service Agents were then under the control of the ''new'' President, they could hardly deny such charges.

In the strangest security move of all, the Dallas Police ended their security supervision for the motorcade one block short of the full route. To repeat. *The Dallas Police decided in advance to conveniently end their security just short of the assassination site* (after the intersection of Houston and Main Streets). This local security decision came to light only after the assassination when the Dallas police publicly disclosed this act in an attempt to absolve themselves from responsibility for allowing the killing to occur.

The Dallas Police Department's excuse for ending their security just before the chosen killing site was that it had determined there would be few spectators in the area. This decision was made in spite of the fact that the White House Staff perceived the area as one of the highest safety risks in the entire motorcade since it was at this point the President's limousine was required to make two, slow, separate turns, making the President an easy target. And, with fewer spectators in the area, the location was a perfect assassin's lair since there would be fewer witnesses.

Whether the Dallas Police advised the White House Staff or the Secret Service beforehand of its decision to abandon local security in this area remains unknown. Logically, this is doubtful because had it been disclosed, the buildings would have been completely checked or the area totally secured by the Secret Service. If the Dallas Police Department's excuse for no protection is to be believed, it still raises the question: "If the police did not plan on securing a perceived high risk area because of lack of crowds, then why have the motorcade go there at all—especially if there was an easier way to proceed?"

The final act in a day of bizarre actions was what happened to the press pool car in the motorcade line up. The press car was loaded with photographers and journalists and was supposed to follow directly behind the car carrying the President's bodyguards, which followed the Presidential limousine. But shortly before the start of the motorcade, it was deliberately bumped to a rear position for no stated reason. This resulting strange line-up change prevented professional journalists and photographers from witnessing and photographing the slaying. While some spectators managed to capture the moment, the question remains: who ordered the press car away from the death scene and why?

29
Obscenity

Obscenity involves public conduct that is indecent, patently offensive, and beyond all moral bounds. While the Dallas Police Department's security protection for the President was bizarre, its actions as a law enforcement agency after the assassination can only be classified as obscene. It was Chief Curry's Dallas Police Department which directly handled the immediate post-assassination investigation. It was Curry's men who "bungled" the interrogation of Oswald. And it was Curry who personally directed Oswald's jailhouse transfer which resulted in his death.

The obscenity of the Dallas Police Department's actions began when John Kennedy and John Connally were taken from the limousine and placed on stretchers at the hospital. Within moments, a pristine unmarred bullet was "discovered." However, no one seemed to know where the bullet came from, nor who found it (some subsequent evidence has linked the finding of the bullet to a hospital employee who has strongly stated that he found it on a stretcher not used to transport either gunshot victim). Subsequent testing disclosed that the bullet had at some point in time been fired from Oswald's rifle. NOTE: It is undisputed that after the assassination a *mint condition bullet was found at the Dallas hospital, somewhere near the victims, and within the vicinity of the*

Police Chief, his officers, and even Lyndon B. Johnson. It is also not substantially disputed that the bullet was a plant. To date, not one reputable ballistics expert has claimed that a rifle bullet, traveling at high speed and going any distance, would not distort, shatter or at least become marred, marked or nicked upon striking any surface other than cotton wadding. And yet, a nearly perfect bullet was found allegedly linking Oswald's rifle to the killing. The only logical explanation that has been advanced is that the bullet had been previously fired at close range into a heavily padded box and then planted at the crime scene to supply hard evidence linking the assassination to Oswald's rifle.

Even the Warren Commission had a difficult time explaining the miracle bullet; but as with all of the other impossible factual obstacles the Commission faced in trying to justify its lone assassin conclusion, it again theorized its way around reality.

The Commission concluded that the perfectly-shaped, nondistorted bullet mysteriously found by some person, somewhere, had managed to penetrate Kennedy's skull and/or strike Connally's ribs and wrist bones and then continue to rattle around to eventually emerge unscathed. Of course, not one subsequent test was able to replicate this feat. Nevertheless, the Commission stated that this is what had happened. The miracle bullet even managed to "clean itself" of microscopic traces of blood, bone, and human tissue. This had to have been the case because if microscopic traces of anything had been found, the Commission would have trumpeted these findings to support its conclusion.

The appearance of the miracle bullet at the outset set the tone of the Dallas Police Department's investigation of the murder. The handling of the "miracle bullet" should have followed standard investigative procedure for evidence. A "chain of evidence" should have been established by not only bagging the bullet, but identifying who found the bullet, when, and where it was found. This was not done and the obvious conclusion is that either the police blundered, or someone deliberately planted the evidence.

The next series of Dallas Police actions on November 22, 1963 become even more unexplainable. As is well known, shortly after the assassination, Dallas Police Officer J.D. Tippit was killed across town in the Oak Cliff area. But, to date (more than 25 years later), no one has offered any explanation why Tippit was sent there. It is known that after the President's assassination in downtown Dallas, patrolman Tippit was dispatched away from the crime scene to Oswald's neighborhood several miles away. He was instructed to "remain at large for any emergency." Neither Chief Curry nor any other Dallas Police official has ever explained, with a national crisis in downtown Dallas and with possible unknown killers on the loose (no one supposedly even knew of Oswald at the time), why Tippit was sent away from the assassination site. Aside from claiming that it was a coincidence, no one has explained why, of all places outside the downtown area of Dallas, Tippit was sent to Oswald's neighborhood to patrol, since Oswald was not even a suspect at that point.

Tippit had been a member of the Dallas police force for over thirteen years, and worked part time as a security guard for wealthy Dallasites. Tippit also had a close relationship with Jack Ruby. According to Ruby's sister and others, the two men were close friends. In the weeks prior to the assassination, eyewitnesses had observed the two spending nights in Tippit's patrol car cruising. All of this makes Tippet's assigned patrol to Oswald's neighborhood immediately after the assassination and before anyone knew of Oswald's involvement highly suspicious.

Equally strange is the post-assassination observation made by Oswald's landlady when Oswald was in his room presumably getting ready to flee. The landlady saw a Dallas police car drive up to the front of her rooming house while Oswald was inside. She saw the police car slow, and then stop, and then she heard the sound of the car horn. After the car horn beep, she saw the car start up and proceed slowly down the street.

Compounding this strange scenario, the Warren Commission summarily rejected the landlady's observation as inaccurate. The Commission's report claimed her recollection and identification of the patrol car's number was in error and therefore her recollection of what else she saw was also faulty. The patrol car number she recalled, according to the Dallas police (if they are to be believed) was for an unoccupied patrol car parked at the Texas School Book Depository at the time. But to completely disregard an eyewitnesses' observation of a clearly marked and easily recognizable Dallas police car, complete with bubble lights on top, merely because the witness may have not accurately remembered the squad's identification number is preposterous! This is like "throwing out the baby with the bath water." Sadly, the police vehicle that the landlady observed stopping and honking in front of her house may have been Officer Tippit's, since he was sent to patrol this exact area and was killed minutes later just blocks away.

After the landlady saw the police car and heard the horn blow, Oswald left the rooming house and was seen walking down the street. He was next seen several blocks away talking casually with Officer Tippit. According to the eyewitnesses, the two men were chatting. Tippit was in his patrol car with his passenger side window rolled down and Oswald was leaning on the car. To some of the witnesses, from the way the two were talking and acting, it appeared they knew each other. But whether Tippit: knew Oswald and wanted him to get in the car; just wanted to stop a stranger on the street to chat during an assassination crisis; was assigned by someone to be Oswald's executioner; or, was to be Oswald's get away driver, remains a mystery. What is known is that after observing the two conversing, the eyewitnesses saw Tippit get out of his car (with no broadcast having been made over the police radio identifying Oswald, or anyone with his appearance as being an assassination suspect) and attempt to draw his revolver. Why he did this is also a mystery because if his intention was to make an arrest his action was in direct violation of Dallas Police Department rules. Such an act required radio notification to the station of his intent, and if so serious as to require the drawing of his weapon, request back up. And, since Oswald did not show a weapon until Tippit got out of the patrol car and begin to draw his own weapon, urgency or self-defense could not have been a reason for Tippit not calling in his intended act. To date, no one has offered a reasonable explanation for Tippit's conduct.

But to the Warren Commission and the Dallas Police Department, Tippit was a hero, slain in the line of duty attempting to capture Kennedy's assassin miles away from the assassination site, when he could not have known from police broadcasts that Oswald was a suspect. The eye witnesses saw Tippet start to draw his gun before an apparent stranger, and the stranger killed him. The mystery is, why was Tippit even there? And why did he draw his gun, if Oswald was a stranger?

At about the same time as Tippit's death, the Dallas Police surrounded the Texas School Book Depository and began combing it. In the southeast corner of the sixth floor officers discovered a perfectly created sniper's post. Book cartons had been stacked up as a shield so that a person could not be seen by those outside the building or by those who may have inadvertently walked up and looked around the sixth floor. Three book boxes were also piled up apparently to serve as a rifle rest.

On a page in the photo section, a photograph depicts this alleged crime scene. A quick review of the photographs discloses again that during the initial stages of investigating, this time at the alleged sniper's post, the Dallas police failed to do their job. For instance, the street level photograph looking up at the sixth floor of the book depository clearly shows that a sniper would have had a clear, close, unimpeded opportunity to shoot Kennedy when the limousine slowly turned the corner from Houston onto Elm Street. The street area directly below the alleged southeast corner sniper post made it a perfect target area. Kennedy would have been at close range when the Presidential limousine was traveling at its slowest speed. But no shots were fired while Kennedy was in this area. The shots were fired after the limousine left this close range area and moved farther down the street and away from the Book Depository. Seasoned investigators would have immediately questioned why a sniper in the Book Depository, if there was one there, did not fire sooner when the target was closest and moving slowly.[24]

The Dallas police investigators, again for some strange reason, completely ignored the human effort required to assemble the massive bulk of book boxes stacked around the sixth floor southeast window to make the sniper's nest. Twenty-eight book boxes were stacked as the outer shield; an assorted number piled up as an inner shield; with three boxes piled together as the gun rest; creating in total over 40 book boxes in all weighing more than a ton. The boxes averaged 50 pounds and each had to be carried, lifted, then arranged, and then stacked. The top boxes had been lifted to head height. If the police had checked, they could have learned that 15 minutes prior to the assassination several employees ate lunch on the sixth floor so close to the window area that one of them left a chicken bone near the scene. This meant that Oswald (assuming he did it) created his nest at the window in front of the workers having lunch without them being concerned, did it after they left and within the 15 minutes remaining prior to the assassination, or he did it in the morn-

[24] Americans should not forget that from November 22, 1963 until recently, the public was not allowed in the Book Depository and could not inspect the location of the sniper's den, the window, or view the street from above. Today, visitation is allowed but the sniper's area is still not completely approachable and the trees outside have matured, changing the views that existed.

ing with no one noticing the strange pile of boxes at the window and with no one missing him from work.

Common sense tells us that other workers would have certainly noticed if Oswald had either spent the morning moving boxes or moved them while they were eating lunch in the vicinity. The fact that no such activity was later recalled by any worker during questioning leads to the conclusion that the boxes were moved and stacked just before the shooting (within 15 minutes of the 12:30 assassination). But would it be possible for Oswald, a man who was 5′ 8″ tall and about 135 pounds, to move and stack these boxes within 15 minutes all by himself? Consider that in a simple test, a 6′ 7″, 268 pound former college football tackle and weight lifter took 21 minutes to move 40 boxes, weighing 50 pounds each, about 30 feet and then stacking them in similar fashion. The test subject, as one could imagine, was exhausted after the exercise.

It would not be logical to conclude that Oswald, who was spotted by a secretary 15 minutes before the murder in a downstairs lunchroom, could have positioned all the boxes by himself in such a limited amount of time. Furthermore, it is not logical to assume that if Oswald did manage to move all the boxes by himself that he would still have enough energy to hold and fire an outdated weapon with better than world class accuracy. Yet remarkably, these points were ignored by the police.

To continue the mystery, the Dallas police found only *three partial fingerprints of Oswald on only two of the boxes* in the area. However, Oswald had presumably opened the window, touched the woodwork and surrounding areas and stacked the book boxes by himself. It is possible Oswald may have worn gloves, but no gloves were discovered. But ignoring the fingerprint question, it still leaves the question of the impossible human feat of moving the boxes in such a short time. Rather than try to answer the question, the Dallas police and the Warren Commission chose to ignore the obvious answer.

Worse yet is the issue of Oswald's magically created fingerprint on the alleged assassin's rifle. Immediately after Kennedy's murder the Dallas police found Oswald's rifle on the 6th floor of the Texas School Book Depository. The Dallas police quickly seized the weapon and had its laboratory perform fingerprint analysis tests on the weapon. On Friday evening, the laboratory tests did not show the existence of any fingerprints of Oswald on the weapon. The weapon was then immediately sent to the F.B.I. laboratory in Washington, D.C. where no prints were found. The rifle was then returned to Dallas and within hours *after* Oswald's murder the Dallas police somehow then found one Oswald fingerprint that everyone had previously missed. The newly discovered print helped link Oswald to the alleged murder weapon. Either the Dallas police laboratory and the F.B.I. botched their original work in this most important investigation or the subsequently discovered fingerprint was planted. The latter alternative is consistent with the acts of someone refingerprinting Oswald after his death in the funeral parlor as was confirmed by Oswald's mortician.

Beyond a ton of book boxes and the lack of, and then subsequent strange existence of, fingerprints, the mystery of the Dallas police actions continued following Oswald's arrest. Upon his arrest Oswald was taken to the Dallas Police Station. He was then quickly taken to the third floor of police headquarters where interrogation began. From late Friday until his death on Sunday, Oswald was interrogated in a number of separate sessions totaling over 18 hours. But *during the entire period of extended interrogations involving a suspect in the biggest crime in Dallas' history—no one tape recorded the sessions, had a court reporter record the interrogation, or at least had someone take contemporaneous notes*. The Dallas police allegedly "forgot" to carry out this basic police practice. If this was truly "forgotten" for an hour, or one session, or even for one day, the inaction may have been excusable because of the excitement and stress. But for 18 hours of interrogation over days? This failure to record what Oswald said was deliberate because within 30 feet of Oswald's interrogation room there was: a *recording* room for interviews; an interview *supply* room; and a communication *equipment* room. The Warren Commission Exhibit demonstrates these facts clearly. At any time during the days of Oswald's captivity by the Dallas police, when he was repeatedly taken to and from these areas to be questioned, someone could have stopped and brought a tape recorder, or asked for a court stenographer to come in, or at least have obtained some paper and a pencil.

As a result of having no contemporaneous record, everyone must rely upon the memories and integrity of the few Dallas police officers and other agents who were with Oswald when he was questioned and who have claimed that Oswald said nothing of consequence during his days of private interrogations while in police custody and kept away from the news media.

However, Oswald did manage to publicly blurt out significant statements. This is because during rare public exposure, while being shuttled back and forth from jail cell to interrogation room, he managed to shout things out to the press. For instance, when Oswald was first arrested he made it known that he wanted the services of a New York lawyer who became famous in the 1950's for representing several criminal defendants in a criminal conspiracy case brought against them by the United States government. This request, made before Oswald was even formally charged with a crime, was *not* an oddball antic as some people originally believed. Rather, journalists and legal scholars have now concluded after research that this was a clue as to what actually may have happened. Oswald, *wanted a lawyer 1,500 miles away* who was proficient in representing persons charged with a conspiracy crime against the government. While Oswald was never charged with conspiracy, and while the Warren Commission found no conspiracy to exist, Oswald at the time of his arrest—by his request for a particular lawyer, disclosed to the world the real criminal charges that he knew should have been issued against him.

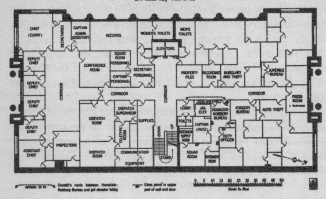

**THIRD FLOOR PLAN
DALLAS POLICE DEPARTMENT
DALLAS, TEXAS**

DIAGRAM 2:1
The third floor of the Dallas Police Department. Within feet of the interrogation area was: an interview supply room; the recording room; the communication equipment room; and the secretarial area.

During another transfer, after he allegedly could not reach the New York lawyer, he pleaded to the press that he needed a lawyer—any lawyer.[25] But, the Dallas Police continued to refuse his request for an attorney. Why? This unanswered question is probably explained by a statement Oswald managed to blurted out during a transfer:

[25] Several people, including the Warren Commission, have implied that Oswald refused the services of a Dallas lawyer who showed up at the jail offering to represent him. However, at that time, Oswald was still trying to contact John Abt as his lawyer. When this was not possible, he began asking for any lawyer.

"I am a patsy!"

And, the patsy who was kept away from the media, not given a lawyer, and privately interviewed without notations of his answers was set for slaughter as early as Friday night. There are no other logical explanations for the actions that were taken against Oswald Friday evening. Dallas Police Chief Curry decided to have Oswald attend a press conference in a police lineup room in the basement shortly after Oswald was charged, in absentia, with Kennedy's murder. However, there was no apparent purpose for this press conference because the reporters who attended were not allowed to question Oswald even though everyone knew he had been charged (except Oswald). Thus, a silent press conference was called. And, for the silent press conference the Chief's order that Oswald be displayed at the conference openly and unguarded like a sitting duck, was completely irrational. The Chief's subordinates protested and suggested that for Oswald's protection he be placed behind a nearby protective screen, but this was not done. All of this makes no sense until one realizes that Jack Ruby was allowed into the room and was standing only a few feet from Oswald with a loaded gun in his pocket. But Jack Ruby did not "act" that night and the exhibition was terminated. Nevertheless, it is undisputed that within hours following the assassination, by the actions of the Dallas Police Department's highly unusual "silent press conference" Jack Ruby had his first opportunity to execute Oswald.

A reason for this strange exhibition of Oswald before Ruby on Friday becomes apparent when one examines Texas law on holding prisoners in jail. At the time, by Texas law, any person charged with a felony crime (murder) had to be transferred from a city jail (Dallas City Jail where Oswald was held by the Dallas police) to the county jail. *By law this had to be completed within twelve hours* from the time charges were filed against the accused prisoner. In Oswald's case, he was in the Dallas City Jail and charged with a felony crime by the evening of Friday, November 22, 1963. Chief Curry (and others) obviously knew the law and knew that by law they had to give Oswald up to the County Sheriff by early Saturday morning. The bizarre Friday night display of the unprotected Oswald occurred during this 12 hour holding period.

When Oswald survived Friday night, the Dallas police then began to break the law by continuing to hold Oswald for more than 36 hours, with Chief Curry refusing to make the transfer.

It was not until Sunday morning, November 24, 1963, that the transfer was made. Contrary to past custom and routine in Dallas where, except for this one case, it was standard for the County Sheriff's office to handle the transfer, Chief Curry took direct charge and used his own men. By Saturday evening it was known all over Dallas that an attempt might be made to kill Oswald during the transfer. The F.B.I., independent Dallas citizens, and even County Sheriff Decker (who was to receive the prisoner), warned the Dallas police of such an attempt. But all such warnings were ignored and the bizarre continued unabated.

The Chief's transfer arrangements of Oswald made no common sense. He ignored the security suggestions from subordinate officers to transfer Oswald in secret and use others as a public decoy. He refused the request of Captain Fritz to transfer Oswald in an armored car. He did not even order a human police shield to surround Oswald on all flanks as was used when Oswald entered the station as a mere suspect.

Rather the Chief ordered an open public transfer of Oswald with only Detectives Levelle and Graves walking on each side. It has never been explained why Oswald as a suspect entered the police station completely protected by a human shield of police officers, and left completely exposed as the charged assassin of the President.

At 11:03 a.m. on Sunday morning, Police Chief Curry ordered the transfer of Oswald, assuring his officers that everything was "all set". However, the basement security was not fully in place, nor was the police transfer vehicle in place.

In fact, about the only thing that was all set was Jack Ruby, who was in place in the police basement, and in an even stranger twist, was so seemingly well prepared that his personal lawyer was waiting in the basement and immediately available to offer him legal counsel.

The Chief did not accompany Oswald when he was taken from the third floor to the basement via an elevator. First, he had a telephone conference with the Dallas Mayor Cabell, and then he ducked out a side door. As millions know, when Oswald took his walk toward the transfer car with live television cameras rolling and photographers snapping pictures, Ruby simply stepped forward and fired a single shot into Oswald's abdomen. As Ruby was wrestled to the ground he cried out:

> *"I had to do it, because they* [the police] *weren't going to do it."*

Conveniently, a fully staffed ambulance was waiting in the basement anticipating the "rare" event. Qualified medical personnel quickly attended to Oswald and an oxygen mask was put over his face and apparently he was then given oxygen. Medical experts have pointed out that this immediate medical procedure was strange. Other than preventing Oswald from talking, some have suggested that the use of a mask and oxygen following an abdominal gunshot wound is contrary to good medical care because oxygen actually promotes more bleeding in a traumatized area (such as gun shot wounds). Nevertheless, the Dallas police in spite of forgetting to get Oswald a lawyer and to record his interrogations somehow managed to plan ahead with an ambulance for Oswald's transfer in the police basement. This allowed Oswald to be whisked away and not publicly disclose his last dying words on national television.

Once again, ignoring this mysterious turn of events and proceeding on, Oswald was taken to the hospital and pronounced dead at 1:13 p.m. Within minutes of Oswald's death,

Police Chief Curry and Dallas District Attorney Henry Wade called a press conference where both men announced that the case was now closed and that Lee Harvey Oswald was the sole assassin.

While the Warren Commission report expressed dismay at much of the Dallas Police Department's conduct, the Commission concluded that Ruby's assassination of Oswald was spontaneous, unplanned, and performed by Ruby alone, just as it concluded that Oswald acted alone. The primary basis for its conclusion that Ruby's act was impromptu was that Ruby had been to the Western Union Station down the street from the Police station on business right before Oswald's transfer. The Commission reasoned that since Oswald's transfer time was unannounced and suddenly initiated by the Chief's order of "all set", Ruby's presence at the shooting had to have been coincidental.

But this is only one way of looking at the facts and the Commission ignored the other. It is undisputed that Ruby was at the Western Union Station on the Sunday morning just before the assassination, close to when the transfer was suddenly started. However, Ruby's presence at, or coming out of the Station may have been the actual "signal" to start the transfer. When one considers that the Station was just down the street from police headquarters and anyone looking out of a third floor window of the police building would have been able to clearly see Ruby (see diagram of third floor on page 182) this certainly is a likelihood. Support for this view are the facts as to what happened just before the transfer. In the middle of an interrogation, Oswald's interrogation was abruptly stopped to start the transfer process just after Ruby finished his transaction and was observed walking out of the Station.

If this view is accepted, then Ruby's shooting of Oswald was not an impromptu event. But he had a perfect defense to a first degree murder charge by being able to claim a sudden, unpremeditated impulse to act out against the assassin of his President. Thus, while Ruby may have failed to execute

Oswald on Friday night because he was concerned with possible pre-meditated criminal murder charges that would be filed against him (or perhaps he could not get the shot off), by Sunday a defense of temporary insanity had been successfully created based on Ruby's "impromptu" visit to the police station.

The actions of the Dallas Police Department described in this chapter when looked at in total defy all logic and common sense. Why did they: never follow up on the miracle bullet; fail to explain Officer Tippit's patrol assignment in Oswald's neighborhood; refuse to say why a Dallas police car stopped in front of Oswald's rooming house; not explain why Officer Tippit was seen casually talking to Oswald before Tippet's death; not investigate how and why Oswald killed Tippit; fail to answer how Oswald could have singlehandedly stacked over a ton of books to create a sniper's nest; not question why they only could find a few of Oswald's prints in the sniper's area; not ask why the sniper did not fire at a closer unimpeded range; not supply an explanation as to how an Oswald fingerprint could surface on the alleged assassination weapon, days later; not allow Oswald to have a lawyer; take no contemporaneous notes of Oswald's interrogations; permit Oswald to be an execution target for Ruby on the late Friday evening; never allow Oswald to publicly talk; not transfer Oswald out of the Dallas jail within 12 hours as required by law; chose to make the transfer of Oswald instead of the sheriff as was customary; permit the Chief to ignore reliable warnings of a possible execution attempt of Oswald; perform a public transfer of Oswald; not use a human police shield to protect Oswald; let Ruby get into a secured area twice with a gun; and, have an ambulance ready in advance of the shooting?

While the Dallas Police Department has never supplied adequate answers to these questions, Police Chief Curry's personal relationship with Lyndon Johnson may offer some insight.

30

The Police Chief and LBJ

Police Chief Curry's activities with Lyndon Johnson after the assassination shed some light on the Dallas Police Department's puzzling actions. Immediately after the assassination the Chief ended up at Parkland Memorial Hospital with President Kennedy and Governor Connally. As both men were wheeled into the hospital, the Chief chose to stay at the hospital rather than return to the crime scene to head up the investigation. While this decision has been criticized, it seems reasonable. But what occurred thereafter was not.

After it was clear that the President was dead and Governor Connally was seriously wounded, Chief Curry still elected to stay at the hospital the entire time that Johnson remained there. However, he did not remain to protect Johnson because under the circumstances, that was no longer his department's job, nor his as Chief of Police. Further, by remaining with Johnson, he was ignoring leading his police team investigating the major crime of the century. When Johnson finally decided to leave for the airport, Chief Curry, instead of remaining at the hospital with the victims, overseeing the search of the limousine for evidence, or returning to the crime scene to lead his men, chose instead to tag along with Johnson.

When the Chief, Johnson and several Secret Service agents

arrived at Love Field, the Chief went aboard the plane with Johnson to "stay a spell." He did this with unknown assassin(s) on the loose in downtown Dallas, following an unsolved assassination of the President which occurred in a motorcade that he had been leading. As such, Curry should have been the busiest man in Dallas. Yet, the Chief volunteered to escort Johnson to the plane and then spent the next 90 minutes sitting with Johnson. When Johnson was sworn in aboard Air Force One, others on the plane complained bitterly that Chief Curry was trying to push his way into every photograph.

These actions do not make sense. Why didn't the Chief return to the crime scene? Why didn't he lead his men? Why did he waste over 1½ hours of his time sitting with Johnson aboard Air Force One? While there seems to be no rational explanation for his conduct, a subsequent chapter will put his actions into the context of other events.

There also seems to be no rational explanation for Johnson's conduct during the same time period. As President Kennedy lay dying at Parkland Memorial Hospital, Johnson stood nearby. The President had just been shot by assassins and, so far as anyone knew, the killing may have been a prelude to a nuclear military attack, a bloody coup, a wipe-out of all government leaders, or even worse. The assassins were "allegedly" unknown and had not been captured. However, despite security staff orders that Johnson immediately leave the area for his own and the country's safety, he flatly refused. In the midst of the crisis, and with himself as a next possible victim, he refused to leave until he made sure that Kennedy was dead. When the news of Kennedy's death was first broken to him, he still refused to leave until another staff member was sent back to reconfirm the death. When he was reassured that the President was actually dead, Johnson finally left for the airport.

But when Johnson arrived at the airport, he did not leave as everyone advised. Bear in mind that in 1963, the nations of this earth were not living in peace and harmony, and it was a frightened America which had just lost its leader. Nevertheless, Johnson again overruled the advice of the security staff, the Secret Service, the White House staff, and even President Kennedy's brother, Bobby, that he quickly get air borne for the good of the nation. Rather, he first demanded that his luggage be taken off his plane and transferred to Kennedy's plane (both planes had the same sophisticated communications equipment and the term "Air Force One" applies to any plane on which a President flies). What Johnson wanted was to fly back to Washington on Kennedy's plane. When the transfer of baggage was finally accomplished, Johnson still refused to leave, claiming he wanted to take Kennedy's body back with him on the plane. After this delaying order was implemented, Johnson delayed his departure even more by stating that he wanted to take his Oath of Office on Texas soil. This required locating a Federal Judge and bringing her back to the plane. During all of this delay in time of crisis, so far as everyone observed, Johnson passed the time by watching TV, drinking bottled water, eating soup, and twice changing his shirt to get ready for his swearing in ceremony. It was hours later before Johnson finally left the city.

During this entire delaying time period Johnson appeared poised and confident, contrary to his later public claim that he was fearful for his own safety and concerned about a "world wide conspiracy!" Since Johnson was not an exceptionally courageous man (just two years earlier he did not want to travel to noncombat zones in Vietnam because he "didn't want to get his head blown off"), his apparent fearless actions during the assassination aftermath were completely out of character. Any reasonable man under the same circumstances who was repeatedly advised to get away from a crisis area for his own safety and the good of the nation would have immediately left. Human nature is such that if one really believed that he was the next victim, he would not wait around to find out.

Unanswered questions remain. Why did Chief Curry not

lead his police investigation, but rather stayed with Johnson? And, why was Johnson so unconcerned about fleeing Dallas? One possible answer is that one or both of these men knew that Johnson had nothing to fear concerning his own possible assassination.

31

Oswald:
The Patsy?

Lee Harvey Oswald claimed he was a "patsy." While not everything about Oswald will ever be known and though rumors of his alleged connections, trips, and political beliefs have emerged, what little is known about Oswald is that he was a perfect "patsy." If one traces his background it becomes clear that he was destined to be a fall guy.

Oswald was born in New Orleans on October 18, 1939. His father died before he was born and his remaining family subsequently moved to Dallas and then Fort Worth. Oswald's mother remarried and then later divorced Edwin Ekdahl. In 1952, Oswald and his mother moved again, this time to New York to live with his stepbrother. At the age of 16 Oswald dropped out of high school and attempted to enlist in the Marines. It was discovered that he was underage and his enlistment was denied. As a result, he spent the next year memorizing the Marine Corps Manual and preparing for enlistment on his 17th birthday. Within weeks after turning 17, Oswald enlisted in the Marines. While younger than most of the men, he graduated 7th in his class as an aviation electronics operator. The Marines considered him more intelligent than the other soldiers and mature enough to handle himself well even in an emergency. Oswald taught himself Russian while in the service and then applied and was accepted to the

Albert Schweitzer College in Switzerland. Oswald planned on studying psychology in Europe after his discharge.

In 1959, a few months before Oswald's active duty status was to end, he obtained an early Honorable Discharge because of a dependency need from his mother. He then obtained a passport with the intention to tour Europe and attend Albert Schweitzer College. However, once in Europe, Oswald migrated northwest into Finland and entered Russia. While there he initially attempted to renounce his American citizenship which, as a former marine, made national news in America. However, after a few months of living in Russia Oswald changed his mind and tried to return to the United States. As early as July, 1960, he unsuccessfully tried to get a Soviet exit visa to leave. He apparently realized there was a marked difference between socialist ideals (i.e. sharing, etc.) and communist practices. From that time on, Oswald always tried to explain to anyone willing to listen that there was a difference between socialism and communism, especially as practiced in Russia.

By September of 1960, the Marine Corps learned of Oswald's actions and decided to change his original Honorable Discharge to an Undesirable Discharge classification. When he learned of the decision Oswald became immensely upset and spent the remainder of his life trying to get the military to return his status to Honorable.

In 1961 Oswald married a Russian woman in Russia and then aggressively renewed his efforts to return to the United States. Eventually, his perseverance paid off and he was allowed to return in 1962 and settled in Texas. He held numerous non-descript jobs while continuing with some efforts to prove to the Marines that they should change his discharge status back.

Because of his military training Oswald had some knowledge of weapons. Further, his trip to Russia created national attention and branded him publicly as a communist traitor to the misinformed (he always insisted that he was *not* a communist, but a socialist). And, because of his intense concern over his downgraded military status from his beloved Marines, Oswald might have done anything to correct this wrong and prove that he was a good Marine. With this background Oswald was a perfect candidate to be a patsy and to be framed as the culprit for murdering President Kennedy.

By 1963 Oswald's conduct can be seen as changing as if to create a noticeable public trail. He regularly appeared to create public scenes, obtain publicity, and then drop out of sight. For example, in *April of 1963* Oswald allegedly fired a rifle shot at retired right wing General Edwin Walker. Oswald's shot from close range completely missed the mark and did not hit the ultra conservative leader. After this he left his wife and child behind in Texas and moved to New Orleans.

Between this nationally publicized shot at General Walker and Oswald's next public performance, he applied for a new passport on June 24, 1963. In his passport application Oswald stated that he *intended to leave the country sometime in November* or December of *1963*. At the same time he demanded that his Russian wife write to the Russian Embassy and request a return visa for herself to Russia. Included with his wife's letter to the Russian Embassy was a separate note from Oswald asking that his wife's request be "rushed." Thus, months before the date for Kennedy's trip to Texas was publicly announced, Oswald was already making plans to get his wife out of the country quickly, and for him to leave the United States in November, the exact time it would turn out that Kennedy would be in Dallas. Additionally, Oswald's June passport request concurred in the time with the Kennedy, Johnson, Connally agreement that the President's Texas trip would be in the fall of 1963.

In *August 1963*, Oswald staged his next public event when he surfaced supporting a *Pro-Castro movement* in New Orleans. The total time involvement with this "cause" was less than two weeks but within this short time frame he managed to obtain press coverage and public notoriety as a dissident supporting Castro. The circumstances of this event were very unusual because within a span of less than fourteen days:

1. Oswald deliberately sought out and befriended an anti-Castro group and indicated an interest in joining;

2. He next secretly created his own pro-Castro group, being the sole organizer and only member;

3. He then "baited" the *anti*-Castro group into a public confrontation by demonstrating and passing out pro-Castro leaflets in front of them; and

4. After he drew public attention by this confrontation to both himself and his pro-Castro cause (through newspaper and radio coverage), Oswald quickly dropped out of sight.

In *September, 1963*, Oswald duplicated his publicity stunt this time in Mexico City. He appeared unannounced at the Russian and Cuban Embassies. After shuttling between the two communist embassies, Oswald created such a noticeable disturbance at the Cuban Embassy that he was thrown out and told that it was "his type who was harming the Cuban Revolution." As before, after creating a public scene and public record and establishing a purported link, Oswald dropped out of sight.

On *October 4, 1963* Oswald returned to Dallas. He obtained a room using an alias. On October 16, he began work at the Texas School Book Depository, a six story building, at the end of the proposed Presidential motorcade route. Using his own name, Oswald easily obtained the job without a specific position being open and went to work in the middle of the week in a "temporary capacity." The job entailed filling orders for various school textbook companies who stored books on different floors of the building. On October 25, 1963 Oswald attended a local ACLU meeting where he was heard stating that: he was not a communist; the U.S. was superior to the U.S.S.R. in civil rights; and, that President Kennedy was responsible for the U.S. civil rights advances.

If Oswald in fact shot President Kennedy, then he obviously changed his mind about Kennedy's leadership qualities some time within weeks of the assassination. This is because it was conceded by all (even the Warren Commission) that Oswald greatly admired Kennedy. By most standards Oswald would have been more likely to vote for Kennedy than shoot him.

Contrasting Oswald's stated admiration for Kennedy to his public statement after his arrest, "I am a patsy," raises the questions: Who was Oswald a patsy for? Why did he do it?

After Oswald's death, the press immediately focused on Jack Ruby as possibly being Oswald's "boss" in the affair. Not only was it recalled that Ruby was seen hovering around the Dallas Police Station during the entire time of Oswald's arrest and confinement, but other known public links placed the two together before the assassination. For instance, Ruby had just recently moved from his upper class apartment to Oswald's lower class neighborhood. Both men frequented or stayed at a local YMCA and held mail boxes close together in a local post office. More important than these coincidences, however, is the number of independent witnesses who claim to have seen the two together. These witnesses include a lawyer, dancer, bartender, waiter, and a tavern customer. Others who have claimed even more personal knowledge of the relationship have said that Ruby's job after the assassination was to have Oswald killed as the patsy in the crime. While proof of this link is not uncontroverted, it should be clear that even if the two could be positively tied together, both were only insignificant participants in the assassination, the planning of which required more sophistication, contacts, and inside information than either man could ever possess.

After Oswald's death, and when the possible connection between Oswald and Ruby began to draw public attention, a new factor was thrown into the pot which turned the focus of the investigation in a completely different direction. Dallas District Attorney Henry Wade and Texas Attorney General Fred Carr informed the Warren Commission that they had information that Oswald was a CIA agent on its payroll as agent number 179 at the time of the assassination. This unsubstantiated news was met with shock and disbelief. Nevertheless, the Warren Commission and assisting government investigative agencies decided to ignore the evidence of possible links between Oswald and Ruby, and also to ignore the claim made by the two Texans. In essence, with such a new allegation surfacing the Warren Commission decided to bury everything. But how Dallas District Attorney Wade and Texas Attorney General Carr managed to get such important top secret information, if it was true, is anyone's guess. To date, no supporting evidence has ever surfaced supporting the claim made by the Texans. As a result, only one of two conclusions is possible: upon disclosure of the CIA link, the government covered it up; or, no such CIA link ever existed. If the latter alternative is correct, then Wade and Carr were given information by someone who was engaged in a deception and who wanted the investigation diverted from centering too close upon a sensitive issue.

Because the link between Oswald and Ruby was never fully explored, even now, decades later, no substantial credible evidence exists linking Oswald to Ruby (or Oswald to the CIA). However, the important question is whether there is any clear and direct evidence linking Oswald to anyone else who could put him in the position of being "a patsy". Fortunately, there is an answer to this question since clear evidence exists linking Oswald to Lyndon B. Johnson.

It is without dispute that in January of 1962, Oswald wrote a personal letter to Johnson's good friend, John Connally, who had been Secretary of the Navy.[26] Oswald asked for Connally's help in changing his downgraded military dis-

---

[26] Connally was from Fort Worth, Texas. He had an association with Johnson that dated back to 1939 when he began his career as an aide to LBJ. The relationship continued and in 1960 Connally was LBJ's Presidential Campaign manager and later LBJ's appointee as Secretary of the Navy. In the late 1960's Connally was indicted in a milk producers influence peddling and bribery scandal and Johnson appeared as a character witness on his behalf (he was not convicted). Recently, Connally went bankrupt owing creditors over $120,000,000.00 in uncovered losses.

charge status. Mistakenly, Oswald believed that Connally still held the post as Secretary of the Navy and that his influence could help. Oswald's misdirected letter was then forwarded on to the new Secretary of the Navy . . . Fred Korth.[27] Korth, had replaced Connally in that post, and just like Connally, he was both a Johnson friend and another Johnson "Texas Appointee." Coincidentally, Korth knew the Oswald family since several years before, as a lawyer in private practice, he represented Oswald's mother in her divorce.

Evidence has also surfaced that just months before the assassination, Oswald traveled to Austin, Texas and apparently went to Governor Connally's office where he created a disturbance. Reports were that the disturbance was over Oswald's discharge status. Since the Warren Commission conceded that Oswald had an above average I.Q., was rational, and understood the American political system . . . the perplexing question is why Oswald went to Governor Connally's office in Texas to complain about a federal military problem which is something over which Governor Connally had no political control? One possibility is that someone, perhaps falsely claiming to represent the interests of Korth or Connally, contacted Oswald sometime after his 1962 letter and represented to him that they could help in having his discharge status amended in exchange for his cooperation.

Beyond this, Oswald's contacts with other close friends of Johnson may have been much deeper. A handwritten note, proven by experts to be clearly in Oswald's handwriting, has recently surfaced. The note was dated November 8, 1963 and was directed to "Mr. Hunt".[28] While the F.B.I. has evaluated

---

[27] Fred Korth was also from Fort Worth, Texas. He replaced Connally as Johnson's second recommendation appointee to the Secretary of the Navy post. In 1963 Korth resigned from the position in disgrace amidst the TFX missile influence peddling scandal.

[28] Some assassination theorists have ignored the obvious and have attempted to link Oswald and the note to the CIA agent E. Howard Hunt of Watergate fame which occurred in the following decade. There appears to be no merit to this attempted link.

the note from the context that Oswald may have directed it to one of oilman H.L. Hunt's sons, others have concluded that the note was actually written to H.L. Hunt, Johnson's close friend. If either view is accepted, the note not only supplies a direct link between Oswald and another of Johnson's friends, but it is consistent with claims that both H.L. Hunt and Johnson knew of the assassination in advance. Just two weeks before the murder Oswald wrote to Mr. Hunt that:

> *"Dear Mr. Hunt:*
>
> *I would like information concerning my position.*
>
> *I am asking only for information.*
>
> *I am suggesting that we discuss the matter fully before any steps are taken by me or anyone else.*
>
> *Lee Harvey Oswald"*

This is especially true when one considers that Oswald's wife, Marina, was observed by H.L. Hunt's personal security director coming out of Hunt's office within a month after the assassination.

Of all of the links, associations, and rumors of connections that have ever surfaced . . . the only clear and undisputed connections are the known contacts between Oswald and Johnson's friends. As such, it is entirely possible that Oswald may have become a patsy for some "good ol Texas boys" who wanted to go "all the way with LBJ."

32
Jack Ruby

With the burials of Oswald and Ruby positive proof as to links between the two may never be established. However, the burials did not destroy the evidence of Ruby's links to other individuals nor of his extremely suspicious conduct immediately before and after the assassination.

By way of background, in 1911 Jack Ruby was born in Chicago to Jacob and Fannie Rubenstein. He grew up in a "tough" neighborhood attempting to provide for himself. During World War II he was drafted into the military where he eventually shortened his name to Ruby. Ruby stayed state side during his term of service and was honorably discharged in 1946. In late 1947 Jack Ruby moved to Dallas where he joined his sister in operating a supper club. From that point on, until his shooting of Oswald, Ruby operated nightclubs and dance halls.

It is from this dance hall and night club environment that Ruby's connections to the underworld arose. Strip tease night clubs became Ruby's front office business probably covering for gambling operations. This placed him into the position of being a small time Dallas "hood" often acting as a liaison confidentially linking the wealthy Dallas establishment to the pleasures of the city's vice.

Ruby's extremely suspicious conduct in relationship to the assassination can be traced directly to the days before the assassination. This is when he visited the Hunt Oil Company building, withdrew a large amount of cash from his bank, and also purchased six one-way tickets to Mexico. The Warren Commission, as usual, explained away the visit to the Hunt building and the large cash withdrawal. But it could not handle the airplane tickets to Mexico, so it just ignored the issue. It also ignored the fact that the day before Ruby actually shot Oswald, he was publicly passing out H.L. Hunts' conservative political literature, talking about his conservative radio show, and voicing Hunt's conservative ideals to others. After the Oswald shooting, a search of Ruby's apartment turned up other ultra conservative literature of the Hunt family as well as the name of "Hunt" written in his personal notebook. The connection between Ruby and this group of Johnson supporters was so direct that after Ruby's arrest the Dallas Police advised H. L. Hunt to get out of town for a while.

One of the most perplexing of Ruby's actions was his appearance at Parkland Memorial Hospital immediately after the assassination. As Kennedy was dying in bay 13, Ruby was spotted in the area. He was seen by people from Dallas who knew him. He talked with reporter Seth Cantor who knew Ruby from a previous news reporting stint in Dallas. In spite of this Ruby later denied being at the hospital. The Warren Commission, as usual, decided that Ruby had not been there because he said so. It therefore excluded all of the independent witness sightings of him at the hospital as unreliable. Besides, the Commission could not determine any possible reason for Ruby being at the hospital.

However, how could a number of independent eye witnesses be wrong as to who they saw? And, what reason did Ruby have for lying about this event? The answer to these questions can again be derived by looking at the facts from another perspective. If one begins by believing the eyewitnesses who saw Ruby at the hospital, then Ruby was lying about not being there. Since there would be no reason to lie about something unimportant, Ruby's lie had to have been related to something significant. And often significant things involve important people. The important people at the hospital at that time included: President Kennedy (slain); Governor Connally (wounded); Vice President Johnson (alive and well); Police Chief Curry (healthy); other high ranking Dallas police officers and some Secret Service agents. If Ruby had gone to the hospital merely out of curiosity, he would not have had to deny it. But if he went to the hospital to talk to one of the important people, or to relay a message to one of these important people, that would constitute a significant purpose worthy of later lying about and covering up.

Assuming this reasoning is logical, it still does not explain what important message Ruby brought, or what important person he had to talk to. However, one reason Ruby would want to talk personally with an important person at the hospital (and later deny he was there) would be if he was involved in an assassination conspiracy and something had gone wrong with the plan. Then, he might go to the hospital to relay the problem or ask for instructions. For example, if Oswald was unknowingly supposed to be a "patsy" and be killed near the assassination site, but got away . . . that would be a disaster to the plan. If Oswald the "patsy" got away and could not be found, the whole assassination plan could be destroyed. If something of this magnitude went awry and Ruby was involved in any way, the very first thing that he (or anyone) would probably do would be to personally report the problem to the more important person and then ask for instructions. While this is speculation, and whether Ruby went to the hospital to personally report a major assassination problem to a person such as Chief Curry, or anyone else for that matter, will never be known.

But what is known is that Ruby's hospital appearance is

consistent in time with Oswald allegedly fleeing the Book Depository and remaining at large. It would also explain why Ruby was seen at the hospital but later lied about it. If this proposition of why Ruby was at the hospital is accepted, it explains a lot of the other apparent mysteries including: Oswald's exhibition on Friday night in front of the armed Ruby; the Dallas Police Department's failure to record Oswald's interrogations; the Police Department's refusal to transfer Oswald; and Ruby's Sunday morning shooting of Oswald ("I had to do it"). While this is merely a proposition, other undisputable facts support it.

For instance, after Oswald's capture and arrest by the Dallas Police Department Friday afternoon, Ruby started to act like a condemned man. This conduct began with a visit to his sister's house where he became nauseous and sick to his stomach. He then began making a series of farewell telephone calls to friends and relatives to whom he had not spoken to in years. He even called his brother Ruben in Chicago, although the men had not gotten along in years. After calling Ruben he telephoned one of his old girlfriends to whom he had also not talked to in years "just to chat." He followed this up with a call to a little boy to make sure that he was enjoying his new puppy. Eventually, Ruby just broke down and began to cry. And, according to his sister, he then decided to lie down for awhile.

Upon arising, Ruby, a nonpracticing Jew, telephoned the local temple to find out the time of the Friday evening worship service. He eventually made it to the synagogue to meet the rabbi and the other worshippers in a post-worship setting. The rabbi, in a subsequent interview, stated that he was flabbergasted to see Ruby since he rarely ventured to the temple. These documented actions of Ruby can only be considered those of a man who knew he had only a short period of life, or freedom, remaining. Ruby's nauseousness and crying episodes are consistent with a man who knew that he was in, or going to be in, serious trouble. His telephone farewells and temple visit were those of a man making his last amends.[29]

From the temple that Friday evening, Ruby traveled to the Dallas Police Station where Oswald was jailed. He was repeatedly seen throughout the weekend going in and out of restricted police areas and offices. This included the office of the main police interrogator Police Captain Fritz. However, these eyewitness accounts of Ruby's activities have always been denied by the Dallas Police Department. These steadfast denials have only been begrudgingly changed to admissions on those occasions when photographs or movies clearly depicted Ruby in a specific area of the police department.

In fact, Ruby's presence at the late Friday night exhibition of the unprotected Oswald probably would also have been denied by the Dallas police if it were not for a newsfilm that captured him there. It was at this needless press conference where Ruby (after just completing a period of crying, nausea, a temple visit) stood in the same room as Oswald. It is undisputed that Ruby had a gun in his pocket. Why Ruby did not use the gun that night one can only guess. Perhaps he got scared or perhaps he could not get close enough. But the more likely answer is that the press conference was abruptly terminated before he could act. The press conference was supposed to be silent with no questions asked. But it had to

[29] In fact, before Oswald was actually killed, Jack Ruby told a Dallas police officer that he was going to have to kill Oswald. There is no evidence that the officer did anything with this information. However, he was subsequently interviewed in Dallas by Lee Rankin, an investigator for the Warren Commission. When Rankin came to address this subject with the officer during his Warren Commission interview with him, Rankin requested a break and sent the court reporter out of the room. He then spent 20 minutes "off-the-record" threatening and intimidating the police officer telling him that if he persisted in telling the truth about what Ruby had told him he was going to be in big trouble. The interview was not completed and the officer's testimony on the subject was not recorded. As a result, the officer complained and subsequently flew to Washington and insisted that the Warren Commission record reflect Rankin's acts and the actual truth. While this testimony is now part of the Warren Commission's record, the Commission ignored it.

be immediat
lence and sh
the newly fil
President (the
Oswald respo
had told him)
terminated and

With this un
the truth. And a
ately, even if t
since with this n
begun talking to
them what he kn
chances would
stepped forward

personal lawyer. Who could not b
overwhelming evidence, that th
wald was part of a premedita
out. Only the Warren Co
The facts also clearl
son's close friends.
made a visit to
political suppo
friend of o
ing Rub
nightc
Jack

...ned Oswald only moments later. Oswald would have died never knowing that he had been charged with Kennedy's murder.

After the press conference, Ruby's subsequent actions for the next few days have been meticulously traced by historians. While the next major event does not occur until Sunday, November 24, 1963, it should be noted that Ruby continued his unusual conduct. He reported to friends that he was thinking about trying to get out of town real fast. He even called his business associate Ralph Paul to advise Paul that he was going to have to kill Oswald. This telephone call was overheard by one of Paul's employees whose testimony the Warren Commission also ignored. Another of Ruby's telephone conversations was overheard by a parking attendant who clearly heard Ruby talk about the transfer and state, "You know I'll be there." Even those close to Ruby began to clear out suspecting or knowing what was going to occur. Larry Crawford, the maintenance man at Ruby's club, just walked right out of Dallas on foot and began hitchhiking away on Saturday evening. And, Ruby's roommate, when hearing the news broadcast of Oswald's execution, but without knowing the identity of Ruby as the killer, immediately stood up in panic in a public restaurant and ran to a telephone to call his

...ieve, in the face of this
...killing of Lee Harvey Os-
...ed plan that Ruby had to carry
...mission!

...show that Ruby knew many of John-
...On the day before the assassination Ruby
...the offices of one of Johnson's strongest
...rters. Even, Lyndon Johnson's Dallasite girl-
...er 20 years, Madeline Brown, admitted to know-
...y and acknowledged frequently drinking in his
...ub. Further, Ms. Brown was originally introduced to
...Ruby through one of Johnson's lawyers. And, as not
...expected, it has now surfaced that many other important
Dallas citizens may have also known Ruby including Dallas
Mayor Earl Cabell and Dallas District Attorney Henry Wade.

The facts demonstrate that beginning with Oswald's arrest
and until his death, Ruby appeared physically and emotionally
shaken by something. The only rational inference that can be
drawn from this is that Ruby had been assigned the task of
"taking care" of Oswald before he talked. Whether this was
Ruby's original job or merely his back up role because the
plan had gone awry is unimportant. What is important is that
after all was said and done, years after the event, as Ruby sat
in jail he would work himself into violent tirades complete
with vile obscenities upon hearing Johnson's name! In letters
smuggled out of jail Ruby declared that Johnson was the
mastermind of the assassination. This is reflected by the following quotation from one such letter authored by Ruby:

> *"First, you must realize that the people here want
> everyone to think I am crazy. . . . isn't it strange
> that Oswald. . . . should be fortunate enough to
> get a job at the Texas Schoolbook Depository
> Building two weeks before. . . . Only one person
> could have had that information, and that man
> was Johnson . . . because he is the one who was*

going to arrange the trip . . . The only one who gained by the shooting . . ."

"They alone planned the killing, by they I mean Johnson and others. . . . you may learn quite a bit about Johnson and how he has fooled everyone. . . ." [Emphasis Added]

Government psychiatrists claimed that these statements and other actions by Ruby demonstrated his insanity. However, these doctors probably never bothered to ask Ruby the true reason for his anger.

33

What Happened to Jack Ruby

QUESTION: How do you set a guilty man free in a scandalous criminal case without creating public outcry?

ANSWER: You try, convict, and sentence the guilty man to the maximum penalty. When public hostility has subsided, you free the guilty man on a legal technicality.

Lyndon Baines Johnson may even have been behind the scenes controlling the criminal murder case of Jack Ruby. Whether Johnson exercised his power is unknown, but Johnson had sufficient contacts to control Ruby's murder case if he was inclined to do so. And, the final results of Ruby's case demonstrate enough irregularities and enough connections sufficient to argue that "Texas justice" may have been at work again.

To evaluate this concept all one has to do is to follow Jack Ruby's criminal case from its inception. At the exact moment that Ruby executed Oswald in the Dallas Police basement on live television, his personal Dallas defense lawyer was only yards away conveniently waiting to undertake Ruby's defense from the moment he was wrestled to the ground and arrested. Before Ruby's arraignment in court for Oswald's murder, a host of additional criminal defense lawyers lined up outside his cell waiting to help. This instantaneous and remarkable array of defense counsel helped guarantee that Ruby's constitutional rights were not violated from the second he committed his crime, but also insured that he did not unwisely talk during any police interrogations.

Ruby was also fortunate enough to be prosecuted by a District Attorney whom he knew personally, Henry Wade.[30] Wade and Police Chief Curry were involved in investigating Kennedy's murder and Connally's wounding. Wade was also involved with Curry in arranging Oswald's unprecedented "silent press conference" (with Ruby in the room with a gun) and on the eve of the assassination received a telephone call from LBJ's aide trying to get him to file only certain criminal charges. Ruby's connection to Wade dated back to 1953. This is because from 1953 to 1963 Ruby had been repeatedly arrested or charged with various crimes, but the charges were always dropped or dismissed. In fact, in one criminal case against Ruby, Wade, as the prosecuting Attorney personally signed and filed a motion to dismiss the criminal case, in spite of the fact that the arresting officers maintained that the arrest and charges against Ruby were valid and the officers never agreed to withdraw the charges.

Ruby's statements to Wade on the evening of Kennedy's assassination ("Hi, Henry, remember me . . .") and even his temporary service as Wade's personal publicity agent in the assassination aftermath (i.e. arranging for a radio interview for Wade and pointing Wade out to television reporters) demonstrated that before Wade undertook to prosecute Ruby, Ruby knew Wade.

Another fortunate advantage for Ruby was that the presiding Judge in his murder case was Joe Brown. Judge Brown

---

[30] Wade also happened to be John Connally's college roommate.

began his handling of the case by hiring a public relations man to serve as a "personal consultant" on his judicial image during the trial. While this act alone was highly unusual, his conduct in the case was even more bizarre. Fortunately for Ruby, reversible error was committed by Judge Brown even before the trial started. Prior to the trial, Ruby's lawyers demanded that the case be transferred out of Dallas because Ruby could not get a fair trial due to local hostility. To buttress their demand, the defense lawyers introduced numerous news accounts reporting about the hostility against Ruby in Dallas. In addition, the defense lawyers paraded in almost 100 witnesses, including many well respected Dallas citizens, who all agreed that Ruby could not possibly get a fair trial in Dallas. It was clear to everyone that the trial site should be moved elsewhere.

In response to this overwhelming evidence, District Attorney Wade could produce only one affidavit from one citizen stating that a fair trial could occur in Dallas. To decide this crucial issue, Judge Brown ignored the overwhelming evidence and remarkably determined that Ruby should be tried in Dallas. To completely insure that Ruby did not get a fair trial in Dallas, Judge Brown refused to exclude as potential jurors those people who witnessed the murder on television. These obvious errors guaranteed, even before the start of the trial, that any conviction occurring at trial would be reversed on appeal.

This is exactly what occurred. Ruby was convicted of first degree murder by a Dallas jury, sentenced to death, and his conviction and sentence was summarily reversed by the Appellate Court in a harshly critical opinion against Judge Brown. Following the reversal, the Dallas District Attorney's office immediately began negotiating with Ruby's defense lawyers about having Ruby plead guilty to a lesser charge in lieu of going through a new trial. The negotiations involved an offer from the District Attorney to completely free Ruby in exchange for a plea of guilty to a lesser offense.

Thus, Ruby was about to walk away free from the Oswald

murder after spending less than three years in jail. Unfortunately, Ruby died in jail before the negotiations were finalized.[31]

All of this may have been just pure coincidence and does not confirm Johnson's involvement in Ruby's trial.[32] However, during the pendency of Ruby's appeal, Judge Joe Brown was caught in a scandal which required his removal from the case for all future matters. It was revealed that Judge Brown had been contacted by Johnson's Texas friends, the Murchinsons, who among other things owned book publishing concerns. The Murchinsons gave the Judge a lucrative book contract and an advance to write a book about Ruby's trial, though the book was never published, along with an all expense paid trip to the Murchinsons' exclusive California hotel.

To come full circle, District Attorney Henry Wade, who prosecuted Ruby and arranged with Chief Curry to put Oswald on display, happened to have been a friend and the former college roommate of LBJ's 1960 campaign manager and was contacted by Johnson's aide the evening of Kennedy's murder. And, Judge Brown, the trial court judge who convicted Ruby in a case that was prejudiced with a clearly reversible error from the start, was later discovered to have been the

[31] Even Ruby's death is subject to debate as to whether it resulted from natural causes or murder. He allegedly died of an extremely rare form of cancer. However, even before discovery of the disease, Ruby told his friends and his prison guards that he was gradually being murdered by the injection of cancerous materials from a prison doctor. After his death, an investigation failed to turn up the name or anything else about any man who allegedly posed as a doctor and gave Ruby injections of an unknown substance.

[32] While the trial court error, the Appellate Court reversal, and the chance to go free for only the short time served may not seem consistent with a plan to murder Jack Ruby, however, it is. While the judicial process may have been working successfully to set Ruby free, Americans should not forget that as 1964 passed into 1965 and onward, Jack Ruby began talking. Initially, he began talking only by innuendos but later he began affirmatively stating that Johnson was involved. If this was true, then Ruby surely had to be silenced.

recipient of a book contract from some of Johnson's other Texas friends.

Thus, the record shows that both the prosecuting attorney and the trial judge in Ruby's murder case were both acquaintances of or were contacted by friends or aides of Johnson.

34

The Hunt Family's Involvement

The one man who was known as Johnson's strongest supporter for his 1960 Democratic Presidential bid against Jack Kennedy was Texas oil magnate H.L. Hunt. Multimillionaire Hunt was so eager to help Johnson beat Kennedy that he committed a federal election law violation in the process. H.L. Hunt was willing to do almost anything to help his friend obtain the presidency.

When Johnson lost the 1960 nomination to Kennedy, H.L. Hunt was among the select few who consoled Johnson in his private hotel suite. Hunt also was among these same select few who advised Johnson to seek the Vice Presidential spot on the Kennedy ticket, rather than completely give up. For Hunt, Johnson, and their other friends, the thought of being only a heartbeat away from the presidency was better than nothing. Like Johnson, H.L. Hunt believed that Johnson was entitled to be President because he possessed superior qualifications to govern and lead. And, while Hunt was an ultraconservative, he continually supported the liberal Johnson. Presumably H.L. Hunt never let politics interfere with making money.

By 1963, H.L. Hunt was one of the wealthiest men in America. He resided in Dallas with his family. To advance his political views he created a nationally syndicated radio show called "Life Line" and was the founder of the ultra-conservative political organization known as "Facts Forum." Hunt had two sons who followed their father's ultra-conservative ideals. In fact, prior to Kennedy's assassination Hunt and his two sons publicly voiced animosity toward Kennedy.

Prior to the President's murder, H.L. Hunt had publicly announced that the President and his staff should be shot since there was "no way to get those traitors out of government except by shooting them out." Similarly, Hunt's son, Nelson Bunker Hunt, partially paid for a full page black-bordered advertisement in the *Dallas Morning News* attacking the President as a pro-communist traitor. The ad appeared on the day of Kennedy's murder and was viewed by many as a "Dallas greeting." However, merely because H.L. Hunt had a strong relationship with Johnson and stated that Kennedy should be shot, is not proof of his involvement in the assassination. But the links between Johnson, H.L. Hunt and those involved in the assassination go much deeper than their common animosity toward Kennedy.

Beginning as early as the 1950's, H.L. Hunt was known to have continuing gambling contacts with Jack Ruby. More importantly, on the day before the assassination Ruby actually went to the Hunt Oil Company building (purportedly to help a young girl obtain a job interview with the Hunts). The same day in the same Hunt Oil Company building, convicted California felon Jim Braden and "three associates" paid a visit to H.L. Hunt's sons Lamar and Nelson. On assassination day, Braden was caught up in a post-assassination dragnet in the Dal Tex building adjacent to the Texas School Book Depository. He was arrested for acting suspicious while being close to the assassination scene and unable to supply a valid reason for his presence. Braden was later released by the Dallas police without further investigation.

After the assassination and after Ruby's murder of Oswald it was discovered that Ruby: had a Hunt family name and number written in his private notebook; had H.L. Hunt's conservative propaganda literature in his possession; and had recently made strong public statements about the positive nature of H.L. Hunt's ultra-conservative "Life Line" radio programs.

Beyond these known contacts, the handwritten November 8, 1963 letter of Oswald to "Mr. Hunt" (previously referred to) is also a significant linking factor. To whichever Hunt Oswald addressed his letter to, it is clear that Oswald wanted to:

> "... *discuss the matter fully before any steps are taken by me or anyone else.*"

If one accepts the word of H.L. Hunt's special security assistant that he saw Marina Oswald coming from Hunt's private offices within the month after the assassination, and that H.L. Hunt also admitted to him that he knew before the murder that a conspiracy existed to kill the President, the picture becomes much clearer.

It is clear that Johnson had ties to H.L. Hunt of Dallas who disliked Kennedy to such a great extent that Hunt stated Kennedy should be shot and was of the opinion that Kennedy was a traitor. It is also clear, by accident or design, one of the major participants in the post-assassination events, Jack Ruby, had direct contacts and ties with H.L. Hunt.

35

LBJ's Admissions & Subsequent Strange Acts

While Lyndon Johnson's links to the pre- and post-assassination events have been examined as well as his potential connections to some of the participants, one more important subject remains in evaluating his opportunity. This involves examining Johnson's admissions and subsequent strange acts. An admission is an incriminating statement made by a person against his own interest or position. A simple example is a criminal defendant in response to an arrest blurting out, "You got me, I did it." Admissions in and of themselves can be used as direct evidence to convict someone of a crime (if given voluntarily). In fact, to convict a defendant in a criminal trial very little, if any, additional evidence is needed beyond an admission. An admission can be either verbal or nonverbal. While a verbal admission is self-explanatory, a nonverbal admission is a more difficult concept.

For purposes of this book, nonverbal admissions are actions that are so unusual or bizarre that while not necessarily absolute proof of wrongful conduct, like a verbal admission, they lend some credence to a defendant's guilt. Perhaps the best example of a nonverbal admission is a suspect fleeing the scene, or better yet, the apprehension of a criminal suspect late at night near the crime scene driving a car with its lights off. While there may be explanations offered for such activity, the act is still relevant to the issue of whether the accused committed the crime. Ordinarily, most criminal prosecutors attempt to introduce this type of evidence at trial as part of the fact scenario.

In Lyndon Johnson's case, according to witnesses, he made both verbal and nonverbal admissions as to his involvement in the crime. Whether the witnesses to these admissions are credible, and whether these admissions can be explained away is up to the determination of others. We are dealing only with what has been reported.

According to Johnson's girlfriend of over 20 years, Madeline Brown, Lyndon Baines Johnson told her *prior* to President Kennedy's assassination that Kennedy was going to be killed in Dallas. While anyone can challenge the girlfriend's integrity, if her word is believed, Johnson's statement alone may have been sufficient to convict him of conspiracy to commit murder. How could Johnson have known about the murder in advance if he was not involved? Further still, even if Johnson was not directly involved in the planning of the murder, his admission would have been enough to criminally charge him with being a party to a crime, since he knew in advance but did nothing. And, Johnson's admission to his girlfriend before the murder certainly brings to the forefront Johnson's argument with President Kennedy concerning seating arrangements in the motorcade. Can any American imagine that someone knew about a planned murder and did nothing? Worse yet, if the admission is believed, how could Vice President Johnson have knowingly let this happen to the nation's leader?

In addition to Johnson's verbal admission are his nonverbal admissions by strange acts. For instance, what was LBJ actually doing at the time of the assassination in the trailing car in the motorcade? Johnson refused to be questioned by anyone under oath as to his activities and he even refused to supply a sworn affidavit. Rather, he had his lawyer prepare an unsworn statement of the facts which he merely signed. The statement did little to explain what Johnson saw, heard, or smelled during the murder.

However, according to Johnson's motorcade seatmate, Democratic Senator Ralph Yarborough (who smelled gunpowder near the grassy knoll), at the exact time of the assassination Johnson had his ear up against a small walkie-talkie held over the back seat listening to the device which was "turned down real low." It was obviously hard for the Vice President to wave and smile at crowds in the Presidential motorcade when he was leaning up against and listening to a small walkie-talkie. But, of course, perhaps Senator Yarborough was mistaken and this did not occur, or maybe Johnson's act was just coincidental and not connected with Kennedy's slaying.

While any feeble excuse explaining away Johnson's interest in walkie-talkie communications during the assassination can be accepted as valid by those seeking to exonerate Johnson, it is harder to explain Lyndon Johnson's rush to refurbish the Kennedy death vehicle. Before Kennedy was buried Johnson ordered the assassination limousine (that had quickly been shipped from Dallas to Washington) to be shipped to Detroit for complete refurbishing. The body and windows of the limousine were replaced and the interior was gutted thereby destroying all evidence of bullet marks, blood patterns, bullet directions, and occupant exact positions. While normally the deliberate destruction of evidence is in itself a crime, if a prime suspect—who happens to be President does it—in America it seems that the activity is not worthy of investigating!

Johnson acted strangely throughout the assassination aftermath. While such strange acts are not admissions and may not necessarily be sufficient to imply that Johnson was guilty of anything, the activities should have been considered. For instance, as JFK lay dying at Parkland Memorial Hospital and his close friend was seriously wounded, LBJ and his wife were waiting impatiently down the hall. And, in the midst of a perceived world crisis, Johnson's wife took out a notebook and began taking longhand notes of Johnson's actions. At 1:13 p.m. when Johnson was told that the President was dead he immediately looked at his watch and then turned to his wife and told her to "make a note of that time." What type of man would do this in crisis if he truly believed it was a crisis?

Eventually, Johnson left Dallas on Kennedy's plane with the body of Kennedy. He returned to Washington. On the return flight Johnson calmly ate vegetable soup and drank JFK's bottled water while everyone else mourned. Prior to the landing in Washington another problem arose. It concerned which President was going to leave the plane first. While President Kennedy was not arguing, Johnson as the new President was. He claimed that as the new President he had the right to depart first and demanded it. Almost everyone else on the plane thought that this was improper and that the slain leader should be taken out first. When Johnson continued to argue about his right to leave the plane first, everyone just ignored him and removed Kennedy's body first. This act enraged Johnson and according to reliable sources he stewed about it for days. Why would the new President be so petty in a national crisis unless he knew something more than the others?

On the day after Kennedy's death, with the nation in mourning and world tensions peaking, Johnson began his Saturday morning as the new President by concentrating on the smaller things in life. While a discussion about this day requires a review of previously described actions it is extremely important from a historical perspective to evaluate this from the time perspective of a nation in mourning. Lyndon Johnson began the day by firing President Kennedy's personal secretary. He demanded that she have her desk cleared out by 9:00 a.m. He then ordered the staff to begin removing JFK's personal effects from the White House (including his rocker). Once this was initiated Johnson hung a gold framed portrait of himself in the White House.[33] Even less tactfully, he insisted that the widow (in the midst of preparing for a funeral) move out of the White House by Monday (the day of her husband's burial) so that he could quickly move in. These types of callous activities demonstrate the cold, ruthlessness of a man who was neither stricken with fear over a possible conspiracy, nor in any way mourning the loss of a leader.

In fact, within one month of Kennedy's burial, President Johnson held his first Presidential Christmas at the White House. He used this opportunity to serve his guests with his new presidential china. Strangely, Johnson bought his presidential china in the early fall of 1963 while Vice President traveling on a political junket in Scandinavia. This raises the question why a man who was not President would buy himself such a product? One possible explanation might be that Johnson intended to give it to Kennedy as a gift. However, Johnson never gave it to Kennedy during his life nor did he give it to Kennedy's widow after his death (i.e. "Jackie, here's what I got for Jack . . . I hope it will help you remember the good times"). But of course, one should not forget that by the fall of 1963, the Kennedy-Johnson relationship had deteriorated so severely that a gift of this type would have been unlikely. Considering the facts presented in this book, another explanation that is just as probable is that Johnson was buying specialty goods that could later be used when he obtained the presidency through assassination succession. If one believes this explanation, then it is just additional proof that Johnson knew of the assassination in advance.

Knowing of Lyndon Johnson's admissions and strange actions before and after the assassination may assist in understanding the true intent of what Jack Ruby was actually saying

---

[33] Johnson quickly removed his portrait when this act was disclosed to the press.

after the event. This is because if one really examines Ruby's public statements during the Warren Commission's questioning and elsewhere, it is clear that Ruby was not only willing to talk but trying to talk, by innuendo:

* * * *

Ruby: *"Gentlemen, unless you get me to Washington, you can't get a fair shake out of me . . . unless you get me to Washington, and I am not a crackpot, I have all my senses—I don't want to avoid any crime I'm guilty of."*

* * * *

Ruby: *"Gentlemen, my life is in danger here."*

Chief Justice Warren: *"I understand you completely. I understand what you are saying. If you don't think it wise to talk, that's okay."*

Ruby: "No, I want to talk, I just can't talk here."

Chief Justice Warren: *"What more would you have to say in Washington?"*

Ruby: *"It's about you, I have something to say about you."* [Emphasis added]

Even Gerald Ford, as a Commission member, grasped what Ruby was trying to say. Ford followed up with a question, "If I understand you, you would be able to tell us more if we got you to the safety of Washington." To which Ruby replied, "Yes, definitely."

Yet, Ruby remained in Dallas and Chief Justice Earl Warren decided not to continue to question Jack Ruby in a "safe place."

What did Jack Ruby want to tell the Warren Commission in safety? What did he want to say to Warren? Did he want to warn the Chief Justice to be careful for his own safety as the head of the Commission, since a powerful conspiracy was involved? These are *not* speculative questions! This is because Jack Ruby did manage to publicly tell parts of his real story to the press.

For example, on one occasion when he was away from his Dallas jail cell Ruby described the assassination as *"an act of overthrowing the government"* and that he knew *"who had President Kennedy killed." And, during one transfer he managed to tell reporters that the Kennedy assassination was a "complete conspiracy . . . if you knew the truth you would be amazed."* Even an old television tape of a brief interview with Jack Ruby proved that he knew a lot more. During a brief recess from one of his court appearances, Ruby turned to the camera and said:

". . . the only thing I can say is—everything pertaining to what has happened has never come to the surface."

* * * *

"[the truth will never come out] because unfortunately, these people, who have so much to gain and have such an ulterior motive to put me in the position I'm in, will never let the true facts come above board to the world." [Emphasis Added]

In applying Ruby's statements to the facts it seems that the only "act of overthrowing the government" that occurred was that Johnson replaced Kennedy as President. The Communists did not initiate a war and no other person or group seized power in America beyond Lyndon B. Johnson. The only thing that could be considered "amazing" would have been if the replacement of Kennedy was intended. And, of the people "who have so much to gain" the only people who gained the most from the murder were Lyndon Johnson and his friends. Lastly, it appears probable that the only one in the United

States with sufficient power to "never let the true facts come above board" was Lyndon Johnson since it was his order that seized all of the evidence and it was his Commission that evaluated the evidence for its public report. And it was Johnson and his Commission who decided that much of the evidence would never be released in our lifetime.

If one combines the admissions and strange acts of Lyndon B. Johnson with the statements of Jack Ruby it becomes crystal clear that Johnson was aware that Kennedy was going to be murdered. He planned his purchases in expectation of his succession to the Presidency. He told his girlfriend it was going to happen, and at the time of Kennedy's death, he acted as a fearless man in complete control of a world crisis because he knew the real cause of the crisis and knew that he had nothing to fear. And, if one believes Ruby, of all the people in the world, it was Johnson, and only Johnson, who had so much to gain and so much power that he would never let the truth surface.

36

The Texas Connection

The right hand man theory is a proven historical fact in assassinations of world leaders. Beginning the day of Kennedy's murder, the right hand man assassination theory should have been considered as one of the most probable explanations for the crime. Many Americans surely thought about Johnson's possible involvement at the time of Kennedy's death, but no one dared to publicly voice the thought. Few people were strong enough to face the risk of public ridicule or even death to bring public and criminal investigative attention to this possibility.

On a practical level America was in the midst of a cold war and American politicians did not want to present to the rest of the world the possibility that a bloody political coup could and did happen in the land of freedom. For all of these reasons, the public stood by and allowed the assassination evidence to be seized and the investigation to be controlled by the prime suspect. And, while Americans sat in silence, many Europeans who were independently observing the same situation, but from the distance of their shores, openly noted the travesty occurring in our land.

However, silence by a nation in a scandal is not unusual. Just a few decades before, Adolph Hitler seized power in Germany. He began to exterminate the Jews. Yet, the German masses did not protest. How could the German masses have allowed the extermination of millions of people when they all suspected or knew the truth? How could an entire country have operated without a conscience? The answer to these questions is similar to what occurred in America following the Kennedy assassination. Out of fear, self-preservation, and national pride, obvious injustices and tyrannical acts were overlooked based on the false hope that what was in fact occurring was not really happening but only being perceived improperly.

Regardless of the final truth as to the Kennedy assassination, Americans just like the German people a few decades before, let one man seize power and do as he pleased. Americans let one man who was a criminal suspect with a strong motive, seize all of the assassination evidence and supply the world with his personally selected Commission's solution to the crime. To simply state this fact is to indict us all. Because of our failure to object, the full truth may never be known. And, the plain truth is that America's continuing fascination with Kennedy's death relates more directly to our own guilt and failure as a society than it does with just this one man's death. This is proven time and again when a new Kennedy assassination book surfaces proposing either a new assassination theory or a new piece of evidence. In such instances, the public clamors for the information hoping to make up for what American silence created in the first place.

For these reasons, many Kennedy assassination theorists have spent considerable time attempting to uncover the invisible. They often get bogged in details trying to trace the small facts. This unearths both minutia and unimportant participants. It therefore confuses rather than clears the major issues. Of what importance is it to the big picture how many paid assassins actually performed the execution, as long as the top conspirator is known.

To end this practice and begin filling the black hole of mystery surrounding the assassination, America must first accept some guilt for its silence. Then and only then can the big picture be established. If one examines the big picture, Johnson was the puppeteer who touched and controlled everything. And, while assassination theorists have written volumes about unexplainable events, none of this should be considered unusual when Johnson was involved. Missing ballot boxes, dead pilots and suicides with a bolt action rifle was the norm! The reality is that the Texas Connection begins and ends with Lyndon B. Johnson.

From the outset Lyndon B. Johnson was involved with the planning of the President's trip. A specific motorcade route was demanded which lead to Kennedy's death.

The connections to Johnson, while regularly ignored, are so clear that undisputable evidence publicly ties Johnson through his friends to not only the Dallas murder, its criminal investigation, but even to Oswald and Jack Ruby. And, it was Johnson, as America's new President, who had the power to order the seizure and even the destruction of evidence by government agencies. Lyndon Johnson's final aspect of control began on November 26, 1963 when he ordered the seizure of assassination evidence and it will not end until 2039 when the sealed evidence is released.

A summary chart of the associations between Johnson and the assassination and its aftermath is set forth on the following page. It may have been through some of these associations that Johnson acquired the needed information to accomplish his rise to the presidency. This raises only one legitimate question: If these connections existed, how come no one has ever talked?

The probable answer involves history. The political history of Lyndon B. Johnson. Throughout his presidency he reminisced about stealing his first election in college using only a few loyal followers. But his reminiscing about the past was really a tip off to the present. With only a few loyal supporters, Johnson had the unique opportunity to acquire information as well as contacts from others and use it to his advantage.

Lastly, people must examine the assassination from Lyndon Johnson's perspective. It was his dream to enter history

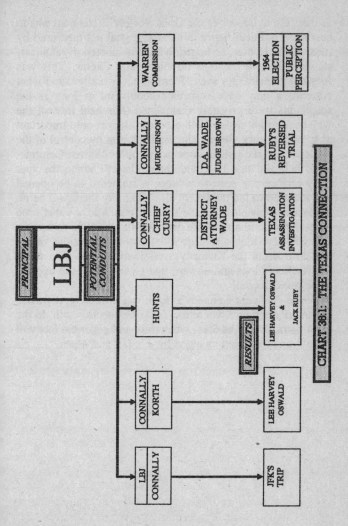

CHART 3B:1: THE TEXAS CONNECTION

as the "Great Leader of the Great Society." His goal was to become a political figure in history, a goal not measured by mere years. Rather, he hoped to be remembered in centuries, standing in time next to Napoleon and Caesar. This was Johnson's desire. As such, Johnson never really cared what Americans may have suspected about him as long as the suspicions were privately maintained (this held true all the way back to his stolen 1948 election). It was only important as to how history viewed him, and Johnson by control of the evidence and the written conclusions of the Warren Commission, believed that he could shape history. When the year 2039 arrives, the sealed evidence is supposed to be opened and released to the public. In all probability there will be no evidence. Johnson will have seen to that. And, by that time the rumors circulating in the decades after the 1963 assassination will have long subsided, with the new generations knowing little about the Kennedy assassination. It is with those future generations and onward that Lyndon Johnson expects to be remembered.

While President Kennedy's death was a tragedy, it will be in America's future where the Texas Connection will do the most harm. It will be then, when truth and historical fact will have ultimately been changed by a bullet and a pen.

SECTION 5

Conclusion

37

Proof of
a Conspiracy

A conspiracy is two or more people acting in concert to commit an unlawful act. President Johnson's Warren Commission found that no conspiracy existed. However, the Warren Commission had to reach that conclusion or the case could not have been closed and the Justice Department under Bobby Kennedy could have initiated an investigation. But a conspiracy did exist because logic, reason, and common sense tells us it had to exist. If the evidence is looked at impartially and with reason, a conspiracy can be proven to have existed for at least nine separate simple reasons. These nine simple reasons do not require extensive scientific tests nor even fancy experts with theoretical jargon. While a skeptical person may deny one, some, or even most of the following reasons which make the existence of a conspiracy a fact, agreement with only one of these reasons is agreement that a conspiracy existed.

One. The Statements of a Known Participant

Oswald repeatedly denied that he killed President Kennedy. He affirmatively stated that he did not have any personal animosity against the President or his family. It was also his opinion that John Kennedy would be recognized as one of America's greatest leaders. For these reasons, Oswald's motive has always remained a mystery. Even Warren Commission member Gerald Ford recognized the troublesome concept of Oswald killing Kennedy without a motive and voiced concern about it.

Of added interest is *Oswald's request for a lawyer specializing in defending conspiracy cases* (Attorney Abt in New York) and his communication to the outside world that "I am a patsy".

If one believes that Oswald was in any way telling the truth when he made these statements, then his statements alone are proof that a conspiracy existed. Further, if it is believed that a person does not ordinarily commit a murder without a motive, then Oswald's lack of one implicitly proves the existence of a conspiracy involving others who were participants with a motive.

Two. A Review of Ruby's Words

While Jack Ruby publicly denied any involvement in a conspiracy, a review of what he actually said and did demonstrated that he only initially spoke the truth by use of underlying meanings. For instance, during questioning he would often volunteer information and hint at associations that he would not have known about unless he was involved in a conspiracy. But after making such remarks, and then questioned about them, he would deny it ("I was never alone at a meeting with Oswald . . . but ask me if I was with Oswald and two other men.").

What Ruby did was out of fear. He publicly lied as ordered, but he indirectly tried to reveal the truth. Ruby even demanded and took a lie detector test to demonstrate his honesty. The results failed to prove that he was telling the truth (the Commission termed this failure as "indeterminable"). This was a stroke of brilliance. While still publicly lying because of fear, Ruby nevertheless proved to the world that it should not believe his public statements. And, of course, by implication this should have told the world to only believe his hints and innuendos.

As time went on and not even the great detectives of the world understood Ruby's clues, he became bolder. In fact, during a recess to one of his criminal hearings, Ruby desperately turned to the press and exclaimed:

> *"This whole thing is a conspiracy. The world will never know."*

If one chooses to believe that Ruby was scared enough to lie when he had to, but smart enough to still speak the truth by innuendo or when in confidence, then a conspiracy existed. And, if Ruby's jailhouse letters, as previously discussed, are believed, then Johnson was one of the conspirators.

Three. The Admission of President Johnson

If one believes that Lyndon Johnson told his close friends about Kennedy's murder in advance, then a conspiracy existed. Since Johnson did not personally fire the shots, his advance knowledge of the murder proves that at least one or more people acted in concert to carry out the crime. This is true even if one continues to accept the claim that Oswald was the lone assassin since Oswald (or someone else) must have told Johnson in order for him to obtain advance knowledge.

Four. The Physical Evidence from the "Known" Participant

No one saw Lee Harvey Oswald put the alleged assassination rifle up to his face, look through the scope, pull the trigger and fire at the President. In fact, no one saw him near the alleged sniper's nest or near the sixth floor of the Texas School Book Depository at the time of the assassination. However, eyewitnesses did see Oswald pull out a revolver and kill Police Officer Tippit. While this itself does not disprove Oswald's involvement in JFK's murder, the gunpowder tests taken after his arrest raise difficult questions.

Paraffin tests taken of Oswald's cheek and facial area established that *no gunpowder residue* could be found in these regions. Yet, the same gunpowder tests taken of Oswald's hand conclusively demonstrated the presence of gunpowder residue in that area. If the validity of the gunpowder tests is accepted (if there was a doubt as to accuracy, the tests could have been easily repeated), then it would confirm what was and was not observed by witnesses. Oswald was not seen firing the alleged assassination rifle and the tests confirmed that he did not. Oswald was seen firing a pistol and the tests confirmed that he did. If one believes the gunpowder tests, then a conspiracy had to exist, since Oswald did not fire the rifle.[34]

Although it can be argued that the Warren Commission ignored the absence of powder burns on Oswald's face because it found that scientific gunpowder tests taken of Oswald were "unreliable," it must be noted that gunpowder tests are standard police tests. They have regularly been used and found to be reliable by both police agencies and district attorneys in the prosecution of tens of thousands of criminal cases across the country. Yet, in this rare instance, strange as it may seem, instead of a criminal defense lawyer attempting to reject gunpowder test results as inaccurate—it was the government, whose prosecutors use it routinely as evidentiary proof of guilt, which claimed its unreliability.

In any other case the absence of facial powder burns in a paraffin test would have been accepted as proof that Oswald

---

[34]Unless one chooses to believe that Oswald killed Kennedy by firing the rifle from his hip which would leave no powder burns on his face.

did not fire the rifle. If Oswald did not fire the rifle, there was a conspiracy because others must have fired it.

Five. The Physical Evidence from Kennedy's Body

It is impossible to completely harmonize the arguments of ballistic experts pro and con about Kennedy's head movements and splatter of brain matter as he was shot. Some experts claim that the spraying brain matter and flopping head prove that he was shot in the head from the front. Others claim that it proves that he was shot in the head from the back. However, we can ignore these disputes and concede that neither side has clearly explained its position. Nevertheless a much clearer and simpler answer is available.

All three doctors who personally examined the President at Parkland Memorial Hospital immediately after the assassination stated that one of Kennedy's wounds was in the throat, at the level of the necktie, and came from the front. Of the two treating doctors who attended the immediate post-care press conference, both repeated these same statements. Also Kennedy's personal physician, Dr. Burkley, the only doctor who examined Kennedy's body both in Dallas and in Washington during the autopsy, has stated that Kennedy's death was the result of a conspiracy (beyond this concise statement, Dr. Burkley has always refused to elaborate).

If one chooses to believe the statements and opinions of the three doctors who examined President Kennedy immediately after he was shot, or that of his personal physician and the only man who saw his body in both cities, and if one believes that such men (a neurosurgeon, an emergency room doctor, the Chief of Surgery at the hospital, and Kennedy's personal physician) were qualified and capable of accurately assessing things and had no reason to lie—then a conspiracy existed. To shoot Kennedy in the throat a bullet had to have been fired from the front and not from Oswald's position in the rear.

Six. The Eyewitnesses

Even if one disregards everything but the eyewitness testimony of three out of every four people who actually witnessed the assassination, then a conspiracy had to have existed. Immediately after the assassination, when government pressure had not yet been exerted on the eyewitnesses, 88% of the witnesses who gave statements or supplied affidavits stating where they saw or heard the gun shots come from, stated that the shots came from the vicinity of the grassy knoll, not the book depository.

Even after the exertion of government pressure through the Warren Commission and others, 58 of 75 witnesses who were asked by the Warren Commission or its investigators to state their recollection as to the location of the gunfire, still felt that the gun shots came from the area of the grassy knoll. Thus, 77% of the witnesses who supplied oral evidence to the Warren Commission offered evidence directly contrary to the Warren Commission's ultimate conclusion (the shots came from the book depository).

However, because statistics and percentages by themselves usually seem cold and not overly persuasive standing alone, to give life to these statistics, on page 238 is a diagram of the assassination site depicted as Diagram 37:1. Contained on Diagram 37:1 are numbers which represent actual assassination witnesses. The Diagram correlates directly to a Chart of Witnesses depicted as Chart 37:1 on the subsequent page. By use of this Diagram and Chart it is easy to fully comprehend the strength of the actual witnesses statements. For instance, witness number 1 in Diagram 37:1 was U.S. Senator Ralph Yarborough who was riding in a trailing motorcade car. His name, location, and observations can be determined by using Chart 37:1 (the Chart of Witnesses). Witnesses numbers 2 and 3 on Diagram 37:1 were U.S. Secret Service agents riding in the motorcade. Their names, locations, and observations can also be determined by using Chart 37:1 (the Chart of Witnesses).

A correlation of the Diagram and the Chart proves that: motorcade dignitaries; government agents; police officers; corporate executives, railroad employees, as well as numerous other reliable individuals, all who were present in different areas at the assassination site, firmly believed that the gunfire came from the grassy knoll area.

If one accepts the proposition that a large number of eyewitnesses to a single event are collectively more apt to accurately perceive an event better than just one or two witnesses, then a conspiracy had to exist because the great majority of the eyewitnesses heard shots or smelled gunpowder from in front of the motorcade (not from Oswald's direction) and, even if one claims that only the observations of a few "trustworthy" eyewitnesses should be accepted as valid (the remainder are unreliable), then a conspiracy still existed. This is because the few "trustworthy" eyewitnesses would still have to include: a U.S. Senator who smelled gunpowder on ground level near the grassy knoll; two trained Secret Service agents in the motorcade who believed that a shot came from the grassy knoll; the Dallas Sheriff who believed from the beginning that shots came from ahead of the motorcade; and, Dallas police officers who believed the same.

If one goes farther and ignores all of the statements by the eyewitnesses, human reflex reaction (i.e. punch is thrown and people flinch) at the time of the assassination still proves that what the eyewitnesses stated they saw was correct. This is because all photographs and movie film taken at the exact time of the assassination demonstrate clearly that almost all spectators (consciously or subconsciously) reacted to the sounds of the gunshots by looking or turning toward the grassy knoll. Statistically 74% of all witnesses to the event ran, looked, or turned towards the grassy knoll (92 of the 124 person identified to have been in the area; not all gave statements).

In fact, even those who dove to the ground in self-preservation still glanced up and towards the grassy knoll. One can always dispute statistics, challenge the opinions of nearly 100

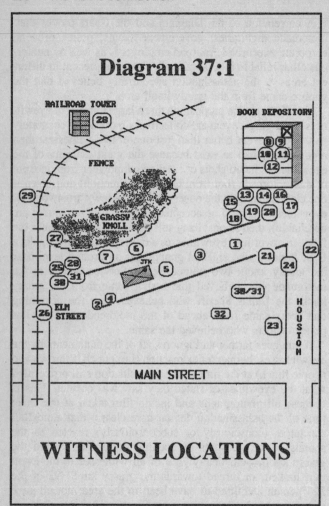

Diagram 37:1

RAILROAD TOWER

28

BOOK DEPOSITORY

8 9
10 11
12

FENCE

13 14 16
15 17
18 19 20

29

GRASSY KNOLL

27

7 6 1
3 22
21 24
JFK 5
25 28 31
30 2 4 30/31
26 ELM STREET 32
23

MAIN STREET

HOUSTON

WITNESS LOCATIONS

CHART 37:1

CREDIBLE WITNESS CHART

NO.	NAME	LOCATION	OBSERVATION/ACTION
1.	U. S. Senator Ralph Yarborough	Motorcade Limo with Lyndon Johnson	Smelled gunpowder at ground level near grassy knoll
2.	Dallas Sheriff Decker	Lead motorcade car	Ordered Dep~ues to knoll and railroad yard area
3.	Paul Landis Jr., U.S. Sec. Serv.	Running board on trailing vehicle	Shots came from the front of the motorcade
4.	Forrest Sorrels	Riding in lead motorcade car	Shots sounded like they came from grassy knoll
5.	Police Officer Robert Hargis	Motorcycle patrolman trailing limousine	Drove bike to curb and raced to the grassy knoll
6.	Abraham Zapruder	Stood in front of grassy knoll fence	Thought assassin was behind him in grassy knoll
7.	Mary Woodward	Stood in front of grassy knoll fence	Heard ear shattering explosion behind her in knoll
8.	James Jarman Jr.	5th Floor of TX School Book Dep.	Shot sounds came from below at street level
9.	Bonnie Ray Williams	5th Floor of TX School Book Dep.	Shot sounds came from below at street level
10.	Victoria Adams	4th Floor of TX School Book Dep.	Ran to knoll where believed shots came.
11.	Dorothy Garner	4th Floor TX School Book Dep.	Gun shots came from grassy knoll area.
12.	Steven Wilson, V.P. of S.W.	3rd Floor tenant in TX School Book Dep.	Shots came from grassy knoll
13.	B. W. Frazier	Steps to TX School Book Dep. entrance	Shots came from grassy knoll/via duct area
14.	Joe Molina	Steps to TX School Book Dep. entrance	Shots came from grassy knoll/via duct area
15.	Mrs. Davis	Steps to TX School Book Dep. entrance	Shots came from grassy knoll/via duct area
16.	Roy Truly, Superintendent	Curb adjacent to TX School Book Dep.	Shots came from grassy knoll/via duct area
17.	Ochus Campbell, Vice President	Curb adjacent to TX School Book Dep.	Shots came from grassy knoll/via duct area
18.	Mrs. Baker	Standing directly in front of TSBD	Shots came from area close to underpass.
19.	Otis Williams	Steps in front of TX School Book Dep.	Blasts came from grassy knoll/via duct area
20.	J. C. Price	Roof of the Terminal Annex Bldg.	Eyes attracted to fence area of the grassy knoll
21.	Mrs. Komas	Southwest corner of Elm & Houston	Shots came from grassy knoll/via duct area
22.	Dallas Deputy Sheriff Oxford	Across Dealey Plaza	Ran across plaza to knoll
23.	Dallas Patrolman, J. M. Smith	Corner of Elm and Houston	Shots came from bushes near overpass. Raced to area.
24.	Deputy Constable S. Weitzman	Corner of Main & Houston	Raced toward grassy knoll and climbed over fence
25.	S.M. Holland	Railroad bridge overpass	Saw puff of smoke near fence and run to area.
26.	Austin Miller	Railroad bridge	Saw smoke from trees in grassy knoll
27.	James L. Simmons	Railroad bridge	Saw smoke from trees in grassy knoll
28.	Walter Winborn	Railroad bridge	Saw smoke from trees in grassy knoll
29.	Richard C. Dodd	Railroad bridge	Saw smoke from trees in grassy knoll
30.	Thomas Murphy	Railroad bridge	Saw smoke from trees in grassy knoll
31.	Clenon Johnson	Railroad bridge	Saw smoke from trees in grassy knoll
32.	Jean Hill	unknown	Thought people were shooting from the knoll.
33.	Lee Bowers, Jr.	Railroad tower	Flash of light or smoke seen by the fence area/knoll.
34.	Dallas Policeman, F.B.I.	varied	All men ran toward grassy knoll area.

separate witnesses, or simply ignore evidence that is contrary to a conclusionary position that is sought . . . but photographs which clearly show instantaneous human reaction to an event cannot be honestly disputed. Within seconds of the assassination all spectators in the area looked toward the grassy knoll, the obvious location of at least one of the real assassins.

Seven. The Target Area

The actual assassination zone, by itself, also clearly establishes that a conspiracy existed. Kennedy was shot on Elm Street *after* the Presidential limousine had already passed by the Texas School Book Depository for a significant distance. The Warren Commission concluded that Kennedy was shot by Oswald sometime after motion picture frame number 207 in the Zapruder assassination movie (the home movie taken of Kennedy during his murder). The significance of this finding is that Oswald, as an assassin allegedly bent on killing Kennedy, passed up opportunities to kill Kennedy when he had a clear shot. Instead he waited to shoot Kennedy until after his limousine emerged, without warning, from a blocking tree. This does not make sense.

Lee Harvey Oswald's best target zone to kill Kennedy was when the limousine slowly turned onto Elm Street and passed directly in front of him. The target was traveling at its slowest point, the target was at its closest point, the target was in clear view and was not blocked by anything.

However, at the location where Kennedy was actually shot, his position was much more difficult for Oswald to hit (as opposed to all other prior areas) from the Book Depository but was an easy target for those on the grassy knoll. This cannot be denied nor disputed. Therefore, reason and common sense tell us that Oswald was not a solo assassin shooting the President from this 6th floor outpost, if he was an assassin at all.

Eight. The Seizure and Sealing of Evidence

Politicians and government employees dislike public turmoil, rumors, and suspicion. It can affect their jobs. This is especially true if there is no valid reason for the turmoil or suspicion. Therefore, if nothing about the Kennedy assassination had to be covered up, hidden, or sealed away because the people in power had nothing to hide the amount of public outcry in this case would have been sufficient to force the politicians to immediately open everything up for public inspection and review. However, following the Kennedy assassination the evidence was seized and despite strong public objection, for unexplainable reasons, much of it was sealed away for generations.

Logically, if such evidence was not damaging to someone important who had the power to see that it could be sealed away, it would have been opened for public review.

The questions of why no thorough investigation was ever conducted, and why the Warren Commission did what it did including sealing evidence, bears not only on credibility, but also on the existence of a conspiracy. A right hand man conspiracy.

Why would Lyndon Johnson not want a thorough investigation if he was not involved, but thought one or more of the other suspects were? He certainly had to be have been aware that he was a logical person to be under suspicion, and if the only way to clear his name was a full blown, "let-er-rip" investigation, does anyone doubt, knowing what we do of him, that he would have hesitated for a moment? The same holds true for Johnson's ratification of his Commission's decision to seal evidence.

Since no true investigation was ever conducted, and because evidence was sealed away, this demonstrates a conspiracy just by the nature of the acts.

Nine. Reason and Common Sense

A great error many people make is to believe education can elevate and improve common sense. The purpose of education is not to learn how to make right answers wrong or make a wrong answer right. Rather it is to examine and understand why the answer is correct, to approach it from a broader horizon. Mankind knew that apples and other things fell to earth because of something long before Isaac Newton. Newton's discovery of the theory of gravity did not change the answer . . . it merely explained it.

In some ways education can sometimes pervert this point. Some of today's most educated people mistakenly believe that they have the capability of perceiving the exact same event as everyone else, but are able to interpret it differently and better because of "superior education" or higher titles in society (i.e. member of the Warren Commission). This is a serious error since it clouds common sense. On any grade level $1 + 1 = 2$, and a crook is still a crook no matter how you state it. Therefore, even if one chooses to completely ignore the detailed facts of the Kennedy assassination and the logical reasons for the existence of a conspiracy which are evident from the facts, a conclusion that there was a conspiracy is still reached by using only reason and common sense.

In fact, this may be the best way to approach the Kennedy assassination mystery, since every person, with their lifetime of everyday experiences, can just feel when something is right or wrong. So for this moment, cast away all past feelings about the assassination, ignore the prestige that the Warren Commission allegedly gave to its conclusions, and instead, merely consider the following simple factual example:

EXAMPLE

A is a leader. B is his assistant and successor if he dies. The two men do not get along. A planned on firing B. B wanted to get A's job.

After planning every detail, B invited A over to his house. A was murdered there by someone. C was caught and then blamed for the killing. However, C had no motive and denied being the murderer. C was then murdered by D.

B took over A's job. B also took over the investigation of A's death. B seized all of the evidence. B declared that he would have his staff investigate the killing. Later, B declared that his staff concluded that C committed the crime and did it alone, and no one else was involved. B also stated that his staff would never release much of the evidence.

The average common sense reaction to this simple example is to believe that B may have been up to no good and may have been involved in killing A. From that initial reaction, the normal mind begins to swirl thinking of other possible answers. But with no additional facts, the reasonable person will finally go back to the initial thought that B may have been up to no good. From this reconfirmed original thought, a person can rationalize more, develop excuses if he knew B, or create additional scenarios for the murder. But the fact is that reason and common sense always leads back to the initial conclusion until it is fully explained away.

If one simply applies the principles of reason and common sense to the events of the Kennedy assassination, it should be clear that a conspiracy of some sort existed. And, that Lyndon "B" Johnson, just like "B" from the factual example, may have been the man up to no good.

38

From a
Different
Perspective

To try to attain the position of American President requires planning, money, and power, in that order. To successfully kill an American President without detection also requires planning, money and power. If Lyndon Johnson, as Kennedy's right hand man, had chosen to attain his life long goal of being President, he had the tools to succeed. He held the position and had the direct connections to participate in planning an assassination by having not only access to the President's time schedule, but arranging it. He had the personal finances as well as the necessary contingent of loyal Texas multi-millionaires to "buy the best and pay off the rest" if that was what he wanted to do.[35] Lyndon Johnson also knew from being a Washington power broker for twenty years that if he could succeed to the presidency, even if the succession was sloppy, he would then possess enough power as the President to cover up any problems and make them appear publicly proper. Therefore, if it is assumed for the sake of argument that LBJ was predisposed to carrying out a right hand man assassination, then an application of this predisposition to the actual facts could result in the following possible scenario:

[35] For instance, his 1960 presidential campaign "war chest" was over one million dollars *one year before* he even announced his candidacy.

POSSIBLE SCENARIO

Within hours after the 1960 presidential election was over, Lyndon Johnson knew that he would probably not be Kennedy's running mate in the 1964 election. This was not only because Johnson initially forced his way onto the Kennedy ticket to begin with, but his presence on the Kennedy ticket was not as beneficial as expected in helping to get Kennedy elected. In fact, in the 1960 election it was only through the use of voter fraud that the Kennedy-Johnson ticket even managed to win in Johnson's home state of Texas. And, when the two men eventually took their respective elected offices in Washington, Kennedy expected grateful silence from his right hand man. However, what Kennedy actually got from Johnson was public embarrassment at home and abroad. And to make matters worse, Johnson was continually tarred with national scandals. Therefore, by late 1962 or early 1963, the handwriting was on the wall that Johnson's probable future involved either resigning from public office in disgrace or being dropped from the 1964 ticket. In any case, Johnson knew that he would never have the opportunity to govern America by popular election.

From Johnson's perspective this was a travesty. He believed that he had greater leadership power in one finger than Jack Kennedy possessed "in his entirety." And, he believed that because of a twist of fate he would not be allowed to reach his destiny. Johnson loyalists held a similar opinion but from an economic standpoint. They knew that what was good for LBJ would eventually be good for them.

To prevent Johnson's downfall, a series of informal discussions occurred among Johnson and his stronghold of Texas supporters. The initial conclusion was that Johnson was in a political predicament that would not allow any action. Even the subject of assassination was initially suggested, but it was rejected since the risks were too great and any killing would immediately point the finger at LBJ and his friends. However, as the months passed Johnson became embroiled in more scandals through his dark associations. From Johnson's viewpoint it was the Kennedys who were airing the scandals and it was the Kennedys who were not playing fair. It became clearer to Lyndon Johnson that only retribution would secure justice for him. As a result, discussions relating to a possible assassination resumed. Eventually, it was determined that to successfully assassinate Kennedy three factors had to be in place. One, a controlled site for the slaying. Two, the hiring of top notch assassins. And three, a patsy who could take the fall in order to remove the light of suspicion from Johnson.

The controlled site for the slaying of President Kennedy had to be outside of his Washington, D.C. stronghold. In all of America the best place for a controlled slaying of Kennedy was in Texas. This was because Johnson and his followers still had sufficient political power in the state to control necessary events. Texas money could shape "Texas Justice". It was capable of buying elections or having obvious murders classified as suicides (i.e. Agricultural Agent Marshall). In 1963, Texas still took pride in its Wild West system, its citizens accepted it, and Johnson's loyalists were still a power in it. However, while the assassination site selection was easy, getting Eastern bred Jack Kennedy to Texas was expected to be more difficult. A reason that appealed to the President had to be created to entice Kennedy there.

It was finally decided that the only way to get Kennedy into Texas was to appeal to his political self-interest. Kennedy was aware that a number of wealthy Texans had richly supported Johnson and other politicians in the past. He was also aware that in 1960 he carried the state only because of voter fraud help from a few high ranking Texans. JFK was casually reminded about this and about the fast approaching 1964 election. And, Kennedy was told that to carry Texas in 1964 would be much harder if he ignored Texas for three solid years followed only by a campaign trip to Texas in 1964. Kennedy had to make it clear to Texans that he needed them at times other than during elections. Therefore, a trip to Texas in advance of the presidential campaign was the obvious solution. The trip would not appear as if Kennedy was pandering for votes. He could remind the Texas voters about how his administration had helped them and through Lyndon he could personally meet the rich and powerful Texans creating first hand contacts and aligning support for himself (before he dumped LBJ from the ticket). With this offered to Kennedy, he took the bait and agreed to go. As with Lyndon Johnson's handling of other political problems, the playing field was now set on Johnson's home turf.

To make more of the opportunity it was suggested that Johnson would help others plan the President's Texas trip, since they knew the important Texans who Kennedy ought to meet, and the places where he should go. Accepting this suggestion was Kennedy's second major mistake, but under the circumstances his error in judgment was understandable. Most likely Kennedy thought that by appeasing Johnson with this small task it would keep LBJ out of trouble and out of his hair. Further, President Kennedy probably thought that Johnson actually believed his insincere assurances that he would remain on the 1964 ticket and therefore would not try to harm Kennedy. By June of 1963, when Johnson, Connally and Kennedy met at the Hotel Cortez, Kennedy had not only unknowingly agreed to enter Johnson's lair but he also agreed to have Johnson plan his activities. Therefore, one of the key elements to the assassination was secured.

At sometime either just before or after the June 1963 meeting between the three men, top notch assassins were hired. According to Hugh McDonald, who claimed to have met one reputed assassin, the independent assassin was hired out of Haiti by a group of Americans who wanted Johnson in power. Whether there is any truth to this specific claim is irrelevant to this scenario. What is clear is that Johnson and his friends had the political contacts and the financial capability to search the world for the best assassins that money could buy. Further, in the overall context of the assassination, it was unimportant to Johnson and his loyalists whether 1, 2, or even more top assassins were hired, nor whether they knew about each other's presence, as long as one of the assassins actually succeeded.

With a trip scheduled in Johnson's locale, with him planning the itinerary, and with one or more professional assassins contractually bound to execute Kennedy, the major tasks were accomplished. Only one problem remained. A person or group was needed to draw attention away from the actual criminals and become the patsy. That person came to them in the form of Lee Harvey Oswald. Johnson had to have been aware of Oswald since he made national news accounts by his journey to Russia. Further, even assuming that he initially forgot about Oswald, Johnson's recollection had to have been "refreshed" when Oswald actually contacted John Connally in an attempt to have his military service discharge changed. By just some small talk between the two men the "perfect patsy" dropped right into LBJ's lap. Oswald was a socialist. He left America and lived in communist Russia. He married a Russian woman and upon returning to Texas held menial jobs, in part because of his downgraded military status. Since at the time the most hated people in America were communists and the most hated Americans were pro-communist Americans, it was determined that if Oswald could even be remotely blamed for JFK's death . . . Americans would eagerly believe it. The perfect "patsy" was found.

The only problem with using Oswald as a "patsy" was to get him to agree to participate and to have him unknowingly establish a more notorious trail of public disturbances in America. This was because Oswald as the "patsy" had to have a publicly known insurgent past. Three probable factors motivated Oswald to agree to act as an unwitting patsy for Johnson: a promise to change his discharge status (he desperately wanted to right a wrong); money (he was broke); or ego (he was told that he was performing top secret "spy" work worthy of a man of his intelligence). With that in place, Oswald was eventually sent on a series of missions before the assassination in order to create evidence for which Americans could subsequently despise him. For instance, Oswald was told to: fire a shot at conservative General Edwin Walker, but not hit him (so he would not be jailed); create a public ruckus in New Orleans with an anti-Castro group; and then finally create a public disturbance at various communist embassies in Mexico City. Oswald willingly performed each assignment flawlessly. And all the while he was leaving a public trail for investigators to later trace. In hindsight, Oswald's quick brushes with publicity and then his moving on to another city for another cause only makes sense in terms of his post-arrest statement that he was a "patsy".

Eventually, the Texas conspirators' plan was fully developed. Kennedy would drive through Dallas in an open motorcade. He would turn off onto a sidestreet and enter an area where no police protection would be planned. His limousine would take another slow wide turn onto Elm Street and would then travel down an incline. Large crowds of potential witnesses were not expected at this point and various sniper posts were available throughout the area.

All that was left was for Oswald to get or be supplied a job in the Texas School Book Depository. And, when the motorcade day came all Oswald had to do was fire one shot close to the President under the mistaken pretense that it had to be done in order to get the President to start accepting greater security protection.[36] Once the first shot was fired to scare the President, while from Oswald's perspective his role was completed, he unknowingly signaled the real assassins to murder Kennedy.

Oswald obtained his job in the Texas School Book Depository as planned. However, prior to the actual day of the motorcade major problems appeared in the plan. One problem was that several of JFK's closest advisors did not want him to make the trip at all. If Kennedy accepted the advice of his

[36]The public should not forget that Kennedy was criticized only one week before his death for ignoring Presidential safeguards when traveling in New York without protection. Further, on the assassination day one "Oswald" shot completely missed the Presidential limousine and wildly struck a street curb.

advisors all of the assassination planning would have been wasted. Additionally, some of the Kennedy's other advisors were demanding that the post-motorcade luncheon be held at a different site. If Kennedy listened to these advisors the motorcade would avoid the planned assassination site by a full block and again destroy all of the assassination planning. And further still, Kennedy's personal advanceman wanted the motorcade route changed to enhance the President's safety. This too would have caused the motorcade route to miss the planned assassination site. However, these problems were solved by the use of "Texas soothing and Texas temper". And eventually through deception, the Texan's planned motorcade route was accepted by the White House.

On the evening before the assassination another problem arose. John Connally was scheduled to ride in the targeted motorcade limousine with the President. This created the possibility of Connally being injured in the crossfire due to his close proximity to the President. Johnson went to Kennedy's hotel suite and attempted to get Kennedy to change the seating assignments. The two men fought. When Kennedy refused, Johnson left and the assassination plans continued unaltered even though there was a serious risk of harm to Connally. Although John Connally was a friend, he was still a subordinate, and therefore a "pissant". He had unwittingly served LBJ's purposes as an information conduit and an innocent supporter to parts of his power plan. Therefore, from Johnson's perspective the risk of Connally unknowingly dying from a Johnson plan was worth "a shot at the Presidency."

For Johnson, beyond the small problem of not getting Connally out of the President's car, the actual assassination went as planned. On November 22, 1963 at 12:30 p.m. the motorcade turned its last corner onto Elm Street. The police protection had ended the block before, the press vehicle had been pushed to the rear of the motorcade, the Dallas motorcycle patrolmen were at the rear of the limousine as ordered and, Johnson trailing safely behind in another vehicle had his ear glued to a secret service walkie-talkie listening to the reaction of the President's security forces. As the motorcade headed down Elm Street, Oswald fired his warning shot at Kennedy. Oswald's shot hit behind the motorcade and as subsequent unrefuted evidence revealed, struck a concrete curb, ricocheted off, and grazed the cheek of a nearby spectator. In response to this signal the real assassins then shot Kennedy. The first sniper's shot struck Kennedy and in subsequent rapid fire a bullet pierced his skull and tore into his brain. This resulted in Kennedy's brain tissue and blood splattering backward across the windshield of a trailing motorcycle policeman. Then the assassins successfully dispersed from the scene. A planted bullet traceable to Oswald's rifle was placed for easy discovery at the hospital. The assassination plan had gone perfectly except for one small and one large detail. The small detail was that Connally had also been hit. The large detail was that Oswald, the patsy, escaped alive from the scene.

Whether Oswald was supposed to be killed in the Texas School Book Depository or shot near his home by police officer J. D. Tippit or executed elsewhere by others is unknown. The important thing is that Oswald as the patsy had escaped and was on the loose in Dallas. While Oswald could not provide any direct links to the top Texas conspirator, he knew enough people and enough about his part in the plan that if he lived to talk and was believed, everything could tumble down like a house of cards. It was for this reason that Jack Ruby went to Parkland Memorial Hospital and later lied about it. Ruby had to report back that Oswald had gotten away alive and that the plan for a "patsy" was about to fall apart. For this reason, Johnson as the successor, in spite of all the requests, refused to leave Dallas. While as our nation's new leader he could not personally kill Oswald, he had to stay close to the scene to ride the mishap through. This was why Johnson refused to leave Parkland Memorial Hospital and when he eventually did leave the hospital, why he created a series of excuses to still remain in Dallas at Love Field.

This was also the reason why the Chief of the Dallas Police in apparent violation to common sense chose to stay with Johnson instead of supervising the biggest crime in Dallas' history.

When Oswald was eventually captured alive by the Dallas Police Department and word of the capture filtered back to Lyndon Johnson at Love Field (with Police Chief Curry aboard Air Force 1), Johnson finally agreed to depart for Washington. While Oswald was captured alive, his custody at least meant that he was under control, not loose on the streets, and all that remained was to silence him.

Permanently silencing Lee Harvey Oswald then became Jack Ruby's job. (It is possible Oswald was to be taken from the School Book Depository and killed, or Tippit was to kill him either as the primary or back up assassin, and that Ruby was the third back up, which is why he went to Parkland Hospital after Tippit was killed, and became sick after the meeting when his turn came up). This job explains why Ruby became nauseous and sick on the evening of the assassination and explains why he made a strange series of farewell telephone calls to friends. It also explains his uncharacteristic visit to a synagogue. Unfortunately, for some reason Ruby missed his chance to execute Oswald at the unusual late Friday evening press conference. However, Ruby eventually accomplished the task two days later in the police basement during the even more unusual public transfer of Oswald.

From the time of Oswald's arrest until his death the only major problem that arose was keeping Oswald away from the public. However, this problem was easily solved by someone's decision in the Dallas police department to: deny legal counsel to Oswald; refuse to take contemporaneous notes of Oswald's interrogations; not allow Oswald to communicate to the public; and not transfer Oswald to the Dallas Sheriff within 12 hours of indictment in violation of Texas law. When Oswald's Sunday transfer eventually came, Ruby got a clear shot at Oswald. With Ruby's one bullet to the abdomen Oswald died and the case was immediately closed. As long as

Ruby kept his mouth shut all that remained was to clean up the extraneous pieces. President Johnson did this when he quickly stepped in and wiped the area clean of all evidence by using his power under a National Security claim and by use of his Warren Commission. All in all, Johnson got his way and became President with only a couple of "piss-ants" killed (JFK, Oswald and Tippit).

CONCLUSION AS TO POSSIBLE SCENARIO

Whether the above scenario is the truth or a close version to it is at best only speculation. However, it fits the facts and rationally explains otherwise irrational and unexplainable acts, particularly by Johnson.

If this scenario is accepted, no matter how distasteful acceptance might be, it fills the void of mystery surrounding the assassination by logically solving the crime and explaining the unanswerable. While some may claim that all of the participants are still unnamed and therefore no proof exists to support the scenario—they are wrong. The key figure is clear and the proof to support it comes from merely evaluating already known and established evidence from a different perspective.

This raises the question, if the "possible scenario" is even remotely true, then why didn't the Kennedys do anything? *However, . . . history demonstrates that they did!*

Immediately after the assassination on the return flight to Washington, some of the passengers refused to sit by or even go near the new President. Even Mrs. Kennedy who was "heavy handed" by Johnson into appearing for his oath-taking, refused to change her bloodied suit, in perhaps a silent protest, and then retreated to the back of the plane to her husband's corpse. It was subsequently leaked that the close members of the Kennedy camp on the plane were "holding Johnson responsible for the assassination."

However, what could realistically be done? Lyndon B.

Johnson was the new President and he now possessed the power. Suspicions and unsupported allegations without proof would not bring Jack Kennedy back nor help the Democratic party. And, within hours of Air Force One's touchdown in Washington, the new U.S. President was already in control of the Dallas assassination evidence.

Therefore, silence remained by decision. This included the President's widow. While remaining publicly mute she eventually departed for Europe in protest for America killing her husband. She told all of us that 'America was no place to raise her children.' But was Jackie Kennedy really angry with us for killing her husband or, was she really enraged with family and friends for immorally trading murder for politics?

A proven tradeoff did occur! On February 5, 1964, William Manchester was contacted by the Kennedy family to write a historic "authorized" account of President John F. Kennedy's assassination (*The Death of a President*). Manchester completed the work after conducting interviews with the Kennedy family and approximately 1000 other people. His first draft was 1400 pages. However, Manchester's thorough and accurate account created political problems. The book portrayed President Johnson as "the forces of violence and irrationality". The original text mentioned: a fight between President Kennedy and his successor over the fatal trip to Texas; the dispute *in* Texas between Kennedy and Johnson; and Kennedy staff suspicions about Johnson.

When Manchester refused to alter his historic account, a lawsuit was brought by the Kennedys attempting to stop publication of the book. The Kennedy family "determined" that the discrediting passages about President Johnson would in fact harm Bobby Kennedy's political career. In fact, the insider word was that Manchester's book was an indictment that would "gut Johnson".

Eventually, the Kennedy lawsuit was settled. The parties agreed to destroy all drafts of Manchester's book, except for the final, "approved" version. Also, by settlement agreement with the Kennedys, an unusual prefatory note had to be inserted into the title page of each copy of Manchester's *The Death of a President*. Finally, after certain "modifications and deletions" (i.e. Johnson) were made that allegedly were not of "historical interest nor narrative power", the book that was supposed to be the accurate historical record of the assassination was released. With release, the public was told that "none of the deletions . . . [were] . . . political in character."

Thus, it appears that the Kennedy family while suspecting that the scenario about Johnson's involvement was true, for the good of their party, Robert Kennedy's career, or other reasons sued to keep their private suspicions from becoming public. This resulted in a publication of an inaccurate historic account involving Johnson.

39

An American
Conclusion

For the author to offer a final conclusion to this American tragedy is impossible. The full facts might not now, or ever, be known. Inferences drawn from glimpses at only partial evidence may result in a false conclusion. Or, an accurate conclusion may have been reached despite false premises. Maybe the Warren Commission reached truthful conclusions and public lust for gossip and scandal has merely tainted the truth. Or, perhaps the reverse might be true and the public continues to sense injustice no matter how hard the government tries to cover it up. For all of these reasons this book will not end with the author's viewpoint on the application of the right hand man theory to the assassination since the viewpoint in itself may be biased or skewed. Instead, it will end with an American conclusion.

The American legal system is based on faith in the wisdom of people. Its foundation is based on individual jurors acting as a group to reach a just and fair result. In this setting individuals, somehow, by their nature get a feel or gut reaction as to what is right. And, individuals acting as a unit miraculously counteract their individual biases and reach a just and fair result.

In the case of the assassination of President John F. Kennedy, you the reader, will be asked to form your own final conclusion. While this book may have presented a skewed set of facts, as an American, you have been exposed over your lifetime to some information about this murder, including, perhaps, facts told in a different way and other theories as to the cause of the assassination. At this time you should not only rely upon the material discussed in this book, but draw on everything else that you have ever learned about the assassination. And, with all of this in mind, using both your reason and common sense, answer these questions:

AMERICAN GRAND JURY

UNITED STATES OF AMERICA,
    Complainant   RE: Assassination of
                             John F. Kennedy

vs.

UNKNOWN CONSPIRATORS,
    Respondents

As an American citizen attempting to determine whether probable cause exists to charge persons with the first degree murder of President John F. Kennedy, I do hereby find and answer the following:

QUESTIONS

1. Whose sole obsession in life was to become a U.S. president?

ANSWER: _____

2. In 1960 who forced his way into becoming John Kennedy's right hand man and publicly commented that he took the position because 25% of presidents had died in office?

ANSWER: _____

3. What Vice President had a short expected life span?

ANSWER: _____

4. Who disliked John Kennedy and hated Robert Kennedy?

ANSWER: _____

5. Who became the target of public scandals and knew that he was going to be dumped from the 1964 presidential ticket?

ANSWER: _____

6. Who had several strong motives to kill President Kennedy?

ANSWER: _____

7. Who was among the few people involved in the intimate planning of JFK's Dallas death trip?

   ANSWER: _____

8. Who ordered the seizure of all evidence after the assassination?

   ANSWER: _____

9. Who created the Warren Commission and who did it report to?

   ANSWER: _____

10. Whose Commission decided not to release much of the assassination evidence in our lifetime?

    ANSWER: _____

11. Who gained the most by President Kennedy's death?

    ANSWER: _____

12. Who was the principal culprit in the murder of President John F. Kennedy?

ANSWER: _____

DATED this _____ day of _____ 19_____.

BY: _____
an American Grand Juror

The Texas Connection Credits

In order to write this book the help and support of many people was needed. Foremost there has been Carolyn Sherris who not only typed draft after draft of this work year after year but based on her expertise with computers produced short cuts that eliminated additional work for everyone else. Working along side of Carol was her husband Bill who I believe was "drafted by domestic demand" to put aside his banking work and create our charts and diagrams as well as solve the technical computer problems.

Additionally, there is Bud Wright who went beyond just trying to produce a quality product to obtaining contacts for me and when the time crunch of Murphy's Law came upon us took this project and pushed it through when even I did not think it could get done.

I also must thank Kimberly Smith for her valuable research, indexing and typing when the workload got too much. In that same extraordinary effort category is Diana McDonough and from years ago Mary Baker of Sarasota, Florida.

The staffs of both U.P.I. and A.P. research and photo departments by their speed and concern demonstrated why they are the best in the world. And, while I am on the subject of the best in the world I would like to sincerely thank all those others who helped put this book together, but by choice insisted that I not mention their names.

Lastly, I would like to thank Anthony Helmstetter, Ed

Helmstead, and Greg Helmstetter of *The Image Makers* of Scotts-
dale, Arizona, for their round-the-clock work in finalizing this
text and reworking it into readable form.

Sources

A Note on Sources

> The volume of material available to Kennedy assassination writers makes the preparation of a complete bibliography impossible for anyone who has done extensive reading on the subject. There is even a book of books on this matter. In preparing this section I attempted to concentrate only on sources that attracted my attention sufficiently enough that I could recall by looking at the book or article if it contained something of importance. Unfortunately, due to the passage of time, that book or article that I recalled may not have always been the first or the best to discuss a particular subject. The sources have been categorized by author or writer, if known, and by title if unknown.

"A County Auction Gets Underway." Sarasota Herald Tribune: January 23, 1988.

"An Editorial: Our Martyred President." Albuquerque Tribune; November 23, 1963.

"Another Grief Stricken Widow Shares Mrs. Kennedy's Sorrow of Widowhood." Dallas: United Press International; November 24, 1963.

"Assassin Shot Kennedy Twice, Sources Reveal." Washington: United Press International; November 24, 1963.

"At Trails and, Cowboys Lament." People Magazine: February 8, 1988.

Averill, John H. *"Kennedy Cancels Plan for Trip to California."* Washington: Los Angeles Times News Service; October 23, 1962.

Baker, Bobby, with Larry L. King. Wheeling and Dealing: Confessions of a Capitol Hill Operator. New York: W.W. Norton & Company; 1978.

Baker, Leonard. *"The Johnson Eclipse—A Presidents Vice-Presidency."* New York: The McMillian Co.; 1966.

"Baker Informed You Must Occupy House He Bought." Washington: Associated Press; November 22, 1963.

Belli, Melvin, with Maurice Carroll. Dallas Justice. New York: David McKay; 1964.

Bishop, Jim. The Day Kennedy Was Shot. New York: Funk & Wagnalls; 1968. [QP]

Blake, Jean. *"Eye Witness Story of Shooting."* Dallas: Los Angeles Times News Service; November 25, 1963.

Blakey, G. Robert, and Billings, Richard N. The Plot to Kill the President. New York: New York Times Books; 1981.

"Bobby Kennedy Resigns Post in Delegation." Atlantic City: Associated Press; August 24, 1964.

Bobealle, Morris A. Guns of the Regressive Right. Washington D. C.: Columbia Publishing Co.; 1964.

Boller, Paul F Jr. Presidential Campaigns. New York: Oxford University Press; 1984.

Boyce, Richard H. *"LBJ Foreign Policy: Afirmness With Russia."* Washington: Scripps-Howard Staff Writer; November 23, 1963.

"British Papers Term Warren Report Honest." London: Associated Press; September 28, 1964.

Bruno, Jerry, and Greenfield, Jeff. The Advance Man. New York: William Morrow and Company; 1971.

Buchanan, Thomas G. Who Killed Kennedy? New York: G.P. Putnam's Sons; 1964.

"Burial of Kennedy to be in Arlington." Washington: United Press International; November 24, 1963.

Burne, Jerome, Editor. Chronicle of the World. Paris: Longman Group UK Ltd.; 1989.

Burney, Peggy. *"I Saw Him Die, Woman Crys."* Dallas: Dallas Times Herald; November 22, 1963.

"Capture: It's All Over Now." New York: <u>New York Herald Tribune</u>; November 23, 1963.

Carlton, Michael. *"Texas Hill Country Formed President Johnson."* Johnson City: <u>Los Angeles Times</u>; July 13, 1986.

Carlton. *". . . Hill Country form President Johnson."* Florida: <u>Sarasota Herald Tribune</u>; July 13, 1986.

Caro, Robert E. <u>The Years of Lyndon Johnson: The Path to Power</u>. New York: Alfred A. Knopf; 1982.

Caro, Robert A. <u>Means of Assent</u>. New York: Vintage Books; 1991.

"Charges Filed Against Oswald." Dallas: <u>United Press International</u>; November 23, 1963.

Cochran, Mike. *"25 Years Later—Kennedy's Death Still Spurs Questions."* Dallas: <u>Associated Press</u>; November 5, 1988.

Collier, Peter and David Horowitz. <u>The Kennedys: an American Drama</u>. New York: Warner; 1985.

"Connally Bankruptcy Sale Draws Lots of Money, A Few Tears." <u>Sarasota Herald Tribune</u>: January 24, 1988.

Connally, John. *"Why Kennedy Went To Texas."* Chicago: <u>Life Magazine</u>; November 24, 1967.

"Connally Told Kennedy Dead." Dallas: <u>Associated Press</u>; November 23, 1963.

"Connally Pursuing Fresh Financial Start." Milwaukee: <u>Milwaukee Sentinal</u>; 1988.

Cormier, Frank. *"LBJ the Way He Was."* New York: <u>Doubleday & Co.</u>; 1977.

"Cuba Calls on UN to Prevent US. . . ." United Nations: <u>United Press International</u>; January 4, 1961.

"Cuba Mobilizes Forces; Castro To Speak Today." Key West, Florida: <u>Associated Press</u>; October 23, 1962.

Curry, Jesse. <u>JFK Assassination File: Retired Dallas Police Chief Jesse Curry Reveals His Personal File</u>. American Poster and Publishing Co.; 1969.

"Dallas Officers Certain Oswald Killed Kennedy." Dallas: <u>United Press International</u>; November 24, 1963.

"Disbelief Greets Estes Tale." Texas: <u>Milwaukee Journal</u>; March 24, 1984.

Donovan, Robert J. *"U.S. Planes Bombing North Vietnam Port."* Washington: <u>Los Angeles Times News Service</u>; August 5, 1964.

Donovan, Robert J. *"Travels With Lyndon."* Washington: Eastern Revenues; August 1987.

Drake, Walter. *"Kennedy, We Need to Defend Berlin."* Harris: Los Angeles Times; June 1, 1961.

Duegger, Ronny. *"The Politician—The Life and Times of Lyndon Johnson."* New York: W.W. Norton & Co.

"End of an Era." Washington: United Press International Telephoto & Caption; November 24, 1963.

Epstein, Edward J. Counterplot. New York: Viking Books; 1969.

Epstein, Edward J. Inquest—The Warren Commission and the Establishment of Truth. New York: The Viking Press; 1966.

Epstein, Edward J. Legend: The Secret World of Lee Harvey Oswald. New York: McGraw-Hill; 1978.

Everill, John H. *"Estes Conviction Upset Because of TV Coverage."* Washington: Los Angeles Times; June 8, 1965.

Exner, *"Mob Boss, JFK Met."* New York: Associated Press; February 22, 1968.

Fensterwald, Bernard Jr., with Michael Ewing. Coincidence or Conspiracy? New York: Zebra Books; 1977.

Fleming, Louis B. *"U.S. Resolution to be Offered in UN Council."* United Nations: Los Angeles Times News Service; October 23, 1962.

"For President Johnson: Understanding." New York: New York Herald Tribune; November 23, 1963.

Ford, Gerald R., with John R. Stiles. Portrait of the Assassin. New York: Simon & Schuster; 1965.

"Four Days." United Press International and American Heritage Magazine; 1964.

Fried, Joseph. *"U.S. Determinhus Must Go, Reports say."* Saigon: The New York News; August 29, 1963.

"From This Window." Dallas: United Press International Photo & Caption; November 23, 1963.

"German Salute Conspirators Who Tried to Kill Hitler." Berlin: Associated Press; July 21, 1990.

Gertz, Elmer. Moment of Madness: The People vs. Jack Ruby. Chicago: Fullit Publishing; 1968.

Goldman, Eric F. The Tragedy of Lyndon Johnson. New York: Alfred A. Knopf; 1969.

Groden, Robert J., and Livingstone, Harrison Edward. High Treason. Baltimore: The Conservatory Press; 1989

"Group Picked Will Help Draft Safety Steps." Johnson City: Associated Press; September 28, 1964.

Gulley, Bill with Mary Ellen Reese. "Breaking Cover." New York: Simon & Schuster; 1969.

Haley, Evetts J. A Texan Looks at Lyndon—A Study in Illegitimate Power. Canyon, Texas: Palo Duro Press; 1964.

Hargis, D. W. "Dallas Policeman Recounts Instant Assassin Struck." Dallas: Dallas Times Herald; November 22, 1963.

Harrell, Ken. "Jack Ruby Is Alive." Boca Raton: The Globe; November 15, 1988.

"He's Rolling Along Like a Tumbleweed." Life Magazine: July 12, 1963.

Hurt, Henry. Reasonable Doubt. New York: Holt, Rinehart & Winston; 1985.

"Initial U.S. Steps in Meeting Crisis." Los Angeles Times News Service; October 23, 1962.

"Investigation of the Assassination of President John F. Kennedy. Book V, Final Report of the Select Committee to Study Governmental Operations. U.S. Senate, 1976.

Irwin, Don. "Flaws Found in Security Procedures." Washington: Los Angeles Times; September 28, 1964.

Irwin, Don. "Johnson's Vet Stand by Goldwater." Newport Beach: Los Angeles Times; August 5, 1964.

Irwin, Don. "Jury Finds Baker Guilty On Seven Counts." Washington: Los Angeles Times; January 30, 1967.

"Jackie . . . Brave and Tragedy." New York: New York Herald Tribune; November 23, 1963.

Jackson, Bob. "Lensmen Heard Shots, Saw Gun." Dallas: Dallas Times Herald; November 22, 1963.

"JFK Co-Stars in New Common Market." Life Magazine: March 29, 1963.

"JFK to Visit Space Center." Washington: United Press International; November 13, 1963.

"Johnson Calls for Day of Mourning." Washington: A Compillation of Press Dispatches; November 23, 1963.

Johnson, Lyndon. "The Vantage Point." New York: Holt Reinhart & Winston; 1971.

"Johnson to Address Congress." Washington: <u>United Press International</u>; November 24, 1963.

"Johnson Takes Oath." Dallas: <u>Associated Press</u>; November 23, 1963.

"Johnson." New York: <u>New York Herald Tribune</u>; November 23, 1963.

Jones, Valerie, and Harrell, Kent. *"Jack Ruby Was JFK's Assassin."* Boca Raton: <u>Globe</u>; September 6, 1988.

"Judge Refuses to Remove Himself From Hunt Case." Texas: <u>Associated Press</u>; unknown.

"Jury To Decide Ruby's Gun Fate." Dallas: <u>Associated Press</u>; October 30, 1990.

"Just a Week Ago, No Escort in New York." New York: <u>New York Herald Tribune</u>; November 23, 1963.

Kantor, Seth *"Party's Spats Play JFK Trip."* <u>Scripps-Howard Staff Writer</u>: November 22, 1963.

Kantor, Seth. *"Oswald says, . . . I was given a short, sweet hearing. . . ."* Dallas: <u>Scripps-Howard Staff Writer</u>; November 23, 1963.

Kearns, Doris. <u>Lyndon Johnson and The American Dream</u>. New York: Harper and Roe; 1976.

"Keep Hands Off Navy Base, Castro Warned." Washington: <u>United Press International</u>; January 4, 1961.

Kelly, Kitty. *"The Dark Side of Camelot."* <u>People Magazine</u>: February 29, 1988.

"Kennedy Had Advance Word of Cuba Break." Palm Beach: <u>United Press International</u>; January 4, 1961.

"Kennedy Nearing Victory." <u>Los Angeles Times</u>; November 9, 1960.

"Kennedy Made Decision." Dallas: <u>United Press International</u>; November 23, 1963.

Kennedy, John F. *"The Burden and The Glory."* New York: <u>Harper & Row</u>; 1965.

Kennedy, Edward M. *"Our Brother, John Fitzgerald Kennedy. . . ."* <u>Parade Magazine</u>: July 3, 1988.

"Khrushchev Tells His Aims." Vienna: <u>Associated Press</u>; June 1, 1961.

"Khrushchev Expresses Condolence." Moscow: <u>United Press International</u>; November 23, 1963.

"Khrushchev Sights Poll to Those Who Seek Peace." Moscow: Associated Press; November 24, 1963.

"Kid Brother Takes Senate Seat: And Teddy Makes Three." Life Magazine: January 18, 1963.

Kiker, Douglas. *"Kennedy."* New York: New York Herald Tribune; November 23, 1963.

Kluckholn, Frank L. Lyndon's Legacy. New York: Devin-Dadar; 1964.

Kraslow, David. *"Democratic Conclave Opens Today; Dixie Clash Grows."* Atlantic City: Los Angeles Times; August 24, 1964.

Lane, Mark. Rush to Judgement. New York: Holt, Reinhart & Winston; 1966.

Lasky, Victor. It Didn't Start with Watergate. New York: Dial Press; 1977.

"Last Seconds of the Motorcade." Life Magazine: November 24, 1967.

"Leading Psychiatrist Give Views on Reason Behind Assassinations." New York: Associated Press; November 23, 1963.

Lesli, Warren. Dallas Public and Private. New York: Grossman Publishers; 1964.

Lifton, David S. Best Evidence: Disguise and Deception in the Assassination of John F. Kennedy. New York: McMillan Publishing Co.; 1980.

Lincoln, Evelyn. *"My Years with John F. Kennedy."* New York: Holt Reinhart & Winston; 1965.

Lincoln, Evelyn. *"Kennedy and Johnson."* New York: Holt Reinhart & Winston; 1968.

Linton, Calvin D. *"American Headlines Year by Year."* Nashville: Thomas Nelson Publishers; 1985.

Lucas, Jim J. *"They Brought Him Home Again Dead."* Washington: Scripps-Howard Staff Writer; November 23, 1963.

MacDougall, William. *"U.S. Forces Ordered on War Footing."* Washington: Los Angeles Times News Service; October 23, 1962.

Manchester, William. The Death of a President: November 20–25, 1963. New York: Harper & Row; 1967.

Manchester, William. *"The Death of a President."* New York: Harper & Row; 1964.

Marrs, Jim. Crossfire: The Plot that Killed Kennedy. New York: Carroll & Graf: 1990.

Mazo, Earl. *"Kennedy-Khrushchev Talks. . . ."* Chicago: Los Angeles Times; May 6, 1961.

McDonald, M. N. *"Dallas Officer Relates How Oswald Arrested."* Dallas: Associated Press; November 24, 1963.

McDonald, Hugh C. *"Appointment in Dallas: The Final Solution To the Assassination of JFK."* New York: McDonald Publishing; 1975.

McNeil, Marshall. *"Lyndon Johnson Is Ready for His Biggest Task."* Washington: Scripps Staff-Howard Staff Writer; November 24, 1963.

Miller, Merlie. Lyndon—An Oral Biography. New York: J. P. Putnam's Sons; 1980.

Model, Peter, with Robert J. Groden. JFK: The Case for Conspiracy. New York: Manor Books; 1976.

Mosby, Alline. *"Reporter Recalls Interview with Oswald in Moscow."* Paris: United Press International; November 23, 1963.

"Mother says, . . . He Helped Me." Dallas: United Press International; November 23, 1963.

"My Secret 21-year Affair with LBJ." Dallas: Star Magazine; July 7, 1987.

"Nation Faces Changes." Washington: Albuquerque Tribune; November 23, 1963.

"New President's First Statement." Washington: Associated Press; November 23, 1963.

"No Foreign Ties Seen in Kennedy's Death." Washington: United Press International; November 24, 1963.

O'Toole, George. *"The Assassination Tapes."* New York: Penthouse Press Ltd.; 1975.

"Oswald Called Expert Shot." Los Angeles: Associated Press; November 23, 1963.

"Oswald . . . Mystery . . . To His Neighbors." New Orleans: United Press International; November 23, 1963.

"Outlook . . . Very Good, . . . Robert Kennedy says." Hyannis Port: Los Angeles Times; November 9, 1960.

"Police Identify Assassin's Rifle as Italian Made." Dallas: United Press International; November 24, 1963.

"Police Certain that Oswald Killed Kennedy." Dallas: <u>United Press International</u>; November 24, 1963.

Polsbyn, Nelson W. and Aaron Wildavsky. <u>Presidential Elections Strategies of American Electoral Politics</u>. New York: Charles Scribner's Sons; 1968.

"President Johnson—The Eisenhower Prediction." New York: <u>New York Herald Tribune</u>; November 23, 1963.

"President Dead, Connally Shot." Dallas: <u>The Dallas Times Herald</u>; November 22, 1963.

"Presidential Broadcast." Washington: <u>Associated Press Photograph and Comment</u>; August 5, 1964.

Price, Raymond Jr. *"The Nation's Problems Remain."* New York: <u>New York Herald Tribune</u>; November 23, 1963.

"Rebellion Quelled; General Walker Seized." Oxford, Miss.: <u>Associated Press</u>; October 2, 1962.

<u>Report of the President's Commission on the Assassination of President John F. Kennedy</u>. 1964; published by U.S. Government Printing Office; and also Doubleday; McGraw-Hill; Bantam; Popular Library; and Associated Press; 1964.

<u>Report of the Select Committee on Assassinations, U.S. House of Representatives</u>. 1979; published by U.S. Government Printing Office; and Report (only) by Bantam; New York, 1979, under title The Final Assassinations Report.

Reston, James, Jr. <u>The Lone Star Life of John Connally</u>. New York: Harper & Row; 1989.

Reston, Richard. *"U.S. Acts to Prevent Major Air Raid by Reds."* Washington: <u>Los Angeles Times</u>; August 5, 1964.

"Retrospect 1964". New York; 1964.

Richards, Charles. *"Dallas Man Says His Dad Killed JFK."* Dallas: <u>Associated Press</u>; August 6, 1990.

Richards, Charles. *"CIA Denials Role in JFK Assassination."* Dallas: <u>Associated Press</u>; August 7, 1970.

Rike, Aubrey. *"Ambulance Driver sees Kennedy, Governor Connally Brought to Hospital."* Dallas: <u>United Press International</u>; November 24, 1963.

Roberts, Charles. *"LBJ's Intercircle."* New York: <u>Delacorte Press</u>; 1969.

Roberts. *"A Report Indepth on Elections 1964."* Washington: <u>The National Observer</u>; 1965.

Sauvage, Leo. "The Oswald Affair." Cleveland: The World Publishing Co.; 1966.

Scheim, David E. Contract on America—The Mafia Murder of President John F. Kennedy. New York: Shapolsky Publishers Inc.; 1988.

Scheim, David E. Contract on America—The Mafia Murders of John and Robert Kennedy. Silver Spring, MD: Argyle Press; 1983.

Schlesinger, Arthur. Thousand Days: John F. Kennedy in the White House. Boston: Houghton Mifflin Co.; 1965.

"Senators Study Time Table for Test Ban Treaty." Washington: Associated Press; August 29, 1963.

"Shame of a Nation—History of Assassination." New York: New York Herald Tribune; November 23, 1963.

Shannon, Don. "Kennedy Study Sending Troops to South Vietnam." Washington: Los Angles Times; May 6, 1961.

Sherrill, Robert. "The Accidental President." New York: Crossmen Publishers; 1967.

"Shocked Nation Mourns Death of Kennedy." Washington: Associated Press; November 23, 1963.

"Shot From a Far, High Up What Secret Service Fear." Washington: Associated Press; November 23, 1963.

"62 Years Since U.S. Had President Slaying." Washington: Scripps-Howard Newspapers; November 23, 1963.

"Slaying Officer Left Wife, Three Children." Dallas: United Press International; November 23, 1963.

"Slaying Shocks Capital." Washington: Associated Press; November 22, 1963.

Smith, Merriman. "Eyewitness Tells of Seeing History Explode." Washington: United Press International; November 23, 1963.

Starnes, Richard. "Awful Truth Hard to Grasp at JFK Home." Washington: Scripps-Howard Writers; November 23, 1963.

Steele, Jack. "Senator Goldwater Chances Fading." Washington: Scripps-Howard Staff Writer; November 23, 1963.

Summers, Anthony. "Conspiracy." New York: McGraw-Hill Book Co.; 1980.

"Teacher says Oswald . . . Loner." Boston: United Press International; November 23, 1963.

"Texan Says His Dad Was One of Three Gunmen Who Cut Down JFK." Austin: Associated Press; August 6, 1990.

"Text of Oath Taken By Johnson." Washington: United Press International; November 23, 1963.

"The Texan Sits Tall in a New Saddle." Life Magazine: December 3, 1963.

"The Police Attempt to Implicate Reds in Task Charge." Moscow: United Press International; November 24, 1963.

"The Full Story . . ." New York: New York Herald Tribune; November 23, 1963.

Theoharis, Ethan. Spying on Americans. Philadelphia: Temple University Press; 1978.

Thompson, Robert E. *"Oswald Slaying!"* Dallas: Los Angeles Times News Service; November 25, 1963.

Thompson, Robert. *"Blockage of Cuba Ordered."* Washington: Los Angeles Times; October 23, 1962.

"Times Starts Series by Johnson Today." Los Angeles Times; September 28, 1964.

"Tragedy No Stranger to the Kennedy Family." Boston: United Press International; November 23, 1963.

"Tragedy Again Summons Kennedy Family Together." New York: New York Herald Tribune; November 23, 1963.

"Troan, John. "New Presidents Health Rated Good." Washington: Scripps-Howard; November 23, 1963.

"Two Bullets Hit Kennedy." Washington: United Press International; November 23, 1963.

"Two Plots Against Ike." New York: Associated Press; November 23, 1963.

"Tyler First VP to Gain Presidency Through Death." Washington: United Press International; November 24, 1963.

"U. S. Indites Texas Police Saw Estes in Alleged Plot to Steal Trade Secrets." Brady, Texas: Associated Press; November 30, 1989.

"U.S. Transfers General Walker to Prison Hospital." Springfield: Associated Press; October 2, 1962.

"US Breaks Off Relations With Cuba." Los Angeles Times; January 4, 1961.

Van Gelder, Lawrence. The Untold Story Why the Kennedys Lost the Book Battle. New York: Award Books; 1967.

Warren, Earl. et al., *Report of the Warren Commission: The Assassination of President Kennedy.* New York: McGraw-Hill; 1964.

"Warren Commission Report: Oswald Acted Alone in Kennedy Assassination." Washington: Los Angeles Times; September 28, 1964.

Wheeler, Keith. *"The Bobby Baker Case: Scandal Grows and Grows in Washington."* Life Magazine: November 22, 1963.

Wieck, Paul R. *"Behind Scenes Thoughts Turn To Power Shift."* Albuquerque Journal: November 24, 1963.

Wilson, Robert. *"LBJ Sent to Power: A Critical View."* New York: USA Today; March 6, 1990.

Wilson, Victor. *"Kennedy Funeral Service 1:00 p.m. Monday in Washington."* New York: New York Herald Tribune; November 23, 1963.

Wisse, David. *"Disbelief Grips Stunned Capital."* Washington: New York Herald Tribune; November 23, 1963.

"World Mourns John Kennedy." Washington: Associated Press; November 23, 1963.

Young, John V. *"Oswald Spurns Lie Detector Test."* Dallas: United Press International; November 23, 1963.

Endnotes

SECTION 1: BACKGROUND

Chp. 1—Transfer luggage: Manchester: Dth. Pres., pg. 239.

Chp. 2—Consideration: W. Comm., pg. 47; LBJ Publicized trip: Summers: Conspr., pg. 29; Hotel meeting: W. Comm., pg. 19 & 48; LBJ's Birthday: LBJ: Vant. Pt., pg. 6; Expanded trip: W. Comm., pg. 48; More plans: W. Comm., pg. 19 & 20; 10-4-63 Paul: W. Comm., pg. 48; Trip to D.C.: Baker: John. Eclip., pg. 240; Fort Worth Breakfast: W. Comm., XXIV; Dallas arrival: W. Comm., pg. 19; Murder at 12:30: W. Comm., pg. V; Connally struck: W. Comm., V; 13th p.m. LBJ told: W. Comm., pg. 70; concern to leave: W. Comm., pg. IX; refusal to leave and delay: Manchester: Dth. Pres., pg. 239, 315, & 318; Swearing in: W. Comm., V; Oswald's call to Abt: W. Comm., pg. 561; silent press conference: Lane: Rush, pg. 191; case closed: Haley: Tex. LBJ, pg. 209.

Chp. 3—Stray Bullet: Buchanan: Who Killed, pg. 93 and Lane: Rush, pg. 57; seizure of tapes: Lane: Rush, pg. 53 & pg. 43 & 50; inexperience doctors: O'Toole: Asst. Tapes, pg. 34; autopsy: Summers: Conspr., pg. 42 & 43; seizure of films: O'Toole: Asst. Tapes, pg. 38; Humes not talk: Lane: Rush, pg. 41 and O'Toole: Asst. Tapes, pg. 35; Connally's clothes: Lane: Rush, pg. 51;

Missing brain: Lane: Rush, pg. 44; seized evid: Mann: Crossfire, pg. 356–357; tax lien: Lane: Rush, pg. 107.

Chp. 4—Federal Law on murder of U.S. Pres.: W. Comm., pg. 43; Convening Texas Grand Jury: W. Comm., pg. 5; Proposal of special Texas commission: McDonald: Apt., pg. 27; Executive order: W. Comm., pg. 4; staff quit: Summers: Conspr., pg. 455; Sealing evidence: Haley: Tex. LBJ, pg. 209 & 210; Tarnished America: O'Toole; Asst. Tapes, pg. 118; Ruby's quote: Summers: Conspr., pg. 455–456; Printing error: Summers: Conspr., pg. 263; Court release date: W. Comm., XXXVIII; Johnson demands: O'Toole; Asst. Tapes, pg. 118; W. Comm. signed report: Summers: Conspr., pg. 68; Report to Johnson: W. Comm., pg. 4; 700,000 copies: W. Comm., pg. I & II; exclude evidence: Haley: Tex. LBJ, pg. 207; report to LBJ: W. Comm., pg. 4.

Chp. 6—Defective weapon: Buchanan: Who Killed, pg. 201; correcting weapon: W. Comm., pg. 181 & Buchanan: Who Killed, pg. 201 & others; Oswald's shooting: W. Comm., pg. 607; Patsy: Summers: Conspr., pg. 130; Ike President: Summers: Conspr., pg. 129; Nothing against President: Summers: Conspr., pg. 129.

Chp. 7—Communists Assassination Theory: Summers: Conspr., pg.435; Conservative Assassination Theory: See Groden among many others; Wealthy Oilmen: Sauvage: Osw. Aff., pg. 304; Harm to Goldwater: See News Sources; Mafia: Schiem: Contract; Saul: McDonald: The Final Sol.; Connally: Reston: Life J. Connally.

SECTION 2: THE CHARACTER OF LBJ

Chp. 10—LBJ's little things: Sherrill: Accid. Pres., pg. 30; Worst elements of mankind: Sherrill: Accid. Pres., pg. 10; Total opportunist: Sherrill: Accid. Pres., pg. 4; LBJ in jail: Caro: Path, pg. 102; Piss-ants: Gulley: Bkg. Cov., pg. 44.

Chp. 11—No Religion: Duegger: Politician, pg. 5; Rotten foundation: Boller: Pres. Camp., pg. 313; Car gift: Gulley: Bkg. Cov., pg. 75; Pope gift: LBJ: Vant. Pt., pg. 180; Penis: Caro: Path, pg. 155; Alice Glass: Caro: Path, pg. 476, 487, 489, & 492; Madeline Brown: Star; Doris Kerns: Lasky: It Didn't, pg. 203; Bootlegger trip: Caro: Path, pg. 121; LBJ alcohol: Gulley: Bkg. Cov., pg. 258; Cutty Sark: Cormier: LBJ, pg. 111; Beer driving: Sherrill: Accid. Pres., pg. 37; Sober up room: Haley: Tex. LBJ, pg. 235; Happy drinking: Cormier: LBJ, pg. 111; Unhappy drunk: Haley: Tex. LBJ, pg. 235; Others waiting: Haley: Tex. LBJ, pg. 235; This is LBJ's concerns: LBJ: Vant. Pt., pg. 93.

Chp. 12—Total opportunist: Sherrill: Accid. Pres., pg. 4; LBJ joke: Lasky: It Didn't, pg. 123; College election: Caro: Path, pg. 190 & 178, 179, 181 & 182 & Lasky: It Didn't, pg. 123; I Campaign: Haley: Tex. LBJ, pg. 12 & Caro: Path, XX; U.S. Senator Campaign: Haley: Tex. LBJ, pg. 22; LBJ's influence in campaign: Haley: Tex. LBJ, pg. 21; KKK: Sherrill: Accid. Pres., pg. 120; Forty-eight Campaign: Haley: Tex. LBJ, pg. 22, 27, 23 & 47 & Lasky: It Didn't, pg. 121; LBJ in jail: Haley: Tex. LBJ, pg. 53; Down in route: Haley: Tex. LBJ, pg. 11, 88, 86, & 87, & Sherrill: Accid. Pres., pg. 239 & Caro: Path, pg. 627; 1960 position on ticket: Lasky: It Didn't, pg. 49; Voter fraud: Lasky: It Didn't, pg. 49.

Chp. 13—See wheeling and dealing by Bobby Baker; Assets: Haley: Tex. LBJ, pg. 56 Lasky: It Didn't, pg. 123; Lady Bird's father: Haley: Tex. LBJ, pg. 56, 57, & 59; Down in route: Haley: Tex. LBJ, pg. 56–57; FCC: Haley: Tex. LBJ, pg. 60, 69, 71.

Chp. 14—Hunting: Haley: Tex. LBJ, pg. 245–247; Marshall: Haley: Tex. LBJ, pg. 245–250; Estes before Grand Jury: MILW. JR. 3/24/84; airplane: Haley: Tex. LBJ, pg. 248–250.

Chp. 15—Footnote references to other obscene practices include Gulley: Bkg. Cov., pg. 54; Caro: Path, 485; Cormier: LBJ, pg. 136, 133, 113, 135, 105, & 197; Haley: Tex. LBJ, pg. 234; & Cormier: LBJ, pg. 39 & 59.

SECTION 3: MOTIVE

Chp. 17—Generally see: Caro: Path, 100, 171, & 535; Marrs: Crossfire; Presidency: Lincoln: Kenn. & LBJ, pg. 153; Travel Together: Lincoln: Kenn. & LBJ, pg. 159; Johnson's practicing: Lincoln: Kenn. & LBJ, pg. 150–151; Vacate premises: Manchester: Dth. Pres., pg. 453–455; LBJ's logo and eagle: Lincoln: Kenn. & LBJ, pg. 15 & 112, Sherrill: Accid. Pres., pg. 20, Cormier: LBJ, pg. 136, & Haley: Tex. LBJ, pg. 231; Bathroom style: Haley: Tex. LBJ, pg. 233; Johnson's feet: Cormier: LBJ, pg. 135; Special chair: Gulley: Bkg. Cov., pg. 31, 33; Brain: Cormier: LBJ, pg. 136; Cost of plane: Gulley: Bkg. Cov., pg. 31; NBC emphasis USA: Haley: Tex. LBJ, pg. 192; LBJ's temper: Baker: John. Eclip., pg. 242, Gulley: Bkg. Cov., pg. 52, Haley: Tex. LBJ, pg. 232; Mad-Ons: Lincoln: Kenn. & LBJ, pg. 65; Swimming Pool: Gulley: Bkg. Cov., pg. 88; Bad side: Sherrill: Accid. Pres., pg. 13; Chicken question: Sherrill: Accid. Pres., pg. 12; See Physiatrist: Marrs: Crossfire, pg. 297; Yacht backwards: Cormier: LBJ, pg. 139; Each count: Roberts: LBJ Circle, pg. 97, 98, 99; Johnson's use of money: Gulley: Bkg. Cov., pg. 55, 35, 38, 36, 33, & 92; FBI: Lasky: It Didn't, pg. 163; Vietnam: Lasky: It Didn't, pg. 164, Theoharis: Spying on Americans, pg. 177 & Sherrill: Accid. Pres., pg. 269; Perverts: Lasky: It Didn't, pg. 178; Special squad: Lasky: It Didn't, pg. 164; Boyfriends: Lasky: It Didn't, pg. 203; Misuse of funds: Gulley: Bkg. Cov., pg. 88 & 90; Government Switchboard: Gulley: Bkg. Cov., pg. 92; Helicopter: Gulley: Bkg. Cov., pg. 90; Massages: Gulley: Bkg. Cov., pg. 90; LBJ Memorial Library etc: Scripps Post & Caro: Path, pg. 777.

Chp. 18—Generally See Caro: Path, pg. 544 & Haley: Tex. LBJ, pg. 75.

Chp. 19—Generally See Haley: Tex. LBJ, pg. 194, 197, 195, 196, & 198, Lincoln: Kenn. & LBJ, pg. 50, 45, 44, 42, 70, 71, 86, & 14; Baker: John. Eclip., pg. 14; Lasky: It Didn't, pg. 29, 30; Sherrill: Accid. Pres., pg. 139–141; Collier: Kenn., pg. 300, 304; Boller: Presid. Camp., pg 302,; Van Gelder: The Untold, pg. 14; along with Sherrill: Accid. Pres., pg. 11; Baker: John.

Eclip., pg. 55; Lincoln: Kenn. & LBJ, pg. 2, 14, 150, 151, 153, & 159; Gulley: Bkg. Cov., pg. 47. Democratic Primaries: Lincoln: Kenn. & LBJ, pg. 45 & 44; Absentee Senator: Lincoln: Kenn. & LBJ, pg. 42; 1960 Break in: Lincoln: Kenn. & LBJ, pg. 70; Lost in Hotel room: Lincoln: Kenn. & LBJ, pg. 86; LBJ's quote as to gambling man: Van Gelder: The Untold, pg. 94 . . . however quotation was supplied by Mrs. Graham of the Washington Post in a news article placed at the time of publication; paranoia Lincoln: Kenn. & LBJ, pg 189.

Chp. 20—Generally See Sherrill: Accid. Pres., pg. 21; LBJ: Vant. Pt., pg. 4; Manchester: Dth. Pres., pg. 5 & 6; Baker: John. Eclip., pges 41, 17, 44, & 69; Lincoln: Kenn. & LBJ, pg. 161; Time with President: Lincoln: Kenn. & LBJ, pg. 161.

Chp. 21—Generally See Sherrill: Accid. Pres., pg. 106; LBJ: Vant. Pt., pg. 2; Baker: John. Eclip., pg. 169, 182, 238, 254 & 505; Lasky: It Didn't, pg. 127; Haley: Tex. LBJ, pg. 73, 7; Lincoln: Kenn. & LBJ, pges. 205 & 183. A question: Lincoln: Kenn. & LBJ, pg 183; JFK's sister: Baker: John. Eclip., pg. 505; Analyst predicting: Lincoln: Kenn. & LBJ, pg. 191; Johnson dumped: Lincoln: Kenn. & LBJ, pg. 197, 200; Last words: Lincoln: Kenn. & LBJ, pg. 205.

Chp. 22—Generally See Lasky: It Didn't, pges. 125, 128, 136, 138, 129; Haley: Tex. LBJ, pges. 224, 135, 145, 130, 129, 137, 125, 144, 121, 139, 122, 128, 133, 119, 117, 120, 115, 175, 224; Lincoln: Kenn. & LBJ, pges. 193, 195, 196; Baker: John. Eclip., pges. 241, 244; Van Gelder: The Untold, pg. 108; Sherrill: Accid. Pres., pg. 14.

Chp. 23—Generally See Life Magazine 11/8/63 and 11/22/63; Johnson quote about Baker: Lasky: It Didn't, pg. 128; Basis for scandal: Lincoln: Kenn. & LBJ, pg. 192; Return from trip: Lasky: It Didn't, pg. 74; Parting with Baker quote: Lincoln: Kenn. & LBJ, pg. 195; Retreat to ranch: Lincoln: Kenn. & LBJ, pg. 198; Life Magazine Team Report: Life 11/22/63; stop investigation: Lincoln: Kenn. & LBJ, pg. 193; Lasky: It Didn't, pg. 129, 138; Sherrill: Accid. Pres., pg. 14.

SECTION 4: OPPORTUNITY

Chp. 25—This overall summary of Opportunity items are more specifically in other portions of the book.

Chp. 27—Trip problems: Bruno's visits and activities in Texas: Bruno "advanceman"; LBJ and Kennedy fight: Manchester: Dth. Pres., pg. 82; Connally unaware: Manchester: Dth. Pres., pg. 157; Connally quotation: Manchester: Dth. Pres., pg. 157.

Chp. 28—Back to crowd: Manchester: Dth. Pres., pg. 33; Ends security short of assassination site: Manchester: Dth. Pres. pg. 33; outriders: Marrs: Crossfire, pg. 244.

Chp. 29—"Miracle bullet" book boxes: Warren Commission Exhibit 399 and others; material available for questioning: Warren Commission Exhibit 2175; Oswald's quote: Summers: Consp., pg. 130; Silent Press Conference: W. Comm., pg. 193–194; Ruby with gun on Friday night: Summers: Consp., pg. 480; Texas Law Transferring from jail: W. Comm., pg. 194; Failure to Transfer: W. Comm., pg. 194; warnings as to death of Oswald: W. Comm., pg. 195 and many others; Transfer decoy in protection declined: W. Comm., pg. 211; Ruby's quote: Gulley: Bkg. Cov., pg. 48; Available ambulance: Buchanan: Who killed Kennedy, pg. 142.

Chp. 30—Pushing into photos: Manchester: Dth. Pres., pg. 325; LBJ relaxing on plane: Manchester: Dth. Pres., pg. 266, 320.

Chp. 31—Oswald at seventeen: W. Comm., pg. 360; sad about military down grade: W. Comm., pg. 363; held non-descript jobs: W. Comm., pg. 379; April firing of weapon: W. Comm., pg. 300; to New Orleans: W. Comm., pg. 379; June 1963 Intent to leave U.S.: W. Comm., pg. 325, 368; incidents between Oswald and Ruby: W. Comm., pg. 710 and many others; Oswald to Connally: W. Comm., pg. 363; Oswald's I.Q.: W. Comm., pg. 357; Oswald to Hunt: Marrs: Crossfire: Photo and pg. 197; Hunt's premonition: Marrs: Crossfire, pg. 278.

Chp. 32—Large cash: Gertz: moment, pg. 61; Conservative literature at all: W. Comm., pg. 319; Ruby seen at hospital: W. Comm., pg. 313 & Lane: Rush, pg. 191, 220, 224, 226 and other books; Ruby armed on Friday: Summers: Consp., pg. 480; Failure to record interrogation: W. Comm., pg. 313; Refusal to transfer etc.: Lane: Rush, pg. 191; Ruby's telephone calls: W. Comm., pg. 317, 315, 316; Ruby's call to temple: W. Comm., pg. 317; Friday exhibition: Lane: Rush, pg. 191; Ruby upset: W. Comm., pg. 315, 316, 317; Ruby on news film: W. Comm., pg. 318; Oswald not told of charges: Buchanan: Who killed Kennedy, pg. 40; Paul: W. Comm., pg. 315, 326; Ruby's quote at garage: W. Comm., pg. 322, 323; Ruby knowing Dallas people: Lane: Rush, pg. 198, 202 and other books; Ruby's quotation: many sources.

Chp. 33—Ruby's pass charges: Gertz: Moment, pg. 5, Lane: Rush, pg. 202; Ruby as a PR agent: Lane: Rush, pg. 220, W. Comm., pg. 319, Lane: Rush, pg. 192; Motion to remove trial: Gertz: Moment, pg. 37, 34; Judge Browns scandal: Gertz: Moment, pg. 211, 212, 214, 219.

Chp. 34—As supporters: Haley: Tex. LBJ, pg. 195; Life line: Sherrill: Accid. Pres., pg. 139; Lane: Rush, pg. 211, Star, pg. 139 et al; add in other items: W. Comm., pg. 343; to offices: W. Comm., pg. 343; Jim Braden: Summers: Consp., pg. 476; Hunt literature: W. Comm., pg. 341, 343; Letter to Hunt: Marrs: Crossfire: photo. and pg. 197; Claim as to prior knowledge: Marrs: Crossfire: pg. 278.

Chp. 35—Statement to girlfriend: Marrs: Crossfire, pg. 298; Refurbishing of car: Marrs: Crossfire, p. 297; Hospital actions: Manchester: Dth. Pres., pg. 234; Actions on Saturday: Manchester: Dth. Pres., pg. 453–455; Ruby's quotation: Summers: Consp., pg. 455–456; Lane: Rush, pg. 207; Ruby's TV statement: Summers: Consp., pg. 495.

Chp. 37—Oswald statements: Summers: Consp., pg. 129, 130, Ruby's words: Lane: Rush, pg. 216; Ruby's quote: Summers: Consp., pg. 492; unpowdered test: Lane: Rush, pg. 125; Statement from JFK's doctor: Marrs: Crossfire, pg. 371; Eyewit-

nesses: Numerous books and sources especially Lane's: Rush;
Sheriffs opinion: W. Comm., pg. 593.

Chp. 38—"heavy hand" oath taking: Van Gelder: The Untold,
pg. 72; "hold LBJ responsible": Van Gelder: The Untold, pg.
72; trade off: Van Gelder: The Untold, pg. 11; "LBJ force of
violence": Van Gelder: The Untold, pg. 34; fight with LBJ: Van
Gelder: The Untold, pg. 59; dispute in Texas: Van Gelder: The
Untold, pg. 60; harm Bobby Kennedy: Van Gelder: The Untold,
pg. 73; "insider get LBJ: Van Gelder: The Untold, pg 68; settlement: Van Gelder: The Untold, pg. 79; booknote: Van Gelder:
The Untold, pg. 81; modifications not important: Van Gelder:
The Untold, pg. 82–83; allegedly not political: Van Gelder: The
Untold, pg. 83.

Index